Praise for
Dallas Murphy's

LOVER MAN

"Clever, intriguing, shocking, touching and funny, this first novel from playwright Murphy inaugurates what should be an outstanding series. *LOVER MAN* will keep readers turning pages at a breakneck pace. Murphy writes with clarity and power; the prison and morgue scenes are shockingly good. His characters are fascinating and unique. . . . One of the Year's best."
—*Publishers Weekly*

"Brave, smart, sensitive, sophisticated, fast, funny—and that's just the dog. The same can be said of his owner, Artie Deemer, and of the wild and hilarious *LOVER MAN*. It's a great debut for man and beast."
—Nancy Pickard, author of the Jenny Cain mysteries

"In a genre of gimmicky heroes, Arthur Deemer is a true original. . . . The frantic, antic humor . . . carries along characterization and narration like twin runaway locomotives. . . . Murphy moves his novel along scene by vivid scene. . . . Most of these scenes are achingly funny—but some are shocking, for Murphy is very good at setting up, then blindsiding his reader. . . . I'm looking forward to the next Artie Deemer novel."
—*Times*

LOVER MAN

Dallas Murphy

POCKET BOOKS

New York   London   Toronto   Sydney   Tokyo

For Marie

POCKET BOOKS, a division of Simon & Schuster Inc.
1230 Avenue of the Americas, New York, N.Y. 10020

Copyright © 1987 by Dallas Murphy
Cover art copyright © 1988 Ron Barbagallo

Published by arrangement with Charles Scribner's Sons
Library of Congress Catalog Card Number: 87-4321

ISBN: 0-671-66188-4

First Pocket Books printing September 1988

10 9 8 7 6 5 4 3 2 1

POCKET and colophon are trademarks of
Simon & Schuster Inc.

Printed in the U.S.A.

My thanks to Marie Allen, Donald Wollner, Barbara Sirota, Joslyn Pine, Louis Serrante, Terry Williams, Vincent Fantozzi, Ray Hayes, Pete McNamara, Barbara Weted Fay, and especially Eugenia Leftwich.

CHAPTER

ONE

MORE THAN MOST ANYTHING ELSE, I LIKED TO DO NOTHing. Peace to me was to pull my Morris chair over to the west window, prop my heels on the sill and, entranced, listen to several hours of selected jazz while I watched the tugboats, masthead lights of red and green, maneuver on the Hudson. I'd smoke a thin bone for concentration and soar out over the black river with giants on my wing. King, Count, Duke, Prez, Major, Fats (both), Chu, Trane, Diz, Chick, Sonny, Bird, Bud, Cootie, and their colleagues— I've flown with them all. My dog Jellyroll shares my enthusiasm. When the wattage kicks in, he curls up on his Adirondack Spruce Bough Dog Bed and licks his parts with contentment. My taste in jazz is broad, but I believe Jellyroll digs bop best of all.

That's what we were doing when they pounded on my door with evil news, and contentment vanished for a long, long time. I peeped out the view hole. Two men, one huge and bullnecked, stood in the hall. The shoulders of their coats were rain-darkened, and water dripped from their hat brims.

"Arthur Deemer," demanded the huge one.

9

"Yes?"

"Police officers."

That's what I thought. If these two showed up at your Halloween party, you wouldn't wonder what they were supposed to be. The giant flashed his shield at the peephole and said, "We want to ask you some questions."

Questions? What kind of questions? Surely hard-bitten types like these didn't come around to bust indolents like me for smoking a bone over "These Are a Few of My Favorite Things."

"Are you going to open up or not?"

Surely. I opened up.

"Detective Cobb," the giant said about himself, "and this is Detective Loccatuchi," a sensibly sized man who nodded at me, a gesture that, when compared to the look on Cobb's face, seemed warm and giving. I nodded back at him. Then they sniffed the guilty air. It seemed to hit them like a felonious assault.

"I, uh, was just listening to some music. Some jazz. Very American. John Coltrane. Elvin Jones on drums, McCoy Tyner on—" I stopped babbling. The cops eyed me coldly.

"You wanna turn it down," Cobb shouted over a great tenor solo.

"Down?" I shouted. "Sure. Absolutely."

I don't keep a lot of furniture in the living room. None, actually. Just my Morris chair. I like to keep the acoustics clean. Jellyroll sniffed the arresting officers' shoes while the officers looked with unmasked suspicion at my bereft living room.

"You gonna turn it down or not?"

"Oh. Absolutely." I hopped to it.

"Hey, Dave," said Loccatuchi, "check this dog. He looks just like the R-r-ruff Dog."

"Huh?"

"The R-r-ruff Dog. From TV."

"That *is* the R-r-ruff Dog," I said helpfully.

"No shit?"

"None," I swore.

It's best I make this clear up front: I live off my dog. I'm not the breadwinner here. Jellyroll is. Jellyroll is the exclusive spokesdog for R-r-ruff Dog Food, his happy face printed on millions of boxes distributed nationwide, not to mention the TV commercials in which Jellyroll says, "R-r-ruff! The full-flavor food!" He is also an actor. He played the title dog in *Blinky's on the Case,* a Disney rip-off that drew them in by the droves. We'll continue to pull down big bucks from that one for years to come. It was just sold to cable television. Jellyroll smiles, that's what makes him commercial. We pass a toddler and his mom on the street and the kid will say, "Look, Mommy, that dog's smiling." That smiling face has made us financially untroubled, but sometimes I suspect that Jellyroll doesn't entirely respect me.

"Wait till the wife hears about this. She loves the R-r-ruff Dog," said Loccatuchi, now down on his knees to ruffle Jellyroll's ears.

Cobb clearly didn't like dogs any better than he liked jazz. "We're from homicide, Mr. Deemer. Manhattan South Homicide."

"Homicide?"

"A Miss Billie Burke was murdered tonight." Just like that he said it, no color, no attitude one way or the other, routine. "I believe you knew her."

I sagged into the Morris chair. My knees just packed up on me.

"Did you know her?"

I heard his question, but it came from a long way off, like a radio station fifty miles down the road.

"You were lovers, right?"

I nodded.

"Do you know her residence to be 47 Sullivan Street?"

"Yes. . . . Is that where it happened?"

"Looks like it. A neighbor called when he observed

water running under Miss Burke's front door. We entered and found her tied hand and foot—you know, like hog-tied. She was drowned in her bathtub. Tell me, Mr. Deemer, did she have strange sexual habits?''

"No.''

"The neighbors say there was a lot of loud talk in her apartment. A lot of people coming and going on the stairs tonight. Was she a professional?''

"A what?''

"A prostitute.''

"Of course not.''

"What about drugs?''

"No drugs.''

"Where were you tonight?''

"Come on, you don't think—''

"It's just routine,'' said Loccatuchi in a voice that had some feelings to it.

"I was here.''

"You sat around all night and blew dope by yourself, that it?''

I began to cry. Jellyroll came over and set his chin on my knee to ask what the matter was. Dogs have emotional lives far more complex than calluses like Cobb could ever know. Cobb stood there in his raincoat and watched me cry as if I were just another of life's annoying little delays, like crosstown traffic.

"You were lovers, you and her?''

"Yes.''

"How long?''

"About three years, but she left a year ago.''

"You lived together?''

"Yes.''

"Where?''

"Here.''

"Why'd she leave?''

"She got sick of being with me.'' That wasn't exactly true, but it was all I could manage.

"So you're saying you haven't seen her in a year?"

"No, I've seen her. We have lunch . . ." I looked forward each week to those lunches and felt sad when Billie had to cancel because of commitments. I never had any commitments.

"We found your picture on her dresser."

"You did?"

"Does that surprise you?"

"Yes."

"Why did you pay her the sum of"—he consulted a black leather notebook—"of $2,158.68 each month?"

"For Jellyroll."

"What?"

"This dog. Jellyroll."

"Is that his name?" asked Loccatuchi. "Jellyroll? That's cute."

"He used to be Billie's dog."

"That's a lot of money for a dog."

"This dog makes a lot of money."

"You mean on TV?"

"And movies," said Loccatuchi. "Blinky."

"So how'd you arrive at the sum of $2,158.68?"

"That's what Billie wanted. I think it was a kind of a joke."

"I don't get it."

"Because it's not a round number."

"So how long have you been paying her that figure?"

"A year."

"Since she left?"

I nodded.

"That adds up to real money as the time goes by."

I saw what he was driving at, the bastard. "No, it doesn't," I said. "Jellyroll makes more than that every week."

"Wow," said Loccatuchi.

"Who was Miss Burke seeing over the last year?"

"I don't know."

"Do you know anyone with reason to kill her?"

"No."

"I understand she had a father in Hollywood, works in the movie business. That right?"

"Yes. She went out there to visit him several times."

"What's his name?"

"Burke, I guess."

"You ever meet him?"

"No."

"Mother?"

"Her mother died when Billie was a little girl. . . . Have you told her father?"

"We're trying. You sure Miss Burke didn't have weird sexual tastes?"

"I'm sure."

"Mr. Deemer, we need someone to identify the body."

"Huh? You mean you're not sure it's her."

"It's just a legal formality," said Loccatuchi. "It's much better for everybody when we have a positive ID."

God, I didn't want to see Billie dead. "When?" I asked.

"How 'bout now?"

"Now?"

"Unless you're too busy."

In a dying Buick we splashed east across the park on the Ninety-sixth Street transverse. Water stood axle-deep under the bridges after ten consecutive days of rain, and the traffic slowed to a cautious crawl to keep the engines dry. Loccatuchi drove and Cobb rode shotgun, me in the back alone. Cobb eyed the city and its movements with malice—potential felons everywhere. Even if I couldn't see his face reflected in the streaked side window, I would have felt the malice convected from the back of his neck.

We turned south on Second Avenue. The Buick's spent shocks set up a nasty swaying motion, like a boat rolling in a seaway. We'd hit a pothole—Second Avenue is an urban moonscape—and the car would reverberate for the next two blocks. I was getting sick. Raindrops on the window glass smeared the city lights like tears in my eyes. I adored Billie. The windshield wiper on Cobb's side had no rubber thing—a metal arm scratched back and forth, scarring the glass deeper with each swipe. We were south of Fifty-seventh Street before anyone spoke.

"So what've we got?" Cobb asked the broken wiper. "A simple sex killing? You say she wasn't weird sexually, but maybe you're wrong. Maybe you're lying for reasons I don't know yet."

I didn't say anything. I had this heavily buttered welder's glove lodged in my gullet.

"Maybe she took the wrong guy home to play tie-up. No sense to it, no purpose. We'll never catch a guy like that unless he does it again or fucks up pretty bad. But maybe it was something else. . . . What'd she do for a living?"

"Photographer," I mumbled. I was getting sicker with each pothole.

"What kinda photographer?"

"Bums," I said.

"What?"

"Bums. . . . You know, homeless."

"What else?"

"Nothing."

"Nothing? Bums don't come back and kill you, they don't like their portrait."

"I'm gonna throw up."

"Huh?" He spun around to look at me. "Sal—pull over! The guy's gonna hoop! Open the door, buddy! Don't blow in the car!"

We jerked to a stop, double-parked. I opened the door and immediately threw up near the tire of a Volkswagen. Pedestrians stopped. I could see their legs hesitate and then hurry on after they realized what they were watching. Cobb never turned around. I wouldn't have either. I hoisted myself up by the window handle and sat back limp. Only then did Cobb look into my face. Would I or would I not blow in his car?

"He's okay, Sal. Let's go." We did.

A staticky woman's voice on the radio said that a robbery was in progress at 108th and Broadway, my neighborhood, but Cobb switched it off. I curled into my corner and rested my head. I remembered the tiny mark, like a fleck of gold ore, in the iris of Billie's left eye, and the thought of it, milky and gray now, made me want to slam my fist into the back of Cobb's neck.

"How do you make a living photographin' bums?"

"You don't."

"So what'd she live off of? The two grand from you each month?"

"I guess."

"You lived with her, right? She have any income then?"

"No. . . . Was she naked?"

"Huh?"

"Was she naked?"

"No. Fully clothed." He stared at me. "I find out you know things you ain't saying, then I'm on your ass like a cheap suit. You hear?"

Bellevue. I should have known that's where it would be. The house of mirth. We turned onto Twenty-fourth Street, turned again between two festering green dumpsters and down a short, steep incline that ended at a closed garage door. Loccatuchi stuck something like a credit card between the jaws of a security device, and the door rose with a clatter. We drove into a sooty concrete parking garage.

Loccatuchi pulled up in front of an open elevator large enough to drive into. Cobb got out, opened my door and led me into the elevator. Was this the way the dead entered? Dented aluminum doors closed in front of us when Cobb pushed the button. We lurched up one floor, and the doors opened onto a long two-tone green hallway. The walls were puckered and peeling from generations of steam leaks like deep, infected wounds. We turned into other hallways, turned about six times through several sets of swinging metal doors, passed exhausted interns with aged eyes, bored cops who seemed to be nursing grudges, and nurses angry at the human condition. We paused while Cobb flashed his badge at a paunchy guard with a drinker's face who showed no sign of seeing Cobb, me, or the badge. Then, abruptly, wordlessly, Cobb stopped. He shouldered open a green metal door. We had arrived.

It was a kind of anteroom built as an afterthought into the large room beyond. The bottom half of the anteroom walls was made of plywood and painted battleship gray; the upper half was glass reinforced with chicken wire. I tried not to look into the big room beyond, but I did. I saw an autopsy table. What else could that thing be? Tools hung neatly on racks within easy reach of the table, their purposes all too imaginable. When I conjured Billie naked on that table, men about to demolish her with those shiny tools, I jerked my eyes away.

A black guy about twenty and a bloated white guy about thirty-five years older sat across from each other at a wooden table and played double solitaire. Cigarette butts floated in a half-dozen different styrofoam coffee cups. Nobody said anything. Cobb filled out a blue form like a library call slip and handed it to the black guy. The fat white guy didn't move, just sat there with his hands folded over his obscene gut and stared at the cards. My knees quivered. I couldn't keep them locked. This was impossible. I couldn't do this thing. I couldn't walk back there, look into Billie's dead face and say yes, that's her; that's the woman I still loved.

The black guy murmured the number, or whatever Cobb had written on the slip, got up, and led us through the door at the rear of the anteroom and into the morgue. The smell hit me hard. At first it seemed a hospital smell of alcohol and disinfectants, but I hadn't smelled anything yet.

The floors were spotless blue tile—that's what I tried to

look at. The black guy led us around a corner. There they were—two full walls of aluminum drawers. Our heels made clicking metallic sounds approaching.

The black guy found Billie's drawer and heaved it open. This was no hospital smell. This was the sort of stench that permeates the tissues of the lungs so deeply that for days you can smell it on each exhalation. When I was a kid, I was given a pet turtle in a plastic terrarium. He soon grew big enough to climb over the walls of his home. One night he did so and vanished. A week later we could smell him under the couch, but it was nothing compared to the stench that hit me when I rolled aside the couch and found my turtle dead in a dry puddle of his own fluids. Turtle or woman, they smell pretty much the same dead.

I hung back. It wasn't too late to bolt. Cobb looked into the drawer. "Christ, buddy," he said, "this ain't her. Shape the fuck up!" He slammed the drawer himself. Even Cobb seemed a little shaken by what he had seen in there. I was glad I'd hung back.

The black guy re-consulted the call slip and marched off down the row of drawers. Cobb followed, and I took a few tentative steps in that direction, careful to keep my eyes on the floor. Observe as few details as possible. It's the details that haunt. He pulled open another drawer and looked in. I knew what he was doing—he was matching the call slip to a tag wired on to Billie's big toe, but I watched that floor. Having got it right, the black guy stepped aside.

Billie's drawer was about neck high, with three more below her and one above. Cobb looked in, pulled back a green sheet that must have covered her face. Then he glanced back at me with a surprised look on his face that said what the fuck are you standing way over there for?

It *still* wasn't too late to bolt. I thought about it. I knew I'd never forget what I was about to see. I knew that years from now the sight of it, on a sunny, happy day, perhaps at the beach, would come flashing back at me. But I couldn't bolt. I approached.

She had no color at all. Even her lips, slightly parted but utterly neutral of expression, were chalky white. Her short black hair, still wet, curled in scallops and wisps on her white forehead. The contrast was shattering. I stood staring at her face. I saw that these weren't drawers at all; they were merely racks with no sides. Inside the dead lay unseparated in their common stink. I remembered her laugh, how the skin around her eyes wrinkled and danced as if she were squinting into the sun. Her laughter, particularly when I could cause it, always made me glad to be near. Her right eye was half open, but only the white showed, the pupil rolled back forever. The other one, the eye with the fleck of gold, was closed. Cobb didn't need to ask if I knew her or not.

"What was her real name?"

"What?"

"Billie Burke. That wasn't her real name, was it?"

"Yes," I said, and I reached up and closed her right eye with my index finger. Cobb made a reflex move to stop me, but it was done. Billie's face was as cold as a bathtub. Cobb folded the green sheet over her, and that was the end of it.

The black guy pushed the drawer shut. I watched her naked feet, which had been so ticklish, pass under my face and disappear.

When we returned to the anteroom, Loccatuchi was sitting on the table thumbing through a skin magazine. The swollen white guy hadn't moved. Loccatuchi stood up and handed me a piece of paper. "Sign here, please. It's a statement that you saw and positively identified her." I signed. "Thank you. I'll get a car going uptown for you."

"No, thanks," I said, "I'll take a cab. Just get me out of here."

"Mr. Deemer—" said Cobb.

I turned to him. He straddled a chair and sat down. I

didn't like the look in his eye. "Stick around town where we can find you."

"You don't really think I did that, do you?"

"Not really. But if you did, we'll find out about it. And we'll send Eugene here after you." He clapped the bloated white guy on the back. His flesh quivered, but he didn't move a muscle, didn't even blink, his fish eyes fixed on the cards.

"You guys got a great act here," I said.

Jellyroll sniffed my pants leg for a hint of where I'd been. I wondered if I smelled of death and if Jellyroll knew the smell in some dark atavistic way. I began to cry again. Jellyroll loved Billie too. She had saved his life— he was a sick little worm-eaten puff of fur when she rescued him from the pound. I sat down on the floor beside him and sobbed into the hair on the back of his neck. He licked my face, and we sat there for a long time in the dark.

My apartment is on the twelfth floor overlooking Riverside Park and the Hudson beyond. No streetlight filters up this high, not even reflection, and no one had seen the moon for two weeks. A total absence of light—except for two tiny red bulbs on my telephone answering machine. One red point of light indicates that the machine is on and taking calls; the other blinks to tell you it has taken one. When I'm feeling reclusive, in a solitary jazz mood, I can go days without answering the phone. Jellyroll has lost gigs because I've wanted to keep at bay the world below, and if things had been normal, I might have ignored that pulsing red light. But nothing was normal. I got up and played the waiting message:

"Hi, Artie, it's me." Christ, it was! It was Billie! "Are you there, Artie? . . . No? Okay. It's nine Sunday night. I'm going to my studio—please meet me there even if it's late. I've got something to give you. Please come. It's important. I'll see you, Artie." For a mindless instant I thought I would see her, that this night was some kind of mistake. All I had to do was go downtown to her studio and she'd be waiting, angry, maybe, because it had taken me so long.

I rewound and played the tape again, then twice more. Jellyroll sat beside me and seemed to listen. What if I had taken her call? I would have met her at her studio—or anywhere else—and she might have missed her killer. Or I might have fought him off. No, I tried to tell myself, I wasn't in her life deeply enough to be responsible for it.

CHAPTER

TWO

THE DAWN CAME UP SUNLESS AND RAINY. I HAD FALLEN asleep only an hour earlier. I had tried everything to make myself sleep, a couple of bones, bourbon. I tried reading about the Civil War, but I couldn't concentrate on General Beauregard's movements along the Rappahannock, and the carnage of Second Manassas took me near despair.

I dressed for the endless rain in rubber boots and an army poncho and took Jellyroll for a walk in Riverside Park. Knowing something was wrong, he hung close and did not stalk squirrels.

When Billie left a year ago, she said life with me was too easy, that it was sapping her ambition. I told her life could be harder. I could attend law school nights in Brooklyn; I could take a day job with a major corporation and work weekends loading concrete blocks. She thought I was kidding. Dreamy moments, I had even considered the future, fatherhood, domesticity, rustic summers in an Adirondack cottage, the young ones splashing in the lake. I held out hope that one day she would return. I didn't believe that business about sapped ambition, but I didn't press her. She'd come back one day, and then it wouldn't matter. I helped her move her stuff to Sullivan Street, and the moving done, she said she hoped I'd take Jellyroll, since there were no grassy parks in the Village. That wasn't the real reason, either. We both knew that by then Jellyroll had become my dog. Dog owning in Manhattan is such demanding work that it almost requires the absence of ambition.

It was April 29, Duke Ellington's birthday, but it didn't feel like spring at all. New buds were nothing more than stunted little kernels on the tips of wintry branches. Jellyroll and I waded through the mud and the wind all the way up to Grant's Tomb. Grant rests beside his beloved wife beneath a marble dome on its own little island in the traffic. Poor Ulysses S. He was not a drunken lout; he was a brilliant, sensitive general prone to bouts with melancholy over the nature of his profession, which he expressed in letters to his wife. Those written after the slaughter at Cold Harbor are particularly stirring. Jellyroll peed on a shiny black cannon, shook himself, and looked into my eyes—what are we going to do now?

Suddenly I knew what I'd do. I didn't weigh the pros and cons, view alternatives from each perspective, then, as usual, do nothing. I would get whatever it was Billie wanted to give me last night. She meant it for me. It was mine. Jellyroll cocked his head suspiciously. There were problems. What was it, this thing she wanted me to have? Could I carry it on my person, or would I need a U-Haul? Would I recognize it when I saw it? Where was it? In her studio, where she wanted to meet me? Or in her apartment, where she was murdered?

I would need to enter surreptitiously and leave without a trace. I needed an experienced person, someone familiar with criminal technique. But I didn't know anybody with those credentials. Except my lawyer.

My lawyer had been evicted from his office several months ago, but it had always been pointless to call him there. I called the pool hall. The deskman, Davey, told me yeah, he was there all right. He was playing nine ball for twenty bucks a game with Too Louis, a porky scumbag who at forty lived with his mother. She paid him to hang around the pool hall instead of around her.

Jerome's Billiard & Snooker Academy, East Eighth Street, third floor, up a set of granite stairs worn concave by the tread of academicians, a red flashing neon sign that says " ILLIARDS." Bums come in to pee under the stairs. I could smell it. And I could hear the magic click and fall of 2¼-inch spheres and the gasps of pain when they didn't fall. I inhaled deeply. I gave up the Game a while back. It's far too demanding and, like life, too revealing of character flaws. But I missed it. I even felt a twinge of sadness when I saw my old cue stick. My lawyer was leaning on it morosely.

Table eleven was surrounded by clots of spectators, some who didn't give a damn, some who only pretended not to, others who openly settled up side bets and talked out the corners of their mouths. Regulars, most of them, they nodded at me. Among the spectators stood Winky, by the drinking fountain. They called him Winky because he had this savage tic in his left eye that screwed up the whole side of his face, the result, someone unreliable told me, of his father's attempt to kill him with a cue stick when he was four.

"Your friend's a dumb fuck, Artie," said Winky.

"I know."

"He's spottin' Too Louis the seven ball and the break for twenty. Is that dumb fuck or what? How come we don't see you no more?"

"I've been working hard."

"The SPCA's gonna get yer ass."

Too Louis was taking aim on the seven ball—his pay ball, a long-rail cut with a danger of scratching in the side, but he missed it. He left the seven hanging in front of the corner pocket. The eight was about to fall in the opposite pocket of its own accord, and the nine—my lawyer's pay ball—was a duck in the side. My lawyer stepped to the table.

"Think you can handle that, pal?" asked Too Louis too loudly.

"I can handle anything you got, Louis," replied my lawyer. "Except your person."

"A fin says he don't get out from there, the dumb fuck," said Winky out the corner of his mouth.

"Winky, a child could get out from there."

"He can't get out with a crowbar."

"Okay, a fin," I said.

My lawyer stroked the seven, stopping the cue ball neatly, shot the eight in with a touch of high right English and rolled down for the nine, straight in the side. He aimed, stroked it—and missed. It jawed between the points of the pocket, where it died. Too Louis giggled, hiked up his seeds, waddled to the table, his thighs chafing, and pounded it in. I handed Winky his fin. "Dumb fuck," he muttered.

Winky had a point. Was this the man I came to consult on a delicate matter of criminal advice, a man who gives away a bad spot to a shark, then gags the pay ball straight in the side? My lawyer let two tens flutter to the table, where Too Louis scooped them up with fingers more like toes. "Wanna go again?" he asked my lawyer. "Yer only eighty bucks down. Yer comin' back." His eyes were all greed. If my lawyer had said yes, I would have left.

"No thanks. Go out and buy yourself a truckload of potato chips."

The spectators began to disperse in search of new action.

"Hello, Counselor," I said.

"Artie. Did you happen to see me miss that duck?"

"Yes."

"It must be this cue of yours."

"Warped, huh?"

"I can't think of any other explanation."

"No, me either. I need your advice."

"Do you mean in the legal sense?"

"No, in the illegal sense."

"Step into my office. Hey, Davey, can I use the office for consultation with a client?" he called to the deskman.

Davy nodded. "Good shot."

My lawyer led me around the back of the desk area and through a door that I knew led to the repair shop. A naked light bulb bounced on the end of its cord when my lawyer pulled the string. There were stacks of disabled cues piled against the back wall along with buckets, mops, and brooms. The room smelled of glue. We sat on the workbench, careful to avoid disturbing a lovely Joss cue clamped in the vise.

"Do you remember Billie Burke?" I asked.

"Sure. Took pictures of bums. You two used to be thick."

"She was murdered last night."

"Did you do it?"

"Of course not."

"As your attorney, I'm behooved to ask."

"I got a phone message from her shortly before she was killed. She said she had something to give me."

"What is it?"

"I don't know."

"You don't?"

"No, but I want it."

"Where is it?"

"I'm not sure."

"You're a bit vague on the specifics."

"It might be in her studio. There's a set of keys to the studio locked in her apartment, but that's where she was killed."

"Are you telling me you want to enter the scene of a murder in order to steal property of the deceased?"

"I'd just as soon break into her studio, but that might be harder."

"Forget the whole thing and smoke some of this."

"Well, thanks anyway," and I got off the workbench.

"Where is this apartment?" my lawyer asked.

"Sullivan Street."

"Old building or new building?"

"Old."

"Elevator?"

"No, stairs."

"What floor?"

"Fifth."

"Doorman?"

"No."

"Street door locked?"

"Yes."

"Basement?"

"Yes."

"You can't enter the apartment through her door because the police seal it up with stickers that say Crime Scene, Keep Out or You Get Stomped. That means you need to come in through the window. Fire escape?"

"Not on her side. . . . Wait, there's a dumbwaiter."

"A dumbwaiter? Where?"

"In the basement. It runs from the basement through each apartment. I just remembered—they use it for garbage."

"As your attorney, I advise you to stay out of narrow places."

CHAPTER

THREE

I LURKED UNDER THE LEAKY AWNING OF A GELATO STAND across the street from Billie's apartment house, one of those long, narrow five-story buildings common to the neighborhood. If you look closely, you notice that each has its own touch of character. Billie's has stone-sculpted stag heads, each different, mounted under the window-sills. I thought about those things to repress my sick fear.

I wore a pair of Con Edison coveralls from the trunk of my lawyer's car, where he keeps phony uniforms. If Winky could have seen me then, he would have said what a dumb fuck, and he would have been right. It's not too late, I told myself. You haven't done anything crazy yet, it's not too late to catch the IRT at Sheridan Square, change to the express at Fourteenth, and in twenty-five minutes be plugged into a classic like "Good-bye, Porkpie Hat." An identification tag in a clear plastic pocket was pinned to my heart. I was Tyrone Washington, Inspector #5533. My glasses fogged up.

I looked both ways. It was getting dark. People were coming home from work. No one looked suspicious except me. I was lurking under this awning in a Con Ed suit. In

New York you don't pay attention to people who seem to be heading somewhere. That's one reason why the pace is so quick. I moved on, two blocks north toward NYU. I didn't see anybody who looked like a cop. But how the hell would I know he was a cop if he was trying not to look like one? I passed a short, wrinkled Italian woman in a black dress, black shoes and socks. That, for all I knew, could be the best disguise on the force.

I turned around and walked directly to Billie's stoop, where I pretended to check the address in a tiny notebook that didn't exist. I tried the door, but of course it was locked. Now I'd have to ring someone's bell. Tyrone Washington here to inspect the old boiler.

"Can I help you?"

"Haw!"

"Didn't mean to scare you. Guess we're all jumpy right now." It was a little man about sixty. The second-best disguise on the force? No, I remembered him. With Billie, I'd passed him on the stairs. He squinted at me. He wore a shapeless yellow slicker, hood up, that made him look like a fire hydrant. "We had a killing in this buildin' last night."

"A killing. Gee."

"Yep. Woman up on five. She was a wild one."

"Look, your boiler's due for inspection. It'll take about an hour."

"I didn't know Con Ed inspected boilers."

"Oh yes."

"I ain't had any heat lately."

"I'll check it out."

"Who the hell should need heat in springtime? Gettin' nastier every year. It's the Second Ice Age we're lookin' at here." He opened the door, and I followed him in. He led me down the hall and showed me the stairway to the basement. I started down, and he made to follow.

"I'm sorry, sir, but insurance regulations prohibit tenants from the scene of an inspection."

"In-surance. Biggest bunch of grifters in the world. My wife fell in a pit over on Bleecker. You think they paid?"

I pretended to begin my inspection.

"Dirty grifters," he said, and then he walked away.

There it was beside the boiler, the ancient dumbwaiter. The door, an unpainted plywood replacement of the original, hung open. I knelt down and peered up the shaft. It was pitch-black and stunk of wet plaster and rotten fruit, but I folded myself in and pulled the door closed behind me. I stood up in the little box—like a miniature sandbox—and I could feel naked brick at either shoulder. Something touched my face. I waved it away. A roach? A rat? I waited for my eyes to adjust, but they won't adjust to total darkness. Fool! Moron! I brought no flashlight! That thing touched my face again. I knocked it away. It didn't feel like something alive. I reached out slowly and grasped it—rope. There would have to be rope. I stood there sweating in my Con Ed overalls and tried to have a talk with myself. *Think,* I told myself. Think or go home. I ignored the fact that if I really *had* thought, I would have gone home. Forget the subway; call a helicopter.

Which rope takes it up? I was thinking clearly enough to understand that there had to be two ropes. I pulled a rope at random. I pulled a lot of rope before I moved upward with a lurch. I kept pulling and began to ascend steadily up the smelly crypt. A thin bar of light appeared at eye level, and I stopped pulling. I listened. Someone was rattling pots and pans. Of course. This would be the first floor. That's how I could tell what floor I was on—just count the bars of light coming from people's kitchens. I pulled onward and upward. The light passed out of sight, and I began to notice that this whole apparatus was creaking and groaning like the soundtrack to *Billy Budd*. What if the rope should pack it in? It wasn't built for this kind of weight. What if right now it was unraveling down to a single strand like a cartoon rope? Then that would be it for Tyrone Washington, and the dirty in-surance grifters wouldn't pay a dime to bury the dumb fuck.

Another light bar appeared and passed. I felt something squishy beneath my boot, but I kept pulling myself deeper into this reverse mine shaft. Another light, then another, passed beneath me. That made four. One more. My stop. But it didn't appear. I should be there by now. Wait. There would be no light in Billie's kitchen. The lower four were full of living people, happy couples cooking something special, telling each other about their day. But Billie wasn't in. I felt the wall for a break in the brick, for the wooden door. It was directly in front of me. The door was barely two feet square. I lowered myself until it was at about waist level and pushed on the door, but it wouldn't open. Was it locked? Was there some kind of hook? I hadn't come this far to be impeded by a cheap piece of wood. I kicked it out. It was no brighter in Billie's kitchen than in the mine shaft.

One entered Billie's little apartment through the kitchen, which meant that the front door—and the light switch—was to my left. I wormed out of the dumbwaiter and half crawled to the door. I rubbed at the wall on either side, but no light switch. Maybe it wasn't a wall switch at all. I hadn't been here for over a year. Maybe it was an overhead light with a string pull. I realized as I waved the air like a deranged traffic cop that I was beginning to panic. I felt little-boy fears. What would I find when I finally got the light on? Who would be there with me, sitting on the couch grinning at me? Maybe Cobb. Or the killer. Maybe Billie herself.

I stopped waving for the light pull and stood still, panting. The stove! I knew where the stove was in relation to the door, next to the refrigerator, and that was to my left with my back to the door. I touched the refrigerator, reached out from there, and found the stove. I turned two dials, and bright blue flame danced in circles. I was alone. At the scene of Billie's murder. I turned on the light by pulling the string that hung near the tip of my nose.

There were only three little rooms, the cramped kitchen, a living room, and bathroom. A sleeping loft that Billie and I built from scratch covered a portion of the living room and the entrance to the bathroom. I always liked this apartment. Seemingly separate from the city, it had the feel of a little country cottage in the Adirondacks, or with its high wooden wainscoting, like the cabin of a sailboat. But there was none of that feeling left. It struck me that this was how I'd remember her apartment, not cozy and warm and vaguely sexual but this way—stuffy and grim.

The keys hung on a nail in the broom closet near the stove. I pocketed them. *Now get out.* . . . The floor was still wet. Did he drown her in cold water? I squished into the living room, and her red carpet bled over my boots. A pair of shiny blue spandex tights lay draped over the sofa. I picked them up and pressed them to my face, but her scent was gone. Still I rolled them up and stuffed them into my Con Ed pocket. Then I walked into the bathroom.

The tub was still full, and everything was smeared with gray-black grease. Had he smeared her body with it, too? Was that part of the fun? Tiles, tub, sink, toilet, even her shampoo, lotions, and things were all caked with grease. Congealed islands of it floated on the surface of the water. My knees unlocked, and I caught myself on the greasy towel rack, leaving a perfect handprint. . . . Fingerprints. That's what the grease was for. The police had left her bathroom this way. I wiped my fingerprints off with a towel. I had seen enough.

I crawled back into the garbage shaft and rode it to the basement. I walked dizzily south to Houston and hailed a cab for home. I'd do the studio tomorrow. Or the next day.

I saw her as I unlocked my apartment door. A long-legged women in jeans and yellow nylon jacket was sitting on the fire stairs.

"Are you Jellyroll?" she asked.

CHAPTER

FOUR

"JELLYROLL IS A DOG."

"A dog? . . . Aw, Jesus!" She stood up. She was about thirty-five or so. Black curly hair sprang from her head like an Afro. She wore those half-rubber, half-leather boots you see in outdoor catalogs. "Who are you then?"

"Artie Deemer. Who—?"

"*You're* Artie Deemer?" She said it as if I were a big disappointment. "Look, this is from Billie." She drew from her back pocket a white business envelope that maintained the curve of her ass when she handed it to me. She turned abruptly and made for the elevator.

Across the front of the envelope in her unmistakable backslanting hand, Billie had written: "To Jellyroll." But the envelope had already been opened. Inside was a single sheet of paper folded twice. A key fell out and dropped on my boot. I picked it up and then quickly read the note. "I'm dead, darling. Get out of your chair, look in the ice tray—Acappella. Always loved you both."
What?

I turned to the messenger.

The elevator door opened. She got in. I yanked her

out, much more roughly than I intended. She kicked me hard in the shin with those damn L.L. Bean boots, and I went down on one knee. She pulled something from her handbag, something black and cylindrical, and pointed it at me. "Keep your distance or I hose you down," she said. Mace. It fit her hand in a sure and practiced way, like a compact in the hand of a seventeen-year-old cheerleader.

"I'm sorry," I said. "I didn't mean to grab you. Okay? I'm going to stand up now. Don't hose me."

The elevator door closed behind her, but she pushed the button, and it opened again.

"Please don't go," I said. "I loved Billie. I didn't hurt her."

"Just stay right there. . . . Billie let me believe that Jellyroll was a person. Why am I delivering a note like this to a dog! That's not so funny." She had a twangy accent.

"No, it isn't. I was surprised too. That's why I grabbed you. I won't do it again. Put that thing away."

Just then Mrs. Fishbein came out of 12C. The frizzy-haired messenger dropped the Mace down the open flap of her handbag and stepped into the elevator. I quickly followed.

"Ar-tee!" screeched Mrs. Fishbein. "Hol' zat car!"

I held it. What else could I do? Mrs. Fishbein dragged her stroke-warped legs into the tiny elevator with Frizzy and me. Mrs. Fishbein wore a yellow poncho that made her look like a crumpled bumper car from Rye Playland. "Zo, Ar-tee, hoz's my Jellyroll?"

"Fine."

"I lof zat animal," she said to Frizzy, as if she offered any indication that she gave a shit. She glanced coldly at Mrs. Fishbein and looked away. Mrs. Fishbein didn't care. She never noticed the response or lack of it from those she talked at. You could be dragging yourself along the sidewalk with two broken tibias and she'd tell you how, when he finally died, her husband's brain was the size of a valnut. "I jus' hope one zing, is all I hope. I hope you younk people nefer get olt. If it ain't za colon, it's za limpfiss glans." That elevator ride seemed to take two days.

When we finally reached the lobby, Frizzy pulled her hood over her hair and bolted.

"Gotta run, Mrs. F.," I said. Ordinarily I'd have walked her to the store or at least as far as Broadway, but not today.

"Yes, you younk people run alonk."

The messenger turned east, and I strode carefully up behind her, but I hung back when I saw her hand burrow into her shoulder bag.

"Just give me an explanation, that's all," I pleaded, but she kept walking, shoulders hunched against the rain. I quickened my pace and came up beside her without making any sudden moves that would get me hosed down. We walked silently to the corner.

"Billie and I were lovers," she said.

"You were?" I said stupidly. "I-I didn't know she—"

"Yeah." She scurried across Broadway against the light.

"What does this letter mean?"

"What it says, I guess."

"What's in the ice tray?"

"I don't know."

"You didn't look?"

"No."

"But you opened the letter—"

"What would you have done?"

"Why did Billie think she might die?"

"Look, what do I know? I just deliver messages to dogs."

"There's a place up Broadway, just a block up. Let's get out of the rain and talk. Please."

"Yeah. . . . Okay."

The River Liffey used to be a grotty sports bar with a

serious game in the back room, but Jim was a man of foresight. He recognized the neighborhood trend toward gentrification and changed his image. "Class, hoss," he told me. "That's how you suck in the upscale master-blasters." I liked it better before. Billie's ex-lover and I took a booth away from the bar and ordered coffee.

"How did you get this note?" I asked.

"Billie left it with my mother."

"When?"

"Yesterday. There was another note that said if she should die, I should deliver the other note to Jellyroll."

"Where is your note now?"

"I threw it away. . . . Is she really dead?"

"Yes. I saw her body at the morgue."

She began to cry silently.

"Did you really think she wasn't?"

"No." She wiped her eyes on a paper napkin. "I just hoped."

"I don't understand why she thought she'd be killed."

"I don't either. I told you." She was squeezing back tears by sheer force of will.

"What's your name?" I asked.

"Sybel."

"Where did you know Billie from?"

"Work."

"You're a photographer?"

"No."

"What are you?"

"I work in the neighborhood. Near her studio. I work for an antiques dealer across the street. She came in about a year ago looking for chairs, but we only sell to dealers. Wholesale. I told her that. We got to talking."

"What's the name of the antiques store?"

"Renaissance."

"She left me about a year ago."

"Yeah, well, she left me six months later."

"For a man or woman?"

"For a man named Leon Palomino."

"You're kidding."

"That's his name."

"What is he, an actor?"

"He's a trucker."

"Trucker?"

"He moves valuable antiques. It's pretty specialized."

A scuffle broke out near the bar. A woman squealed, and two upscalers dressed out of the Land's End catalog shoved at each other's chests, Reeboks shuffling for traction.

"Quit that fightin', hoss," Jim shouted, but they didn't. Jim produced a Louisville Slugger and rapped the bar with it. "Quit fightin' or I slap you shitless." The upscalers quit shoving each other, and the woman stomped out.

"Nice place," said Sybel.

"It used to be. . . . Do you know what this means? It means somebody killed Billie for a reason. I mean, as opposed to some freak who killed her for kicks."

"No kidding?"

"Pardon me. I'm slow. You're way ahead. You already knew that."

"Look, if somebody gets killed after leaving a note saying they expected it, then it's likely not random. You don't need Paul Drake."

"So who did it? Leon Palomino?"

"For all I know, you killed her."

"Same here."

"Right. We've got the basis for a beautiful relationship."

I wondered for an instant who, given the choice, Billie would rather have slept with. "Do you want to look in that ice tray?"

"No, I do not. I did my part. I delivered the letter. I don't want to hear about it again. I should have taken it straight to the police, but instead I did what Billie wanted. What else is new? Anyway, you're on your own.''

"Maybe we could be a little less hostile for now."

"I'm not hostile. I'm angry."

"At Billie?"

"Sure, wouldn't you be?"

I didn't even know. "This Palomino person, was Billie still seeing him?"

"She dumped him, too."

"Man or woman?"

"For his twin brother."

"What?"

"You don't know about Billie's exploits?"

"No." And I didn't want to hear about them.

"You lived with her, right?" Sybel asked. "Well, maybe she changed."

"What do you think's in the ice tray?"

"Listen to me: I don't know *anything*. I've got to go." She picked two quarters from her purse. I saw the Mace next to a fluffy stuffed whale. She laid the quarters beside her coffee cup.

"What kind of guys are these Palominos?"

"Freddie's okay. Leon's a dolt. Freddie's wife left him; took the kids and moved to Latin America somewhere. Freddie was always kind of mopey most of the time. Vulnerable. Leon's got these two plastic nudes standing in the back window of his Camaro. Their boobs rotate as the car moves." She stood up.

"How can I get in touch with you?" I asked.

"Why would you want to do that?"

"In case I think of something."

"Think fast."

"Can I call you at Renaissance?"

"No, stay away from there."

"Why?"

"It ties up the lines."

"How about at home?"

38

She peered at my eyes, looking for angles, then rummaged in her purse for a broken Bic and a crumpled cash-register receipt. She scrawled her number. "So long, Jellyroll," she said. Two horny yuppies at the bar discussed her ass as she walked out.

Go home, I told myself. Listen to something with Dexter Gordon in it.

CHAPTER

FIVE

UPPER BROADWAY SEEMED HAPPY IN THE RAIN. LIGHTS twinkled. Arm in arm under single umbrellas, happy white couples strolled from *The Stranger,* playing at the Thalia. Smiling Hispanic couples in party clothes gathered outside the Tropical Ballroom, from which floated purple light and salsa. A black couple waited at the stoplight in a gas guzzler that shook with their laughter. Those of all races out for a good time. Even the Korean grocers giggled, hacking carrots. I pulled my hood up and hailed a southbound gypsy cab, told the driver Eleventh and Broadway, please.

Acappella Productions was on the third floor of the old Hotel St. Denis. Abraham Lincoln stayed there soon after John Brown seized the Federal Arsenal at Harpers Ferry. Lincoln walked from the hotel in a chill February drizzle to Cooper Union, where for the first time he addressed the big-city audience: "All they ask, we could readily grant, if we thought slavery right; all we ask, they could readily grant, if they thought it wrong." Except for a handsome, curving marble-and-wrought-iron stairway, nothing of the old St. Denis remained. The six floors are chopped up into tiny offices leased by therapists, raggedy-ass lawyers, mail-order book operations, and Central European émigré organizations maintaining a low profile. Billie was the only photographer.

I stepped from the cab into a four-inch gutter torrent bound for the sea. Two winos sheltering under the awning watched me wade up onto the sidewalk. One nodded gravely at the torrent and said, "We got a severe drainage problem here."

"Fuck the circus," said his associate.

I squelched up the steps and unlocked the street door with Billie's key. Was I being watched? I looked around. Only winos. There it was, Renaissance Antiques, across the street, a square four-story ex-warehouse or factory from the days of light industry in Lower Manhattan. Cages were drawn down over the new, incongruous plate-glass windows full of furniture, but I was supposed to be looking for people. I saw none.

I walked up to Billie's floor and stopped on the dark landing to listen. Somewhere water slowly dripped. ACAPPELLA PRODUCTIONS, said the hand-carved wooden letters. Billie photographed bums exclusively, no smiling vacations, no puppies (not even Jellyroll), no sunsets or sailboats. She published a slim volume of horrific faces so stark and real, so diseased, one could feel the wet pus in their untended sores. Staunchly, admirably, noncommercial—that was my insightful view. I never said, "Look here, lover, why not a cuddly puppy in the fucking sunset every once in a while?" I wonder if Billie resented my blindness.

The lock had been drilled out. I fumbled with her key in the dim light before I recognized that there was a hole the size of your thumb where the cylinder should have been. I pushed the door open. The light was still on.

The room had been ransacked. Something had picked it up, given it a violent rattle, and put it back down. Photographs and contact sheets covered the floor ankle-deep. Stubbly, grimy, and damaged faces stared up at me without hope. All the photos on the wall, Billie's favorites, had been twisted from their frames and demolished. Two tall filing cabinets lay on their sides, empty. Stripped of drawers, Billie's desk had been flipped on its back. The darkroom door hung ajar. I looked in. Ransacked. Plastic developing trays, chemical bottles, drying racks, and all the other arcane apparatus hurled about. Even her enlarger had been torn apart. The destruction was total but not mindless. Somebody had searched for something. You didn't need Paul Drake.

I knelt down in front of Billie's little half refrigerator and opened the door. It was full of clothes. What an unusual place to store your laundry, in a refrigerator. . . . Gradually I understood. There were clothes in there, all right, but not laundry. These clothes were being *worn*— by a very dead man all curled up. Somebody must have levered him in with crowbars. You couldn't have fit a box of Arm & Hammer in with him. His knees were drawn up tight under his chin, and his back and neck were bent in a way no living man could stand. His forehead was pressed hard against the freezer section, a little box mounted in the upper corner. That forehead—I only saw it for an instant, but I'll never forget that forehead frozen blue-black and frosted all the way down over his eyebrows. Where the black skin ended, a band of fire red began—as if all the blood in his dead body had been somehow sucked by the cold into his face. Even the whites of his eyes were flaming red like the demon's in bad science fiction.

I ran in animal terror. I slipped and skated over the downtrodden and, out of control, slammed into the door headfirst. I managed to get my hands up fast enough to protect my face but not my glasses. They struck the door a blow that bent them flat and bruised the bridge of my nose. Once out, I sprinted for the stairs.

When you don't do much besides listen to bop, you tend not to experience mortal terror. I had no idea what it does to the muscles. They get a squirt of juice that causes them to contract out of control. I could have run right up the wall, but I didn't. Instead, I stopped dead at the top of the stairs. I had heard a noise. Footsteps. The tap-tapping of hard heels. From where? Coming up the stairs, heading my way. I stood panting, waiting for rational thought to catch up. I dove through the men's room door. The footsteps reached the top of the stairs, then grew louder still. Right outside! I leaped into a stall and latched the door.

He entered the restroom after me. I sat on the seat so my feet would be positioned convincingly. Think! What would I do if he tore the door off the stall? Kick him in the nuts. My only hope. He ran water in the sink. Probably to cover the sound of my screams. Cautiously I peeked out under the stall.

What? Red stockings? Thin, shapely ankles and high-heeled shoes? She washed her hands, dried them on a paper towel, and walked out, heels tap-tapping, fading to silence. I unlatched and pushed open the door of the stall. For a quarter, I noticed, I could get reliable feminine protection from a vending machine on the wall. I sat there for a long time, trembling. The right earpiece of my glasses stuck straight out to the side, and my nose hurt. I don't know how long I sat there before I was capable of reshaping my glasses and considering my next slick move. I still didn't have what I'd come for, assuming it was still there. No, forget the whole thing. The only sane move was to find the nearest phone and call the cops. I couldn't go back into that office. No. Out of the question. . . . Yet I had come a long way to get here—here in the women's john with my hands twitching, my glasses perched at a drunken angle. It was the surprise that had devastated me. That only happens once; I knew now that in fact there was a corpse in the fridge. If I were to return, I wouldn't feel that same mind-altering terror. Would I? Naww. Hell, I wouldn't even need to look at him. I could cover the fridge with my poncho and reach in for the ice tray. I could even call the cops after I'd done that. At least then I'd know what it was Billie had left for me. I *wanted* to know that.

The poncho slid off as I was reaching in for the ice tray, but I averted my eyes from the frozen face. The ice tray contained no cubes. Instead, the little molds held thirty-five-millimeter negatives, each individually cut to fit. I crouched beside the corpse and emptied the negatives onto the eight-by-ten glossy face of a ragged and clearly insane bag lady. There were about a dozen of them, but I didn't stop to count. I stacked them in a single pile and put them in my shirt pocket, where they would be safe from the rain. I replaced the now empty ice tray and closed the refrigerator door.

Wait. There's a body in your murdered ex-lover's ice box. Can you close the door on it with no effort to determine its identity? I reopened the door and coldly studied the contorted form. He was sitting on his wallet, which meant I had to move him—assuming, of course, I was up to the morbid task.

I grasped folds of his brown leather jacket and pulled. He didn't budge. I tried several sharp, short jerks to crack him loose, but that didn't do it, either. I sat on the floor and braced my boots against the frame of his coffin to get my back into it like an oarsman. That dislodged him with a sickening rip.

When I was a dumb little kid about nine, an older boy whom I idolized because he had a paper route told me that to sled his hill with the other paperboys, I would first have to touch my tongue to the naked steel runner. When I withdrew my tongue, I heard the skin rip as if made of cloth, and seeing the little circle of it frozen to the runner made the pain seem doubly intense. I've never forgotten that ripping sound. And that's exactly what happened to this poor dead man's forehead. A big pocky, bloody bowl of skin stuck fast to the aluminum side of the freezer box. I never did look square at this forehead, but I saw it peripherally—white bone from his hairline to his brow. He was nearly halfway out of the refrigerator.

His right cheek hung over the edge. If he was right-handed, that's where he'd carry his wallet. If he was left-handed, I decided, I'd forget the whole project. I removed his cold wallet and a black Ace pocket comb with flecks of dandruff in it. I searched his wallet in a kind of crazy compulsive haze. It held four tens and a five, a scuba diver's certification card, a membership to a Y in Queens, a condom in a foil packet, a poorly exposed photo of a kid on a tricycle, and a New York driver's license that said he lived at 2150 Woodlawn Avenue and that his name was Frederick Palomino. Billie's ex-lover. For whom she dropped Leon. For whom she dropped Sybel, for whom she dropped me. Now dead as a frozen claw hammer.

A person can act, move, perform tasks while the brain has checked right out. That's probably what happens in combat. Utterly repulsed, the brain says *adiós,* you're on your own if you plan to keep messing with this madness. I was *aware* of what I was doing—that I was leafing through a dead man's life, that I ripped off his forehead to get at it—but my brain wasn't making any judgments about it. I was brewing up a pot of coffee, toasting an English muffin, tasks, nothing more.

I slid the chilled black leather back into his pocket, and with my feet I shoved him back into the tiny crypt. His head went in crooked, protruding, but I forced the door closed and gave it a sharp rap with my boot, then another, until I beat Palomino's skull in far enough for the latch to catch.

After you toast the coffee and brew the bread, then what you do is wipe your fingerprints off the appliances. Routine. Do it every day. Get the fingerprints off the light switch and off the doorknob. With the back of my hand I pushed the studio door open a crack and listened. I stepped out into the empty hall and realized I was soaking wet—even my feet were sweaty—but I was out of that charnel house with what I came for in my shirt pocket. Now I was just a guy walking down the hall on the way home after a long but rewarding day spent in the furtherance of his chosen career—frozen foods. Then I heard footsteps. I stopped. Another fresh jolt of seemingly inexhaustible adrenaline shot through my body, but I walked on innocently toward the stairs. The footsteps came closer. These weren't the sounds of the delicate heels I'd seen in the women's john. These had a heavier sound.

He was a shrimp of a guy about sixty, with horn-rims and two comical tufts of hair above each ear but nowhere else. He looked like a tall midget. He passed me and turned down Billie's hall. As he did so, our eyes met for an instant. I saw a flash of surprise or fear—whatever it was, it was plainly not the intentional disinterest of strangers passing in a hallway. I looked back. So did he. Then he turned around and accelerated. I watched him go. He stopped in front of Billie's door and turned to me.

"Where's Barnett Osley?" he demanded of me.

"Who?"

"Are you part of this photography crowd?"

"I—no—"

"I beg your pardon." He turned and headed for the back stairs.

What? I stood rooted stupidly in my spot as he turned out of sight.

I ran down the central stairs and reached the lobby in time to see Stretch hurry out the front door into the street. He turned right. I hurried to the door and looked out. Stretch crossed Eleventh, and for a moment I thought he was heading for the front door of Renaissance Antiques, but he turned left onto Broadway.

I crossed Broadway to follow more discreetly from the other side. *Was I part of the photography crowd?* He scurried across Thirteenth and continued north without looking back. But then suddenly he stopped dead in his tracks and turned to survey the street behind him. Just in time I ducked down in a crouch behind a parked car. Walking arm in arm, two fellows under a giant golf umbrella turned from Thirteenth onto my side of Broadway. When they saw me, their conversation ceased in mid-sentence, and they hugged the building to give me, clearly a drug-crazed hub-cap thief, a wide berth. I pretended to be very concerned with my wheel well, but Stretch spotted me. He ran north toward Union Square. Tiny arms and legs churning in a wet blur, he made it across Fourteenth against the light, and he vanished into Union Square Park, a menacing patch of darkness in the middle of the traffic.

Picture books of old New York show Union Square Park as an elegant, sunny refuge from one of the city's busiest intersections. Couples, now dead, stroll arm in arm in dapper suits and frilly ankle-length gowns. Vestiges of its former state—mature English planes and elms, a bronze statue of George Washington astride a huge horse, and a monument to the Union with the entire text of the Declaration of Independence printed in noble bronze letters—still remain, but at night it's no place to be. Bands of small-time dopers, dealers, and chain snatchers own the place after sundown, and the Declaration of Independence is graffitied into nonsense.

The park and most of the surrounding square were slated for restoration. Several of the old buildings you see in the picture books already lay in confused piles of rubble. Two hulking, dirty bulldozers sat near the park entrance like great yellow crustaceans feeding on muddy chunks of sidewalk, and rolls of chainlink fence were stacked like firewood nearby, ready to encircle the park, once the thugs were driven out. I walked into the darkness.

You're a damn fool, I told myself. People were getting killed; besides which, I had no clear idea of the purpose of this trip. What was I going to do, tackle Stretch and sit on him until he told me what the hell's going on? I stopped ten yards in, waiting for my eyes to adjust. I listened. I watched Cobb draw a chalk line around my spread-eagled dead body. It didn't mean a thing to him, routine. Then the rain washed away the lines. I saw movement, a dark shape, darker than the background.

"Help!" It was Stretch, the same squeaky voice that asked if I was part of the photography crowd. "Help me! Please!"

"Hey, assho'—" This was a different voice, a deeper one, a mean one, and it came from behind me. I spun. "Why don' you pick on a man y' own size?"

There were four of them, dim, huge shapes moving to encircle me. "Who are you?" I asked stupidly.

"We jus' members o' the community, tha's all, an' we don' like to see assho's like you beatin' up on dorfs."

"Oh, you don't understand," I said. "That's my old man. He's been drinking—he's been on the sauce, you know. Mom—uh, Mom wants him home. She's sick. Very sick. Colon trouble. That's why the old man's been on the sauce. This is just a domestic problem, but I sure do appreciate you looking out for the old man."

"No! No!" squealed Stretch from somewhere back behind the Declaration of Independence. "That man means to kill me!"

"Oh, come on, Dad. It's me, Frank."

"Don' you fret, Pop. You get on outta here. We take care o' this assho'."

On any given evening in Union Square, these thugs would be delighted to stomp Stretch into the cobblestones for his loose change, but not that evening. They were suddenly public-spirited citizens. "Hey, assho', why don' you pick on Slicer here. He's 'bout yo' size." A hulking form about the size of George Washington's horse stepped toward me. I could hear that rotten little Stretch sprinting north out of the park, leaving me with Slicer and the Merry Men of Sherwood.

I turned and ran. Ran hard. For about six strides. Until

I hit a fence, a solid little wrought-iron welded bastard of a fence about thigh-high (except to Slicer, to whom it would seem a croquet wicket). I went ass over canteen, struck a tree trunk and landed in the mud at its base. I was hurt, and I had felt negatives brush my face when my shirt pocket was upturned. The shadowy figures peered over the fence at me lying in the mud.

Conversations about urban violence aren't uncommon in New York. At a dinner party, say, someone might tell you how their doorman found this headless, limbless torso in the air shaft. In one such dinner conversation, I heard a very attractive woman say that what you want to do in the face of imminent assault is to fake a fit. "You mean like an epileptic fit?" asked a diner interested in specifics. "Hell, any kind," the woman said. "Most muggers don't have medical degrees." That's what I did. Faked a fit. *All* kinds. I screamed in unbearable agony and bowed my spine in seizure, I made claws of my fingers and twitched them, I bellowed, gurgled, and I slapped my shoes together.

"Th' fuck's he doin'?"

"Dyin' looks like."

"Just what the assho' deserves pickin' on dorfs. Hey, assho', you goin' straight to hail."

I sustained convulsion, and just before I exhausted myself, the Merry Men faded into the darkness. Then I rolled over and started digging in the mud. On hands and wounded knees I groveled in the mud for negatives, like Silas Marner searching for his stash. I was out of character to the point of derangement. As I found one, I shoved it hysterically into my shirt pocket along with gouts of mud. I wasn't sure how many I found. Maybe all of them; probably not. When I could search no more, I dragged myself back over the fence and out of that miserable park. I tried to hail a cab from the northern end near the subway station.

Five passed me. Then two more, even though I was

waving wildly. I realized why—they thought I was a madman. I wouldn't have disputed them. I pulled bills from my pockets and waved them at the next cab.

"I'm a mud wrestler," I told the driver when he gave me that New York are-you-nuts? glance.

"Ya lost, huh?" he said.

CHAPTER

SIX

I REMOVED MY CRUSTY CLOTHES, THEN WASHED THE NEG-atives in a pasta strainer. I laid them side by side on a glass table and put a desk lamp on the floor beneath them. Too much glare. I put my muddy T-shirt over the lamp.

People, singly and in groups. All strangers to me. I felt let down and frustrated. What did I expect? A face with a sign held beneath its chin saying *I did it?*

Sybel could tell me about these Palominos. I fished her number from my pants and phoned her. I tried to figure out a way of questioning her without mentioning that at least one Palomino was frozen stiff. It wasn't so much that I didn't trust Sybel, more that I wanted nothing to place me at the scene. But I was in no condition to plot, so I decided to wing it:

"Haw-wo?" An Oriental woman, probably old—I woke her up.

"May I please speak to Sybel?"

"Ha?"

"Sybel."

"No See-ball! No See-ball!"

"I'm sorry."

I hung up. Maybe I didn't trust Sybel, after all. I'd have to call again to be sure I didn't misdial.

"Haw-wo!"

Why didn't I call the police? Billie had placed in my hands major evidence. Billie hadn't sent it to the police. She sent it to me. She was trying to communicate with *me*. Duke Ellington's birthday was the start of a long flight from my Morris chair, and if I called in the cops, I'd never get off the ground.

Like a twisted old arthritic, I got up at eight, because Jellyroll had a nine o'clock call. Ordinarily, he doesn't have to audition. They know him. If he's the right type, they just phone with the gig. But today we had to audition—for a TV movie called *Dracula's Dog*. The way I heard the idea, Dracula had this dog, a pet that he took everywhere and that, I guess, lay around the coffin all day and pissed in the hometown dirt. They originally wanted a mean-eyed rottweiler with rabies, but then some dork decided "to go the other way!" Get Dracula a cute and cuddly dog and film the whole thing in Samoa. The dog is so cute and cuddly that Dracula, moved, mends his bloodsucking ways and joins the Polynesian Legal Aid Society. Or something like that. When the alarm went off, I almost called to cancel, but . . . Jellyroll had always wanted to see Samoa.

"Hey, Artie, how's it goin'?"

"Hi, Vinnie." Vinnie was lame. His knee didn't seem to work. He lay nearly supine on the black leather couch in the reception room at ABC over on Sixty-ninth near Columbus. A buff-colored cocker spaniel named Roger sat at Vinnie's feet and panted nervously.

I told the receptionist at her little window that Jellyroll was here. Everyone hops to when he shows up. Sometimes it's embarrassing. She asked me if I wouldn't please have a seat for just one moment; then she went off to pass the word to the heavies—Jellyroll's here to save your asses.

I took a leather seat beside Vinnie. Jellyroll and the blond cocker sniffed and circled and wagged their tails.

"Hello, Mr. Deemer," said a fleshy woman from across the room.

"Oh, hello, Mrs. Sackley." Mrs. Sackley was a professional handler who always wore gloves, as if she didn't want actually to *handle* an animal.

"I see your Jellyroll every time I switch on the set," she said with a frigid smile. Jellyroll moved over to sniff her schnauzer, but Mrs. Sackley didn't approve of sniffing. She shielded the schnauzer with a mammoth leg. "Isn't your Jellyroll sweet," she said. Her eyes said, "I hope the fucker gets distemper and cashes his check." I called Jellyroll back before Mrs. Sackley slipped him a ground-glass burger.

"Hey, Artie," said Vinnie. "Last Hurrah in the fifth at the Meadowlands. Great mudder—best mudder I ever saw in twenty years. Pontoons for hooves. A sawbuck on the nose'll land the smart man two bills. I just wanted you to know."

"Okay, thanks, Vinnie," I said, but I knew he'd never leave it at that.

"I got pals in the paddock. They showed me his hooves. The size of your head!" His eyes, the left one clouded with cataracts, pleaded with me to show interest. "Last Hurrah could water-ski, you had a boat big enough. Roger ain't been workin' all that much or I'd put down my own twenty."

"I tell you what, Vinnie, here's forty. Put it down for both of us." What else could I do?

His good eye sparkled, and he excused himself to go in search of a phone. I ruffled Roger's ears.

"Yes," said Mrs. Sackley, "every time I switch on my set."

"Right this way, Mr. Deemer." The receptionist smiled. Of course it's unfair, but what can I do about it?

The receptionist led us into a chilly black TV studio.

Three fellows wearing headphones argued intently but silently up in the control booth. I knew one of them, but he was too busy arguing to return my wave. Idle camera operators stood drinking coffee and talking about sex. Camera operators, I've noticed, talk about sex a lot. Then three producer types, identical in every respect, approached me with three big smiles, sincere-looking smiles that made you want to believe them. But you can't. They each in turn shook my hand with equal firmness, after which they kneeled down to fuss over Jellyroll. One looked up at me and said, "Could we just get to know him for a while?"

I said sure and ruffled Jellyroll's ears before I left him to the sharks. Sometimes I think Jellyroll sees this crazy scene as just a lot of happy humans who want to pet him, but sometimes I think he sees through it—sees that at bottom there is me selling him out after giving his ears a hypocritical ruffle. Those three guys were walking him around, calling him here and there and generally acting like they'd never been near a dog. I went to talk to one of the camera operators.

"Hi, Phyllis."

"Artie. I heard you were coming to save the day." Phyllis was a blond woman with a weather-beaten face, as if she'd recently returned from a sailing trip or an expedition to the Andes, and she had about her the quiet self-confidence of people who do that sort of thing. We sat on some coiled cables in the corner, and though people bustled around pushing mike booms and things, they paid no attention to us. "So you met Larry, Curly, and Moe," she said.

"Yes, what's their story?"

"Fear."

"Do they test every dog that comes in?"

"In film *and* video. We've been here nine to five for two weeks."

"Well that's good for you." I liked Phyllis.

"I'm sorry about Billie."

"Yes. . . . I had to identify her body."

"You did?" She looked squarely into my face, looked with unselfconscious concern into my eyes. "You look bad, Artie. Why don't you take some of your dog's money and go to an island somewhere it doesn't rain."

"Will you come with me?" The idea of us scantily clad on a dry island was very appealing, but I knew she wouldn't do it.

"I work, Artie. Some people do, you know."

"Jellyroll would be honored to pick up the tab." She put her hand on my forearm and made it tingle, but that was just a way of saying no. "I have some negatives, Phyllis. About ten. I thought you might know somebody who could print them for me. Fast."

"How fast?"

"Immediately. They were Billie's." I wanted to tell her everything, lie down like a little boy with my head in her lap and tell her the whole rotten story.

"Color?"

"No, black and white. Thirty-fives. I'll pay a hundred dollars if I can get them this afternoon. Is that reasonable?"

"Sure. Let me think—It'd be nice to get the money to somebody hungry." She pulled a black address book from her back pocket, where I wanted to be. For a troubled instant I thought about Palomino and his cold wallet.

"Phyllis, what did the *Post* say?"

"The *Post*? Jesus, why?"

"I don't know. I guess I'm scared to see it by accident—in the subway or blowing in the gutter. I'd rather hear it from you."

"It said in those ugly black letters: BOUND-DROWNED. . . . The article said some unnamed source in the police department told the *Post* that one of Billie's former lovers was under suspicion."

"Oh."

"Billie had a lot of lovers, Artie. I guess you know that."

"Yes."

"I'm sorry," she said, but I couldn't answer. "I'll go make a few calls for you." She left the studio.

Did the police really suspect me? Was I being followed? Two hefty guys came for the cable I was sitting on. I stood up, and they took my seat away.

The producers were heading my way in a rank, led by Jellyroll, wagging his tail. They wore bright, expensive smiles of good cheer. "That's quite some dog you have there, Mr. Deemer," said Moe. "Quite some dog indeed." Larry and Curly vouched for that.

"Just between us, Mr. Deemer, we have Barnaby Price playing Dracula. We're very excited about working with Barnaby."

I had never heard of Barnaby Price, but I didn't say so. I nodded vigorously and enthusiastically, I hoped.

"*And* Prudence Akroyd is playing the girl."

"Oh, great," I said, but I'd never heard of her either. It makes people nervous when you tell them you never heard of the folks they think are hot shit.

"*And* we're very interested in Jellyroll." Larry and Curly concurred. "Can we call you Arthur?"

"Artie."

"Well, Artie, we're very interested in Jellyroll. Of course, we have to see some more dogs, but between us, we're *interested*. Sincerely. . . . Are you his handler, Artie?"

"Yes."

"Well, between us, Artie, Samoa is paradise this time of year." Moe clapped me on the shoulder like a guy who had just gotten off a neat one at the smoker.

"So I hear," I said.

"Say, Artie, tell me, does Jellyroll always cock his head to the side like that when you talk to him? I mean, could we count on him doing that? Regularly, I mean?"

"If you ask him questions."

"Then you think we could get it on film right now?"

"Sure," I said. Samoa is paradise this time of year.

Phyllis returned to the studio. I tried to catch her eye for a sign, but I should have known she'd give none while I was talking to the boss.

"Could we get this, please?" asked Moe to the studio in general, and he seemed frightened some technician would tell him no for reasons he couldn't understand.

"Quiet, please," someone called, and Moe seemed relieved. Camera people took their places.

Jellyroll sat center stage in the hot lights like a lamb for the slaughter. I stood out of the camera range, and Jellyroll pivoted to watch me. His handler. I began to ask him questions, nonsense mostly, since it's the intonation, not the words, that counts. He cocked his head from side to side with each question. His ears were pricked, his eyes bright and expectant. The producers hugged each other with glee.

"Do you want to go to Samoa?" I asked Jellyroll. That killed them.

Moe took my arm and escorted me to the door. Larry and Curly pumped my hand. Then they all clapped Jellyroll on the sides. He sniffed their shoes for a clue to their identity.

I waited for Phyllis out in the hall. The receptionist ushered Vinnie and Roger into the studio. "You can *bank* on Last Hurrah," said Vinnie as he passed me. Phyllis came out as Vinnie went in.

"I got somebody. Her name's Marsha. She'll meet you in the lobby near security. I told her to look for Jellyroll."

"Thanks a lot, Phyllis."

"Is there going to be a funeral or anything like that?"

"I don't know. Her father's in California. I guess that's up to him."

"Call me if you hear." She kissed my cheek in a warm,

friendly way, then patted Jellyroll's head and said, "So long, you sweet little gold mine."

Marsha called me at home at one o'clock to say the prints were ready. She phoned from the subway at Times Square and offered to deliver them anywhere I wanted. I asked her to meet me at the Greek coffee shop on Broadway at 104th.

On the way out, I took the elevator to the basement and went looking for Fidel, the super. He wasn't in the furnace room or the laundry room. I heard salsa from his workshop and followed the numbing beat. Fidel was glaring at an electric motor he had clamped in a vise. He held a long screwdriver as if it were a bayonet with which he was about to kill the motor. A short, balding man with a coarse brush of a mustache, Fidel had been superintendent of this building for thirty-five years. He could do everything. He could weld and plaster, he could repair air conditioners and elevators, he could place a bet for you and put a fresh motor in your juicer, and he could, I suspect, speak a lot more English than he let on. I knocked on the wall, but he couldn't hear me over the music.

"Hi, Fidel."

"Ey, ey, Artee. Refrige." He pointed at the motor. "Focker. I keel." Then he looked at me, ready to take my beef. My bathroom ceiling fell in last month due to an upstairs leak, and Fidel had been dragging his feet on the replastering job. You come out of my shower smelling like a spelunker, and Fidel figured I was down to press him on it.

"I'd like to have a key to the back entrance," I told him. The tenants' entrance is on 104th Street near the corner, but around on Riverside is a service entrance, a huge spiked gate that leads down a flight of rough steps to a narrow, dark courtyard, not much more than an air shaft between buildings. From there, with another key, I could get into the basement and up to my apartment unseen by anyone watching the front entrance. I was being prudent and farsighted, and I felt momentarily proud of that.

Fidel's expression didn't change, but his black eyes kind of glazed. "Not allowed, not allowed," he said. "Landlor', call landlor'."

I laid a twenty on the bench near his vise. He peered at the bill. You could see him weighing the danger of his position should I do something crazy against twenty for doing nothing. "You a good one," he said, by which he meant I didn't dog him around like Mrs. Fishbein, and that seemed to tip the scales. He opened a drawer and handed me two keys. "No loose, no loose," he warned, holding the keys next to his heart. I pocketed the keys, he pocketed the twenty, and I shot the motor with my forefinger.

"We keel," he said. "We keel together like *Magnificent Seven.*" I appreciate the straightforward nature of my relationship with Fidel.

Marsha was waiting in a booth, her hands folded demurely over a manila envelope. When I sat down across from her, she opened the envelope and proudly passed me a short stack of eight by tens. I noticed she had little-girl hands, unmarked by the world. "It was nice," she said. "I got to use the darkroom at NYU. My boyfriend works there mixing chemicals. I made three sets for you."

I hoped she wouldn't notice how my hands trembled as I shuffled through the stack. People. Strangers to me. . . . No! Not all of them—there he was, unmistakably. Stretch.

A waiter arrived and stood over us silently, saving his voice. "Coffee, please," said Marsha. I said the same.

Stretch was making a phone call. His face was furrowed with worry or frustration as he stood on tiptoe at the phone station. He was utterly unaware that Billie was taking his picture. Then I saw the pictures of Renaissance Antiques—taken from across the street and up several floors.

I looked up at Marsha. She was smiling happily at my apparent enthusiasm for her work. "Very good," I said, and passed her an unsealed envelope holding $150. She counted it avidly, and when she got to the end, she giggled with delight. "Hey, thanks a lot, Artie. Artie, right?" Marsha said. "I sure appreciate it. Look, I want to show you something—" She slid around the table to sit beside me. "See these?" She isolated four photos from the others and found the negatives to match. "These are very weird." She held the negs up to the light. "Do you see why?"

"No."

The waiter arrived with the coffee. Marsha took a twenty from the envelope I gave her. "Allow me," I said.

"These are photos of old snapshots, like from somebody's album. They've been rephotographed with a micro lens—to get real close."

"Why would anyone want to do that?"

"I can't think of any reason. Except that you come out with a thirty-five-millimeter negative."

"I see." Then you cut the negative from the strip and you hide it in the ice tray in case you get killed.

"Look at this one," she said, pointing to a picture of a pilot, World War II era, standing in front of his fighter plane. "This is a photo of an old *Life* magazine cover—you can see the bottom of the letters, and see, here's the date." As she was pointing out these things, I was thinking with a dry, hollow feeling in my stomach about how many photographs I lost in the mud of Union Square Park.

"Listen," said Marsha, "I'm having a show. I mean, it's just in my boyfriend's apartment, but some biggies are coming. Maybe you'd like to, too." She took from her backpack a hand-lettered flier that said: "Marsha Cook, Fragments of a Vision." The address was way the hell over in Alphabet Land on East Fourth Street.

"I'll try to make it."

CHAPTER

SEVEN

I PUT PROFESSOR LONGHAIR ON THE BOX, TURNED HIM well up, double-locked the door, and spread out Billie's bequest on the floor. Jellyroll sniffed each in turn, and for a moment I imagined he smelled Billie on them. I grouped the photographs according to age, the old "family snapshots" in one pile, the "new" in the other.

I looked first at the old:

He is a fighter pilot. Handsome in the fresh, downhome way so common in World War II faces, he poses before his airplane. He can't be much over twenty, and his pose is jaunty. He leans against a vertical propeller blade, big smile, his arms folded, legs crossed at the shins, one foot pointing straight down into the tarmac. His plane, I happen to know, is a P-47 Thunderbolt, a powerful, fat-bodied fighter that weighed as much as some light bombers. Not a handsome airplane, but strong. Pilots called it the Jug. Back near the bubble canopy, glinting sunlight, there are painted two rows of black swastikas, his "kills." The boy is an ace. He radiates confidence, his white silk scarf tied like a cravat and bloused up around the scratchy collar of his flight jacket. There is the feel of a high school yearbook about this picture. The star half-back, he might have been posing against the whitewashed leg of a goalpost more congruously than against one of the deadliest single-seat airplanes of the war. Just over his head, beneath the half-cropped title of *Life*, it says July 18, 1944.

As a kid, I'd pore for hours over photos of the war. My father was killed in a P-51 when I was six months old. Two weeks after the Germans surrendered, he flew into a railway bridge over the Meuse while playing dogfight with his squadron mates. They had at their hands and feet the fastest fighter in the world, but they were born too late to use it as its bred purpose; but my father was no less dead, leaving me to look at photographs as a way to understand what it was like to have a father.

I turned to another:

A young girl in a stiff organdie dress crouches on her knees, trying to induce a cute spotted puppy to jump over a stick that she holds about three inches off the ground, but the puppy is uninterested in tricks. He seems about to chomp on a dandelion.

The same little girl in the next photo:

She stands between two adults, holding their hands at the beach, the ocean lapping gently around their ankles. The little girl's mother, if that's who she is, is beautiful, long, light hair touching her shoulders, a slim, sexual body in one of those modest 1940s bathing suits with the little skirt pieces so you can't see the curve of her crotch. And the father—the father is the ace on the cover of *Life* magazine! No question about it.

The same family appears again:

Christmas. Ace, Mom, and the happy little girl are gathered around the decorated tree, a manger scene laid out at the base on a white sheet as if Christ were born in the snow. Rumpled, as if they just got up, but smiling, Mom and Ace are watching the little girl open a present.

The spotted puppy is the present. The little girl's glee can almost be heard from over the years.

Two birthdays ago Billie gave me a good camera. I got it from the closet, removed the lens, and used it like a magnifying glass to examine the little girl's face . . . Billie? Did she have a tiny fleck of gold in her eye? The old photos were too grainy to tell. But suppose it were Billie; suppose that the ace and the beautiful blond woman were her father and mother? What kind of sense would that make? You have this suspicion that you might get murdered, so what do you do? Do you rephotograph some scrapbook pictures of your childhood and stash them in your ice tray for your ex-lover to find? Sane people don't do that.

Suppose Billie weren't sane. Suppose the purpose of sending me into that fridge wasn't to find photographs at all but to find Frozen Freddie. Professor Longhair was singing about some wild women on Rampart Street, and I smoked half a gasper to ease my ugly thoughts, but it didn't do much good. I put Billie's childhood in a single pile, and then I turned to the rest of the photographs from the ice tray, but I was interrupted by someone pounding on my door. I hoped it was a neighbor—Mrs. Fishbein or someone—come to tell me my music's too loud, but it wasn't.

"Cobb. Open up, Mr. Deemer."

I shoved the photographs back into their envelope and hid them under the stove.

Cobb and Loccatuchi looked mean. They wore the same raincoats, only wetter than the night before last. In unison they sniffed the air.

"What are you, Deemer, some kind of doper?"

"No, I—"

"Go ahead, Sal, read him."

"You have the right to remain silent; everything you say can and will—"

"Wait a minute! You're arresting me?"

"Yep."

"For what? For marijuana? It's a misdemeanor in this state, and you have to have a search—"

"Who said anything about marijuana? We're arresting you for tampering with evidence in a murder investigation, obstructing justice, and generally being a shithead. Then we'll come back with a warrant and turn this place upside down. We find dope, we'll tack that on too. Turn that *down*. What are you, deaf from all those drugs?"

I turned it down. "Listen, why don't we have a seat and discuss this like gentlemen?"

"Have a seat *where?*"

I brought in two chairs from the dining room, but neither cop sat down.

"The deceased kept a studio at 88 East Eleventh, that right?" Cobb asked.

"Yes."

"The place has been ransacked. What do you know about that?"

"Nothing."

"Bullshit, Deemer. The superintendent of the building says a man fits your description was there about midnight. He says this guy was wearing an army-surplus rain poncho." He pointed over his shoulder at my poncho hanging guiltily behind the front door. "So what were you looking for, Deemer?"

"Nothing." What about *Palomino?*

"All right, Sal, read him—"

"I was there last night."

"That's better." Cobb sat down, and Loccatuchi imitated him. I sat in my Morris chair.

"But I couldn't get in."

"Why not?"

"The door was locked."

They stared at me. "Locked? It was midnight, what the fuck did you think it would be?"

"I thought I had a key, but it didn't fit."

"Let's see it."

I went to the foyer and picked up what I knew to be a key to a neighbor's place down the hall. I handed it to Cobb, who examined it, but I figured that was phony—he was just trying to trip me up. I decided to try not to commit myself to anything definite before he sprung the Palomino business on me.

"Why'd you go in the first place?"

"To get some photographs. I was feeling very low about Billie. I went to her studio to get some photographs—as a remembrance. But the key wouldn't fit. Maybe it's the wrong key, or maybe Billie changed the lock."

"So you tried the key, then gave up and went home?"

"Yes."

Cobb lit a cigarette and peered at me through the blue smoke, a hot-browed gaze. He stood up and took a stroll around the living room. He looked at things, the stereo most intently; he even stuck his head in the bedroom. I figured it was a ploy to unnerve me, and it was working. But I wanted to keep those photographs for a while. Billie meant them for me. "I been seventeen years on the force, Deemer, and I developed this itch. Sal can tell you. I get this itch right here—in the back of my neck—when some guy's tryin' to bullshit me." Pretending to examine my preamp, his back to me, he made exaggerated scratching motions with both hands. "The lock was drilled out. Gone. Totally. So don't feed me that bullshit about the wrong key."

The answer to that seemed so obvious I was scared to try it. But my confidence was growing. He wasn't going to arrest me. If he were, I'd be down there right now, phoning my lawyer at Jerome's Billiard Academy. "Couldn't the lock have been drilled out *after* I left?"

Cobb stared at me for a long time before he said, "Sharp one, huh, Sal? Oughta be on the force. Why did the deceased take pictures of bums?"

"She felt sorry for them."

This, clearly, was a difficult notion for Cobb to grasp. "Renaissance Antiques. That ring any bells?"

"No."

"Cooperative, ain't he, Sal?"

"Oh," I said as if I'd just remembered, "it's across the street from Billie's studio."

"Good. What else?"

"Nothing. Just a store. Isn't it?"

"Yeah, right. Just a store. Anybody else been around asking questions?"

"Like who?"

"Like who? Like anybody in the whole fucking country!"

"No."

"You must think we're a bunch of chuckleheads, Deemer. Sal, he must think we're both simple fucks."

It's true, I was beginning to think they missed Freddy altogether.

"Let's go, Sal. This guy's useless." Then he turned back on me. "One day, Deemer, we'll be comin' for you, and we'll remember how cooperative you were."

But Sal changed the subject: "What do you know about Billie Burke's father?"

"Just that he's in the film business."

"You know that because she told you? You never met the man?"

"No, never."

"We don't find any Burkes with daughters at the major studios. We'll keep trying, but if you could supply any further information—"

I said I was sorry, but I didn't know any more, and that was true.

"What about the name?" Loccatuchi continued. "Billie Burke was an old-time actress. It seems odd she should have the same name. Maybe that was a career name, like a synonym."

I said that it was the name I knew her by, and that, too, was true.

"Yeah, well, I still think you're bullshittin' us, Deemer, but I don't know why. Yet. When I find out, I'm gonna have your hair on my belt."

I'd heard about this routine before, good cop-bad cop. The bad cop led the way to my front door. Was that *it?* No Palomino?

I ventured a question: "Why do you think someone would ransack Billie's studio?"

"Gee, I don't know. Why do you think someone would ransack a place?"

"Because they were looking for something?"

"Good idea. They were looking for something. What?"

I said I didn't know, and that wasn't true. I knew what they were looking for. It was in an envelope under my stove with the Roach Motels.

"Yeah, that's what I thought, lover man. Sort of blows to hell the theory that she was the random victim of some asshole who likes to watch women drown, wouldn't you say?"

"Yes."

"Christ, Sal! The guy actually said yes to something. You got thoughts on that, Deemer, you know who you're gonna call?"

"Yes," I said.

"Yes again. Now we're getting somewhere." Cobb laid a card on my foyer table, and they let themselves out.

I smoked the other half a gasper to quell the twitching hands. I put Eric Dolphy on the box, playing exquisite pain, and soon I began to feel safe again. I focused on the notes, finding refuge in concentration. I sat in my Morris chair, put my feet on the sill, and watched the river. I pretended it was the lake outside our rustic Adirondack cottage. All I needed to do was to give myself over to the music and there would be harmony between reality and imagination. Jazz could turn the world into a happy place. Jellyroll sensed the potential. He stretched his spine with a long sigh, circled, and flopped on the Spruce Bough.

But I got up—even though the music was working, I got up. I drew the envelope out from under the stove with a mop handle and studied the "new" photographs.

CHAPTER

EIGHT

I DON'T OWN A SUIT. I HAD ONE, BUT I DONATED IT TO A thrift shop when bell-bottoms passed from style. So I helped myself to one of Jerry's. He's a master-blaster mergers and acquisitions lawyer who lives next door to Mrs. Fishbein. His was the key I showed Cobb. Jerry's always flying off to the Sunbelt in a hurry with a litigation bag filled with gibberish to tap dance around the Securities Exchange Act of 1934, as amended, and he hits me up to feed his cat. So I figured he owed me use of a suit.

After Cobb and his sidekick left, I'd spent two hours over Billie's photographs, staring at them, trying to make some sense of them separately and as a group. I also brooded over those I might have lost in the sooty mud under that tree. I was in an ugly mood when I changed into one of Jerry's four blue pin-striped suits and headed downtown. I stopped at the Strand Bookstore to acquire some antiques jargon.

Renaissance Antiques seemed larger in the daylight. I stood under my umbrella on the opposite side of Broadway and watched the building as if close scrutiny might reveal its secrets. It occupied the corner of Broadway and Eleventh and nearly half the block in either direction. It was a lovely Depression-era building with a great deal of masonry detail. The ground floor served as a showroom, with large plate-glass windows in which were displayed chests of drawers. There must have been twenty of them. I walked around to the entrance on Eleventh and peered in through the glass door. Antiques of every time and kind were stacked helter-skelter, one atop the other. It looked like the last Xanadu scene in *Citizen Kane*. I rang the bell beneath which an elegant brass plaque said "Dealers to the Trade."

I waited a long time before I saw a man approaching the door, winding his way through a tunnel of furniture. He opened the door a crack no wider than his face, which was narrow and hawky with an Ichabod Crane nose, and he said, "I'm sorry, we only deal to the trade."

I recognized the face—I had been staring at it in two of Billie's photographs—but I covered my surprise with a big grin. "Hi," I said, "I'm Seth Klimple. Klimple's of Sausalito. Perhaps you didn't receive my wire?"

"Mr. Klimple? No, I don't believe I did."

"I'm not surprised. It's been that kind of trip thus far. May I come in nonetheless?"

He held the door for me and said with a warmthless smile, "I'm Mr. Jones. Manager." You wouldn't buy a subway token from this guy. The air inside was musty and damp, like a grandmother's cedar chest. Jones watched me with little black eyes as I surveyed the stock.

"I specialize, Mr. Jones, in Art Nouveau. *Fin de siècle* is very big on the Coast."

"Yes . . . I believe we have a rosewood settee."

"A Selmershein or a Plumet?"

"I'll have to check."

"May I browse? I'm eclectic."

"Certainly. Excuse me, I'll check on the settee."

"Take your time."

What was Jones to Billie that he should show up in her

70

photographs? Her killer? There was no reason to think so, except that he had the eyes for it. I struck off through the maze in search of Sybel, and suddenly I had a vision. Heart pounding, I stood apart and watched myself kill Jones, a total stranger. Perhaps it had something to do with all that old furniture looming over me like the walls of a dreadful canyon. I killed Jones with an ax. Night before last I was lounging in my Morris chair relatively free of stress, and today I struck Billie's killer—chosen on appearance alone—a terrible two-handed blow that split his head from crown to chin like an overripe honeydew. Both halves rolled sideways over his shoulders and bounced on the floor at his feet. Only when the two halves came to rest on their ears did his body crumple in a pile. Jesus. Where did that come from?

"Get out of here!" hissed a female voice and every muscle in my neck contracted about two inches. For a mad moment I was terrified that she'd witnessed my lethal clout to Jones. I couldn't see all of her, only her face. She had hissed at me through a hole in a stack of matching chairs. Her dark, curly hair was drawn dramatically away from her face and tied behind her head. She wore a simple gold chain wrapped tightly around her throat.

"You gave me a phony phone number," I squeaked. "Why did you do that?"

"Because I didn't want to talk to you. I thought you'd get the message."

"Not good enough." I was beginning to collect myself. "Some things have happened. You talk to me or I go straight to Cobb and sic him on you."

"Are you crazy? I can't talk now!"

"When do you get off?"

"Five."

"Meet me somewhere."

"Nowhere private."

"How about the public library?" I wanted to go there anyway.

"Which one?"

"The one with the lions. Do you know where the Map Room is?"

"No."

"Ask. I'll see you there at five-thirty. If you're not there by six, I go to the cops."

"All right, I'll be there, but you cut this Klimple bullshit and get out of here." Sybel vanished.

"Mr. Klimple?" It was Jones calling me. I made two left turns around a fifteen-foot-high stack of dining tables, and there he was. "I found the settee, Mr. Klimple. Right this way." He indicated a forking tunnel and led the way.

It was a monstrosity. "Oh, it's marvelous!" It had gaudy carved lion's paws for legs, and up near the seat the lion's head appeared growling from a jungle of vines that coiled up the arms and over the back. You wouldn't want to sit in the lumpy thing, not without one of those suits they wear when training attack dogs. "My partner adores jungles. How much are you asking?"

"Seven hundred."

"I'll bring her in to see it. May I have your card, Mr. Jones?" He didn't seem to care a bit about my Klimple act. He seemed nothing more than an ordinary merchant doing his work with superficial courtesy. I was relieved at that and sorry I had killed him on such short evidence. His card said, "Mr. Jones. Antiques."

"May I have your card, Mr. Klimple?"

"Sorry, I can't oblige. My hotel room was burglarized last night. Took everything."

"I'm sorry."

"However, I don't blame it on NYC. Could happen in Sausalito. Could happen in Anytown, U.S.A. Let's face it, the traditional values are on the skids today. Sad but true." I was getting a little overconfident. "I'll be in first thing in the A.M. with my partner."

Jones nodded.

I didn't see Sybel on the way out. It was raining steadily

as I walked up Broadway to Union Square Park, where I began to root around in the mud at the base of the tree. I clawed and sifted earth like a crazed archeologist, and once I thought I'd found a negative, but it turned out to be one of those glassine packets street dealers call nickel bags. I was being watched, I realized, by a throng of punks and loiterers. They seemed nervous, skittish and wary, like a flock of shore birds. When I rose up on my knees, they cringed and shrank back in silence at the sight of this obsessed antiquer from Sausalito groveling in the mud in a pinstriped suit. I stood, trembling, and they faded back a few more steps. "Did anybody find any negatives under this tree?" I asked. "You know, like photographs." But they disappeared. It was time to get out of this business.

There was a single piece of mail for me at home. Bright Bay Nursing Home, said the return address. I give away a lot of Jellyroll's money because we don't need it all, so I'm on everybody's list. But this wasn't a request for money. It was a bill:

Dear Mr. Deemer:

Pursuant to our agreement with Ms. Burke, we are sending you the statement for May. Fees for resident patient care are payable in advance on a monthly basis.

We at Bright Bay are distressed and saddened to learn of Ms. Burke's death. However, given Mrs. Burke's tenuous condition I have elected not to inform her of the tragic news.

I would be happy to discuss this and any other matter relating to Mrs. Burke's care at your earliest.

Sincerely,
Elwood Dibbs

Total Amount Due: $2,158.68

CHAPTER

NINE

I GOT TO THE LIBRARY WELL BEFORE FIVE AND MADE OUT a call slip for *Life* magazine, July 18, 1944. I stood anxiously at the periodicals desk as an indifferent young clerk went to look for it. I was still feeling crazy and frustrated, and sure enough, she returned empty-handed and lazily muttered something at me.

"What!"

She jumped. "It's on microfilm," she said. "Microfilm. On the third floor."

I spun the old machine to the table of contents—there it was, the caption to the cover photograph:

> Maj. Danny Beemon, Fifth
> Fighter Group, Eighth AF,
> after his return from an
> escort mission over the
> German heartland.

I spun to the article. It was general rah-rah typical of wartime press, about what a terrific job the Eighth Air Force was doing in Europe, how D-Day couldn't have come off without them, and what a fine leader Jimmy Doolittle was. This Danny Beemon was mentioned as being among the top pilots in the European Theater. Though I'd never heard of Beemon, I'd heard of the others, of Gentile, Blakeslee, Zemke, Johnson. If dreaming of doing a thing were the same as doing it, then when I was twelve I flew with them, searching out FW-190s on the frigid upper edge of the atmosphere where vision is endless.

I returned the reel of microfilm and hauled down the *Official History of the Eighth Air Force*. Beemon, it told me, had destroyed nineteen German fighters in air-to-air combat by the end of the war. In the bibliography, I found a newsletter called "The Big Eighth." It had a New York address and was listed in the phone book. I called from a booth in the marble hallway.

"Hello. I wonder if you can tell me anything about Major Danny Beemon, about what happened to him after the war, his present whereabouts. I'm writing a book."

"A book, ey?"

"Yes, sort of a *Boys of Summer* approach."

"Good for you. Danny Beemon, ey? He was a hot one, all right. Hang on, I'll ask Buzz." *Buzz?* There was a guy actually called Buzz? "Buzz is remembering. Gotta give him a second." We waited while Buzz remembered. . . . "Buzz says Beemon survived the war, all right. Buzz says they sent him out to the Pacific. Saipan, but he didn't see no action. . . . Buzz says he don't know what happened to him after the war—Wait—he just remembered: Beemon got killed testing jets in California."

"He's dead?"

"That's what Buzz says."

"Does Buzz remember about what year that was?"

"Fifty-one, fifty-two, thereabouts. If you wanna come in and talk about that book, we'd be happy to see you."

"Should I call for an appointment?"

"Naw, just come on in. Most of us are dead, you know."

"Pardon?"

"I'm just saying you better hurry it up with that book."

The Map Room is beautiful, richly wooden, with an elaborate map of the world painted on the vaulted ceiling. In fact, the entire library is an architectural treasure, but the Map Room is my favorite, and I used to use it as my personal retreat until I realized it made little sense to commute to one's retreat when one's own apartment would suffice. I wished as I entered to see grizzled, bearded explorers planning expeditions to Borneo or the Karakoram, but there was only a bored clerk sitting at the front desk, listening to her Walkman and reading *Shogun*. Then I saw Sybel, the only other person in the room, sitting at a table in the far corner and eying me with mistrust and resentment as I approached. Before I even put down my umbrella, she snapped, "Look, don't come around the store anymore."

"Why?"

As an answer, she stood, gathered up her bag and umbrella, and banged her chair in.

"Okay," I said, "I won't."

She looked into my eyes to see if I was lying, which I was, then sat back down. "So?" she snapped.

"There were photographs in that ice tray. Negatives. I had them enlarged." I tapped the manila envelope as portentously as possible and sat down across the table from her. Her eyes were beautiful, deep and dark, but hostile. It's tough, even under the best of circumstances, to deal with the person, man or woman, who shared your lover.

I removed the photographs from their envelope and showed her the one on top. It was a shot of Renaissance Antiques taken from across the street and up about three stories—from Billie's studio, I believed. Sybel looked at it expressionlessly, then looked back at me.

I tried the next one in the stack—I had arranged them in the order I thought most effective—but this one elicited no more response than its predecessor. It was a picture of

Jones standing in front of Renaissance Antiques. His stance seemed to suggest that he was waiting for something or somebody.

"Maybe you don't understand," I said. "These are the pictures Billie left for us in the ice tray. Important. Get it?"

"What do you mean *us*?"

"Yeah, *us*. Why didn't Billie just leave a message on my phone machine? 'They're in the ice tray.' No, she sent word through you. Why? Because she wanted us to meet. You know what else I think? I think she was killed over these photographs. So could you cut this hostile attitude and *say* something about them?"

"I don't know you. Why should I trust you?"

"Because Billie wanted us to meet. . . . Never mind, just look at the pictures." I passed her the next one: Renaissance Antiques from the same elevated angle. Jones stood at the curb in front, only now there was a big panel truck in the frame. Two burly men were muscling a chest of drawers down a ramp from the rear of the truck, the arrival of which Jones might have been awaiting in the previous photograph. "Who are those guys?"

"The Palominos," she said.

"Which is which?"

"The big one is Leon."

He was considerably bigger than Freddy. Leon would never have fit in that refrigerator.

I passed her another photo quite similar to the previous ones. Jones still stood near the stern of the panel truck, and the Palominos were still on the ramp with the chest of drawers, only here a long black car was parked behind the truck.

"What are you doing?" Sybel asked. "Practicing to be a blackjack dealer?"

"What?"

"Just show them to me. I'm sick of you dealing them out one by one and watching my reaction."

I passed her the stack. ''Who is the cheery fellow behind the wheel?'' He wore mirrored sunglasses and a dark scowl.

''Ricardo. He's Jones's assistant.''

''Is Ricardo his first or last name?''

''I don't know.''

''Is that the whole staff? Jones, Ricardo, the Palominos.''

''And me.'' Her tone defied me to make something of it. She looked at the next photo. It was of Stretch at the phone booth.

''Who's he?''

''I don't know.''

''I ran into him last night in the hall outside Billie's studio. He asked me if I was part of the photography crowd. Then he asked me if I knew a guy named Barnett Osley. Then he ran from me.''

But Sybel said nothing. She looked at the next photograph. It returned us to curbside, Renaissance Antiques. The van was gone, but Ricardo, Jones, and the black car remained. A gray-haired man in his late sixties was addressing Jones forcefully, index finger pressed into Jones's chest. ''Who's that guy?'' I asked.

''I don't know.''

''No? Then what's going on at Renaissance Antiques? Do you know that?''

''Nothing.''

''Nothing? Then why did Billie leave all these photographs of the place and all its people in an ice tray before she was murdered?''

Still she said nothing, just stared at me. She wasn't even trying, so I decided to haul up the bigger guns.

''Freddy's dead,'' I said. ''Murdered.'' That drew some reaction. Her jaw dropped, and her black eyes blinked as if I'd just thrown a handful of sand into them. ''I found him stuffed into Billie's refrigerator like a hundred and

78

eighty pounds of seedless grapes. The studio was ransacked. I think they were looking for these photographs."

Sybel began to cry, and my anger evaporated.

"Was Freddy a friend of yours?"

"Sort of. . . . He took me to a Mets game with his two sons. I liked the way he treated them, bought them caps and things, banners." She clenched her eyes, squeezing out heavy tears. I don't own any handkerchiefs, but I passed her a Kleenex. She balled it up and threw it at my head. "Drop dead, fucker! *All* the men Billie screwed were brutes!" She snatched up her belongings and made for the door.

I caught her arm as she came around my side of the table, and I think she seriously considered clouting me with her umbrella. "Please don't go," I pleaded. "I'm not a brute. I'm a wreck. I've been through the wringer since Billie died. Please sit down. I'll tell you everything. The whole truth."

She stood there for a moment before she sat back down and regarded me through teary eyes. I told her everything step by step just as it happened. No other two days in my entire life had been so filled with events. They took a long time to tell. But when I finished, I felt tremendous relief. Not only had I shared with someone my grief, anger, and fear, I had put the events in order, made connections in that objective way required to tell anything. I told her about Billie's bathtub and the wreckage of her studio, about Freddy's forehead frozen to the aluminum, about Cobb and the stench of death in the morgue, I told her about Stretch and the mud of Union Square, about Danny Beemon, and the letter from Dibbs. And I felt as if I had just emerged from a terrible trek through the jungle. My shoulders, from up around my ears, drooped down to a saner level. I felt such a pleasurable easing of tension that I wanted to smile, but I didn't—only a true brute would crack a smile after telling a story like the one I just told.

Sybel sat back heavily in her chair as if I had shifted

the weight from my shoulders onto hers. She held both hands over her mouth. Then she said so quietly I had to ask her to repeat it, "We didn't even know Billie."

I said nothing.

Sybel picked up the next photo in my stack—an old woman wearing a terry-cloth bathrobe standing in a doorway. Nothing of the building was visible, just a weary old woman in a doorway out of all context. She clutched a Raggedy Ann doll against her breast. The doll's battered head flopped over her shoulder sideways. "Do you think this is Billie's mother?"

"Yes."

Sybel placed the old woman in the doorway beside Danny Beemon on the cover of *Life*. Then she placed the Raggedy Ann lady next to the photographs of the happy family at the beach and around the Christmas tree. Beemon was the father of the family—there was no question about it—but time had scoured away all resemblance between the smiling young mother and the old lady hugging her doll. I had already tried that matchup.

"Billie told me her mother was dead and her father lived in California," Sybel said. "Why did she lie like that?"

"I could take the family photos out to the nursing home and show them to Mrs. Burke. She could tell me if this little girl with the puppy is Billie or not."

"She looks so happy, doesn't she, the little girl with the puppy. . . . I wonder what happened to her. We've got to take these pictures to the police. We have no choice. I bet just having them is some kind of felony."

"It is. . . . I've got to think Renaissance Antiques has something to do with this," I said. We were going off the track—I wanted to *know* something.

"And since I work there, I ought to know something about it, right?"

"I didn't say that. But if you do, I'd like to hear it."

"If I did, you would." Sybel's eyes hardened under her

tears. "I just work there. I don't know how the owners run their private lives."

"Who are the owners? Jones?"

"He's the manager. I don't know who actually owns it. Look, I'm just a drone employee. It's just a way to support my kid."

"You have a kid?"

"A girl. Five years old."

I gave that some thought. "You're married?"

"I was, but it didn't take." She sat silently for a long time, maybe trying to decide whether she wanted to tell me anything about her life, then without color in her voice, she said, "I married an idiot of an actor and got pregnant. I was an ignorant girl from a dairy farm in Plattsfield, Wisconsin. Two days after Lisa was born, he left to do *Measure for Measure* in Texas somewhere and never came back. Last Christmas he showed up with presents for me and Lisa. He'd had his teeth fixed. He brought boy's toys— he forgot his child was a girl. I threw him out. I was living with Billie then. My husband is bringing a custody suit against me on the grounds I'm an unfit mother."

"He hasn't got a leg to stand on," I said stupidly.

"What are you, a lawyer?"

"No."

Suddenly Sybel glanced over my shoulder at the doorway and inhaled sharply, her brows popping up into arches. I spun around, but no one was there. "Leon—it was Leon Palomino!"

"Did he follow you here?"

"How would I know? But he's not here to do a book report."

"What did he look like? I mean, did he look surprised or angry or what?"

"Hell, I don't know. He's nuts. He's a hyperactive."

"You didn't see anybody behind you on the way over?"

"For all I know, he followed *you* here."

That had just occurred to me, too, but I didn't see how he could have known—

"Leon has this tattoo of the Grim Reaper on his arm. Inside this balloon, like the Grim Reaper is speaking, it says: 'Ia Drang 1966. It Was a Bitch.' "

"Vietnam?"

"Yeah, only he wasn't even there. His brother was—Freddy was. But Leon goes around talking about the war all the time. Sometimes he goes all rigid and trembles and says, 'I'm gettin' a flashback.' " Sybel pulled a notepad from her purse and wrote on it. "This is my real phone number. Let me know what the police say." She collected her bag and umbrella, ready to leave.

"Wait," I said. "I don't even know your last name."

"Black," she said, and she walked out.

Sybel Black. I wondered what her real name was, her dairyfarm name.

My lawyer was playing alone, practicing rail shots, shooting the same shot over and over, center cue ball medium hard, then the same shot with high right English. He looked pretty good, rolling the cue ball cleanly, not striking it. But he had no character.

"Artie. What say? You get in?"

"Yeah."

"Another satisfied client." He leaned down to shoot another rail shot, but I removed the object ball as he pulled the trigger. The cue ball struck the empty rail. "Very rude, Artie, and very immature."

I laid two twenties and a ten on the spot where the object ball had been. "Ahh," said my lawyer, "a retainer. Modest, but a retainer still."

"I might be in danger," I said. "Maybe not, but just in case, I'd like to hire a friend. A big friend."

"If you're in danger, as your lawyer, I advise you to seek help from the authorities."

"Okay, thanks anyway." I reached for my money, but my lawyer shot the six ball at my hand.

"I'm required to say shit like that, Artie, in order to maintain my standing in the professional community. If you don't want to take my advice, okay. I certainly won't leave you without legal assistance. Besides, I'm on retainer." He folded the retainer into his shirt pocket. "You want a weighty friend. No problem. What kind would you like?"

"Well, I'm not sure. I don't want a guy to walk beside me like I'm Frank Sinatra."

"Check."

"Did you read *Tinker, Tailor, Soldier, Spy?*"

"You mean you want Alec Guinness?"

"Smiley wanted someone to 'watch his back,' someone to follow behind, stay out of sight, and make sure Smiley wasn't being followed."

"An ass man. No problem, but they cost. You can't get the average psychopath for a position like that. You need a thug with intellectual prowess."

"I might need two. One for a woman."

"No problem. We can get you a whole commando unit if you want."

"Just the one to start."

"Better give me a deuce down."

I gave him the cash.

"Want to play some nine ball for old times?"

"Nah, I have things to do."

"Come on, Artie. One game. You can even have your old cue back. . . . For old times."

We played for two hours.

"Feels pretty good, huh, Artie? Feels like law-school days, back when we thought the world was round."

"Yeah," I said nostalgically.

CHAPTER

TEN

I STOOD ON THE BOW OF THE STATEN ISLAND FERRY AND watched the Statue of Liberty slide by on the right until the rain on my glasses ruined visibility. I went inside where, shivering on a fiberglass bench with the universal ass molded in, I sat brooding on that family in the photographs. If it was Billie's, it lay in wreckage, two-thirds dead, the other moldering in a grubby, overpriced Staten Island nursing home. If not Billie's, what was she trying to tell me by putting someone else's family snapshots in that ice tray? What was she trying to tell me, anyway, and why the fuck didn't she tell me when she was alive!

"Excuse me," a woman seated nearby asked a man passing up the aisle. "Where does this ferry go?"

"It'ly," replied the stranger.

As we docked, I watched a half-eaten watermelon bob red side up in our backwash like a huge disembodied wound. Dibbs promised me an easy walk up Bay Street from the ferry slip to the Bright Bay Nursing Home. On a fair day it might have been pleasant enough—the Statue glinting in the sun, the towering Lower Manhattan skyline, and all that shiny water—but today it was a nasty slog into the wet sea wind.

I passed six other nursing homes on the way to Bright Bay. This seemed to be the dying district. You linger here for a while; then, when you finally cash your check to everyone's relief, they truck you over to one of the huge cemeteries in Queens, a view of Manhattan available from both places. I arrived at Bright Bay in a bad funk. The place was no different from the others, a central lobby with rows of numbered doors reaching out on either side to nearly touch the neighboring nursing homes. They were all low-slung single-story buildings that looked like budget motels on a southern interstate. She might have posed in any of these doorways to have her picture taken with her Raggedy Ann doll.

If you were casting an old western and you needed an undertaker, Dibbs would be your man—long buzzard neck, sallow, sunken cheeks, and hooded eyes. When he met me in the lobby, his hawk hand outstretched, I thought this trip would exceed all my expectations of gloom. This grim little bastard was making nice to my money while he kept the old folks drugged stupid and lost in their own filth. I'd read about guys like him and his Medicare racket. No, when he shook my hand, I saw that his eyes were kind—you can't fake eyes—and his home was warm and spotless. Cheerful fresh flowers stood on end tables, and the old folks, neatly dressed and groomed, sat around in soft sofas and smiled in conversation.

Dibbs ushered me toward a door with his name on it. He paused en route to talk to an elderly woman with blue hair who entered from the hallway. She supported herself on an aluminum walker. Dibbs patted her gnarled hand and asked, "How are those feet, Mrs. Florian?" I didn't hear her answer, but it made Dibbs chuckle. He pinched a white mum from a vase and stuck it in the top buttonhole of her sweater. Mrs. Florian giggled like a girl.

Dibbs's office was no bigger than a commodious walk-in

closet. He had a plain metal desk with an extra chair and a Mr. Coffee machine. There was no room for anything else. Dibbs turned his desk chair around, offered me the extra one, and we sat knee to knee, his back pressed against his desk, mine against the wall. "Coffee, Mr. Deemer?"

"Yes." I passed him a check for $2,158.68.

"Ah, I'm much relieved. Frankly, I was frightened you wouldn't or couldn't assume care for Mrs. Burke. The hardest thing I do is send these people off to municipal care. Harder than watching them loaded into the funeral car. Mrs. Burke, you should know, is quite thoroughly senile. She's in no physical pain, but for her, reality is a moot point. Would you like a splash of rum in that coffee, Mr. Deemer?"

"Yes."

He poured us both a big splash from a bottle of Mount Gay.

"Old age is nature's cruelest joke, Mr. Deemer. Makes one angry at one's own God." He poured us another splash.

I showed him the picture of the woman with the doll. "Is this her?"

"Yes. Not a flattering likeness, however. You've never met her?"

"No. I promised Billie that if anything happened to her, I'd take care of her mother." Dibbs nodded. "That is her mother, isn't it? The woman in the picture?"

"Yes. Ms. Burke came regularly to visit. She called her 'Mom.' But I have no legal proof of their relationship."

"Did Billie or her mother ever mention the name of Beemon?"

"Beemon? Why, no."

"Billie told me that her father lived in California. The police haven't been able to locate him. He should be informed—you know."

"Mrs. Burke did mention her husband once or twice,

not recently, though. She said he was killed in an aviation accident.''

''She did? She said that?''

''Yes, she has her lucid moments.''

''Have you ever seen this?'' I showed him the photograph of the *Life* magazine cover. ''That is Danny Beemon.''

He looked at Ace and looked back at me, his eyes full of questions. I think my excitement was making Dibbs a little nervous. I drank up to collect myself. Billie lied about her mother and father. Her father was dead, her mother alive. And her father's name was Beemon.

''You see, Mr. Dibbs, if her father's dead, then there's no one to claim her body. Except her mother.''

''It would be a cruel thing, Mr. Deemer.''

''Yes. I'll take care of the arrangements.''

''Is it likely that the authorities investigating the murder will want to question Mrs. Burke? In my opinion, that would be most undesirable.''

''I'll try to prevent it.''

''You have that power?''

''No, but the police think Billie's mother died when she was a child.''

''And why is that? If you don't mind my asking.''

''Because that's what Billie told us all.''

''I see.'' He didn't, of course, but he seemed willing to let it ride, and I appreciated that.

''Could I speak to Mrs. Burke?''

''Certainly. . . . She leads a very tranquil life, Mr. Deemer. I think the best service we can do her is to keep it that way.''

''I'd like to show her these photographs, that's all.''

''Finish your coffee.''

The recreation room was adjacent to the lobby. We entered through a set of French doors with crinkly-clean drapes. Five old guys in suits played stud for money and smoked mean-looking black cigars. Intent, none of them looked up when Dibbs and I walked past the table. A man and a woman played Ping-Pong with a badly dented ball; they giggled and rolled their eyes each time it took a crazy bounce. Other old folks sat before the big picture window and watched the shipping maneuver in the harbor.

She was sitting alone watching a televised baseball game. On the field the sun shone cheerfully. She held the Raggedy Ann doll to her chest with both hands.

"Hi, Eleanor," said Dibbs. "How are you doing today?"

"Fine. Gooden's pitching. The Mets just scored four, and it's only the second." Her wrinkled cheeks twitched with glee.

"Well done, Mets. Eleanor, I'd like you to meet someone. This is Arthur Deemer."

"Artie. How do you do, Mrs. Burke?"

"Eleanor. How do you do?" We shook hands. Her eyes seemed clear and cogent to me.

"Artie would like to watch a few innings and chat awhile."

"Oh, how nice."

I sat beside her. I could smell her perfume, floral, lilacs perhaps.

"They're at Atlanta. Top of the third, four-zero."

The count went three and two on Dykstra, while I watched her profile and Raggedy Ann eyed me ambiguously. Mrs. Burke still owned pieces of Billie's face—the masculine cleft chin, the steep forehead, and the long, narrow nose. Dykstra fought off several tough pitches, then walked.

"He's good," Mrs. Burke nodded her approval. "Now they can do all kinds of things with a four-to-nothing lead."

Billie might have said that. I looked away from her mother's beautiful cleft chin before it made me sob. I looked to the game, but there was no refuge on the sunny field. I looked into Raggedy Ann's button eyes. Backman bunted Dykstra to second.

"May I show you some photographs, Mrs. Burke?"

"Pictures?"

"Yes. Billie gave them to me."

"Billie takes nice pictures. Clear. Sad, though."

I laid the four Family Snaps side by side along the edge of the glass coffee table at her knees. Memories seemed to cross her face like fast-moving mountain clouds across the sun. I pointed to Mom beside the Christmas tree and at the ocean's edge. "Is this you, Mrs. Burke?"

"That was a long time ago. There's Billie. Sweet little girl." She petted Billie's childhood face with her index finger. "Oh. There's Petey."

"Petey?"

"Petey the puppy. He lived to be eighteen."

"Oh."

"Yes. Petey. He was sweet."

"Mrs. Burke, this man in the pictures, was he Billie's father?"

"Sure," she said.

I pointed to Danny Beemon on the cover of *Life*. "He must have been famous."

"Oh, yes. A hero. He traveled all over with the stars. Who are you, Mr. Deemer?"

Good question. "I'm a friend of Billie's. She gave me those pictures, but I don't exactly know why."

"Why don't you ask her?"

"Well, I think she wanted me to find out on my own."

"Billie's an odd one, all right. She takes after her father." She giggled.

"Did you remarry after he died?" I asked.

"What?"

"Please pardon me for asking."

"Died? You said died. He didn't die."

"He's alive?"

"Of course."

"But the man in the pictures is Danny Beemon."

"D.B.! Of course. I know who my husband is. Don't you think I know who my husband is!"

"Yes. I'm sorry. I didn't mean—Danny Beemon is alive?"

"Yes! There he is right there!" She very nearly shouted it.

"Where?" I asked in a frightened whisper. She was pointing at the television. Keith Hernandez stroked a line drive two feet fair to right. Dykstra scored easily.

"He's a Golden Glove first baseman!" Her eyes filled with tears.

I knocked on Dibbs's door. He wore a pair of Walkman earphones down around his neck. We assumed our places, he against the desk, I the wall. I told him about my talk with Billie's mother, and he nodded sadly. Then I asked, "Who brought her here, Mr. Dibbs?"

"Woody."

"Pardon me?"

"Woody. My name, alas, is Elwood, but you can call me Woody."

"Thank you."

"Her daughter did."

"How long has she been here, Woody?"

Woody computed on his fingers. "We're coming to a year in May."

"A year?"

"In May."

"I see."

"Do you like music, Artie?"

"Yes. Jazz mostly."

"Splendid. I have some Charlie Parker here, classics from the good years. 'Relaxing at Camarillo.' Would you like to hear a little? I have double headphones." He poured us a mug of rum with a splash of coffee, and there we sat, knee to knee in his closet office, listening to Bird, who wailed.

CHAPTER

ELEVEN

IT WASN'T QUITE DARK WHEN I GOT BACK FROM STATEN Island, but a heavy mist brooded over the neighborhood. I took Jellyroll for his evening walk down to the river, where the mist had turned to genuine sea fog. Jellyroll chased a few soggy squirrels, which, when treed, chattered angrily down at him, their little hearts pounding visibly. Why did Billie put childhood snapshots in that ice tray?

We were alone on the promenade that edged the river. I could hear evening commuter traffic, bumper to bumper on the West Side Highway, but I couldn't see any cars. New Jersey was likewise invisible. It seemed as if I were standing on the edge of a great sullen ocean. Suddenly I felt isolated and anxious. Where was Jellyroll? I'd heard him ranging ahead only moments ago, but I couldn't see or hear him now. I whistled. He didn't respond. I whistled again.

"Hey, buddy," called a voice from the murk. "The dog's right up here."

I walked toward the voice until I saw a man leaning over Jellyroll. Something was wrong. Though in the fog it looked as if the man were petting him, Jellyroll was not happy. His tail was down, ears back. That's not how he responds when strangers fuss over him. I moved closer. Leon Palomino.

"We got to talk, pal. We gotta talk right now." He had Jellyroll by the collar, and in his other hand he held a knife blade against my dog's throat.

"We'll talk, Leon, but not until you let go of that dog."

"How'd you know my name?"

"I know a lot. If you hurt my dog, I'll bring it down on you like a ton of shit."

"Who are you!"

"No talking until you let him go." I made no move that might jeopardize my dog, even though that now familiar flood of adrenaline was washing through me.

Leon was considering his alternatives. Maybe he recognized that if he hurt my dog, I'd kill him—or hire it done through my lawyer. He released Jellyroll, who scurried over to hide behind my legs, and the adrenaline valve shut down, leaving me limp. Yet I still had to deal with this nut with a knife who faced me across ten feet of wet concrete—about three steps, one second perhaps, before he was on me. He made no move at all. We stood watching each other for a long time before it dawned on me that he was as frightened as I.

Leon Palomino was tall, loose and gangly, about thirty-five, and he had a roughened, weathered look like a man who did real work, the sort you see in the South behind the wheel of a dented pickup, gun rack in the back window and a six-pack on the seat. He wore jeans with a thread-bare hole in the knee, pointy cowboy boots, an army fatigue jacket with the name tag torn off, and a Mets cap pulled low over his brows. But Leon wasn't from the South—he spoke in a thick Queens accent. "I seen you all over the lot. I seen you at Billie's in a fuckin' Con Ed suit. After that you go over her studio. Then yesterday I seen you at the Antiques in a hotshot suit. Who are you, pal? Who you with?''

I stood silently, because I had no idea what to say.

But Leon wasn't prepared to wait. "You in this with her? You thinkin' about pickin' up where she left off? You do, you end up just like her."

"Did you do that to her, Leon?"

"Course not. I felt like it. But I never did it. She was a turncoat bitch, but I never hurt her. I loved her."

"Me too," I said.

"Yeah? That right? Then we got that in common." He twisted the knife around and around in his right hand, but it seemed an unconscious, nervous action, not a threatening one. "You were lookin' for pictures, right?"

"Right."

"Find 'em?"

"No."

"You want to know what I think? I think they never existed. I think she made 'em up."

"Why would she do that?"

"Hell, why would she go blackmailin' guys like that? You don't blackmail those guys."

"What? Blackmail?"

"You don't know nothin' about that. You just happenin' to be lookin' for some pictures, fill out your album, right? Let's talk straight, pal, or we gonna stand here in the wet like we don't have shit for brains?''

"Who killed her?"

"Hell, coulda been anybody. Get in line. Coulda been you."

"I told you, I loved her."

"Yeah, get in line for that too. So maybe that puts you in the deep shit right beside me and Freddy."

"How do you mean?"

"How do I mean? I mean maybe you shot your mouth off to her as loud as me."

What was he telling me? That he had told her something

she used to blackmail somebody? Only the lower portion of his face was visible. It was pitted by old acne scars.

"You with Pine?" he asked.

"Pine? . . . Yeah," I ventured, "I'm with Pine."

"Maybe you are, maybe not. Let's pretend you are. You tell Pine something for me, you bein' so tight with him. You tell him me and Freddy never told her much. Nothin' important. Look, we're just delivery boys. We fucked up, sure, we know that, but we couldn'ta told her about clients. We don't know none. We just move the stock. Tell Pine to check out Jones. Did you know she was shaggin' Jones? Well, she was. Jones knew the clients. All Pine's got to do is think. He'll see me and Freddy don't mean a thing." He paused to stare at me. I tried to look like I was with Pine. "We're in the wind, me and Freddy. Tell Pine we're gone. We just vanished."

"Was she working with Jones?"

"Yeah"—he chuckled ironically—"only he didn't know it."

"What do you mean?"

"I *mean* she was shaggin' everybody."

"What about Ricardo?"

"He's a tagalong, far as I know. Carries a gun, but who don't?"

"What about Sybel?"

"What about her?"

"Is she involved in the blackmail?"

"She don't know shit. Well, she knows, but she don't want to know. You know what I think? I think she shagged Sybel first."

"First?"

"For starters."

"Pine wants to know who killed her."

"I said—I don't know."

"No, you said it could be a line of people. Name them. Pine'll appreciate it."

"You with Pine, huh?"

94

"Yes, I told you."

"Yeah, you did, but I always been a dubious kind of guy. Maybe you're still with Billie, in which case that's you out there floatin' facedown. Maybe you're with the hoods."

"Hoods? What hoods?"

"Course they don't hire a lotta dog walkers."

"What hoods?"

"What hoods? *The* hoods. Let's say you're an undercover dog walker for the Godfather. You tell 'em that same message. Me and Freddy don't know a thing, plus we're about to vanish, plus we never talk to cops. My grandmother was a saint from Calabria. Maybe you're workin' for yourself. Maybe you got the pictures, sell 'em to the highest bidder. Good idea. You know what she told my brother? She goes, 'As long as I got the pictures, nobody can touch me.' Good move, bitch."

"Who do you *think* killed her?"

"I don't know, but look how she died."

"What do you mean?"

"Somebody tied her up and held her head under the water till she told 'im where the pictures were. Did she or did she not say? Meanwhile, I don't think you know Pine from Robert Fucking E. Lee. I think you're nothin' but another chump hangin' off her bra straps, and it ain't gonna do me no good whatsoever talkin' with you. But just in case you're some kinda hard ass in disguise, you tell your boss I'm gone. Me and Freddy both, gone. We're gone to Norway or somewhere, make pots. He's got zero to fear from me and Freddy." Leon turned and walked into the murk.

He stopped when I called his name. "It's not only Billie," I said flatly. "They killed Freddy, too."

"Bullshit."

"I saw his body."

"No."

"Yes. In her studio. Somebody stuffed his body into that little refrigerator in the corner."

Leon stood statue-still for a while; then he drew three quick sucking breaths and squealed like an injured little animal.

A railing, bent and broken by time and the members of the community, runs along the walkway at the river's edge. Designed to resemble a ship's rail, it has a curved wooden cap bolted to the top and fitted along its length with neat scarf joints. Leon reared back and plunged his knife into the wood. The blade snapped beneath his hand and remained imbedded in the wood. When he dropped the bladeless handle, blood spurted from his palm. He didn't seem to notice he was cut. He grabbed his face in his hands. His Mets cap fell off the back of his head. When he removed his hands, his face was smeared with wet, glistening blood. He began to sob, his shoulders heaving and jerking. Blood and tears and rainwater streaked down his cheeks. I had never been in the presence of that kind of emotion.

He clutched at the railing, and for an instant I thought he meant to hurl himself over the top into the slate water, but he didn't. He needed the support to stay on his feet. "I went back there! Christ, I *sat* on that thing!" I had too.

Blood dropped off his fingertips and puddled in the creased toe of his cowboy boot. He hung on the rail for a while before he turned to face me. He pointed his hand at me—I saw the long cut flap open with a belch of blood. "I was in 'Nam, man, I know what killing means." And he backed away, fading to nothing in the fog.

I stood quivering. Blackmail? Is that what this madness spun around, a cheap blackmail scheme by the woman I loved? *No.* That was just not possible. Why did I tell Leon his brother was murdered? Though I hadn't planned it, the reason became clear even as I stood there, trying hard to gain control of my knees—I wanted to sic him on the killers like an attack dog. Good luck, Leon.

I picked up the bloody knife handle and used it to pry the blade out of the wood. Then I picked up his Mets cap and tossed those three things in the river. Then I asked myself why the hell I did that.

I realized I was being followed as I crossed Riverside Drive. It was a big black man, far bigger than Cobb. He carried a woman's umbrella, the collapsible kind, which barely covered his head. I walked right past the entrance to my building and gave Jellyroll a little jerk when he started to turn up the steps. He looked at me quizzically as we hurried on toward West End. Was I just imagining the man? I turned south on the avenue. He turned the corner as if attached to me by rope. I crossed West End and walked to Broadway, where I bought a newspaper. I pretended to be interested in the window of a secondhand paperback bookstore. I glanced left and right, but he was gone.

I turned abruptly from the books and walked west on 104th, back toward West End. Mist hung around the streetlights, dimming them. When I was halfway back to the Drive, I saw him over my shoulder, heading my way, a black glacier under an absurdly tiny umbrella. At Riverside, I turned right and began to run. Jellyroll thought that was good fun. I clenched Fidel's service entrance key tightly in my fist. I unlocked the spiked steel gate and slipped in before the glacier turned the corner. I lay down on the wet concrete steps and tried to look out under the gate for a glimpse of him. Jellyroll didn't make a sound as the footsteps approached.

I saw his feet—high-cut black basketball shoes, 15½s easy, no socks, Bermuda shorts, legs like muscular filing cabinets. I put my face sideways in the gap at the bottom of the gate, but I could see only as high as his belt. He walked past. I lay with my cheek on the wet concrete and imagined myself squashed like a Dixie cup beneath those Pro Keds.

Sealed in my apartment behind about three hundred dollars worth of locks, I fed Jellyroll, then put on some thinking music. Bill Evans, the Vanguard Sessions on Milestone with Scott LaFaro and Paul Motian. I sat in my Morris chair and thought hard, I thought about what I knew and didn't know, what made sense and what didn't. Billie didn't. But thought shriveled without a chance against all that fear. Someone had come for me. He waited in the rain. Biding his time. I brooded on vulnerability. Strangers kill. Didn't Leon Palomino say the Mafia was involved? The Mafia had fuckers ready to kill me for a few loose joints and carfare. They'd give me to some small-time hopeful because I'd be easy to kill. I didn't know the Mafia was an equal opportunity employer.

A tug, cheerily lighted, red, green, and white, pushed a barge upriver. Sluggishly, I realized that meant the fog had lifted out there, but not in here. It would be cozy and warm in that wheelhouse. Men in flannel shirts would be drinking coffee and talking about the observable, the measurable—the air temperature, current, the RPMs, and the manifold pressure. Only fear and dread were clear in my house.

I needed to go to the john, but I didn't want to. It was dark in there, and I was a boy after a scary movie. The sound of my own activity could cover their approach from behind. No killer could sneak up on me while I was in my Morris chair. I drew up my knees to my chest and gripped them. Would some firepower make me feel better? My neighbor Jerry kept guns. I could build a bunker around my Morris chair, pee through the gun ports.

I padded warily into the foyer for the number Cobb had left and dialed it. No answer. Probably out drawing chalk lines around corpses. They'd be right back. There were problems with telling Cobb the truth. I had knowingly withheld evidence, but an indictment was better than a .22-caliber chunk of soft lead bouncing around inside my brain pan. I'd wait. I had all night before Jellyroll had to go out. Perhaps he'd get the *Dracula* gig, and after my release, I'd join him, burn off grief and anger and fear under the Samoan sun.

I played a blazing Sonny Rollins-McCoy Tyner duet and smoked half a bone to smooth the waters while I waited. I felt better now it was over, now that I had decided to bring in the police. I'd had enough time with Billie's photographs to know they carried implications beyond a message to me, and now it was time to pass them along. Yes, that was the sane thing to do. So what the hell, I decided. Might as well smoke the rest, now I'm near the end, only a phone call away.

Billie sat down on the red Iranian carpet beside Jellyroll. Warm morning sunlight glinted on the ends of her short black hair. The sound of her voice was lush and soft. She whispered in Jellyroll's ear, "I love Artie. We both love Artie, don't we." His tail thumped twice in agreement against the floor. Billie had just gotten up. There remained the vague imprint of a sheet fold in her cheek that I found enormously erotic. She wore only her Mets jersey. She smiled up at me, and the fleck in her iris shone like a chip of sunlight. She sat in my lap and put her arms around my neck. I could smell her hair. In a moment she would remove the shirt with her cross-handed grip of the bottom hem and drop it over her shoulder. I would feel her breasts compress, nipples hardening, against my own bare chest. This was what I always wanted, a sweet retreat; never mind that it precluded real awareness. She would sigh contentedly. So would Jellyroll. Me too. We'd return to the bedroom soon, but meanwhile someone would sing "Lover Man," Lady Day or Ella, and we'd have before us a lifetime of sunny summer mornings.

CHAPTER

TWELVE

I SNAPPED AWAKE RIGID WITH FEAR IN THE MORRIS CHAIR.
Nightmare images—dead faces, ashen faces, bodyless,
floating up from the river-bottom ooze, breaking the surface, crossing the park, and pounding on my door. They
came for me, faces, the kind of faces you just don't blackmail, their foreheads ripped away. Time to make the call.

The room was dark and silent, so I switched to
WKCR and cranked up the power on Duke's birthday
celebration. "Do Nothing Till You Hear from Me."
Ray Nance on cornet, Russell Procope on alto, Gus
Johnson on drums. I waited until Ray Nance ended his
solo, then I went for the phone. But the wait was just
long enough. I had heard that piece many times before.
I even owned two outtakes from an earlier session before Nance joined the band. If I'd not listened, if I'd
gone straight to the phone, things would have happened
differently, I guess, but that's the same old story, barely
noteworthy. Paths converge and diverge again at random; had you hurried some more, you might have
missed that E train on the morning the aggrieved sprayed
it with machine-gun fire.

The phone rang.

Two words in and I knew the voice. It was squeaky and nasal. Stretch said, "Are you the gentleman who visited Acappella Productions?"

"What's it to you?" I pretended to be tough. For all Stretch knew, I was tough.

"If you should be that man, we may have grounds of mutual interest."

"Yeah? Where are you now?"

"Ten minutes away."

"From me?"

"Yes."

"I'll be here." I actually wanted to talk to him because he'd be able to tell me things, I decided. Besides, he was the smallest person I knew in a position to tell me things.

I went into Jerry's apartment, fed his lonely cat, and then searched for a gun. I found two in the foyer closet—a shotgun and a powerful-looking rifle. One weekend a year Jerry and a carload of other sports motor up to the Catskills to murder deer, and I feed his cat. I figured he owed me use of a gun. (I reminded myself to have his crusty suit cleaned.) Considering the pros and cons of rifles and shotguns, I settled on the latter, because accuracy was less crucial. The hefty weight of the shells I found in a box near the gun surprised me. I'm ignorant of guns, but a lot of assholes use them effectively, so how hard could they be? I worked the pump thing back and forth several times. Nothing came out. I shoved in three fat shells and wondered if it was now ready for use. Who did I intend to shoot? I ignored that question as I removed a pair of Jerry's pants, hung fastidiously in the pants section of his bedroom closet, and stuck the loaded shotgun down one leg—it makes people nervous to see their neighbors roaming the halls with heavy firepower.

I returned to my place and leaned the shotgun out of

sight behind the French doors that, when closed, separate the dining room from the living room. Then I changed my mind—the whole idea of deterrence turns on your enemy's knowing you're not to be fucked with. So I leaned it up against the middle of the white living-room wall, where it stood out like a shotgun against a white wall. I had the tiniest taste of a gasper for clearheadedness and a sense of context.

When Stretch rang the downstairs door, I buzzed him in. He stood tiny and dripping in the hallway. He seemed to be alone, no nightmare faces hanging behind him. Without showing myself, I opened the door a crack barely wide enough for the little man to sidle through and planted my foot behind it. After he squeezed in, I shoved the door shut and bolted it twice.

His plain shapeless raincoat was saturated to the point of uselessness. Little puddles were forming at his feet. His eyebrows, stiff and brushy, met in the middle.

"Still on the sauce, Dad?"

"My name is Dr. Harvey Keene."

"How do you know mine? You had to know my name to call."

"May I remove my outerwear?"

I pointed to the hook behind the door. Keene wore a tiny tweed sport coat over a blue shirt and crumpled pants soaked from the knees down. I sat on the windowsill. Stretch was dwarfed in my Morris chair.

"Are you a sportsman, Mr. Deemer?"

"Me? No. Why?"

He gestured at the shotgun.

"Oh, that. That's just the tip of the iceberg. I've got bazookas in the bedroom." I'm tough on dwarfs. "How did you know my name?"

"I've been following the man Palomino. He led me to you only a short while ago in the park. I followed you back here."

"That doesn't get you my name."

102

"That wasn't difficult, merely tedious. I wrote down each name on the buzzer in the lobby, then I looked up and phoned each party. Inevitably, I came to you. Are you aware that you are being followed by a large Negro man?"

"Yeah, I'm a regular mother duck."

"Pardon?"

"Why were you following Palomino?"

"In the hope that he might lead me to Barnett Osley." He said the name with quiet emphasis and stared into my eyes from under his steel-wool eyebrows.

"Am I supposed to know him?"

"I hoped you might."

"I don't. Who is he?"

"He's my partner."

"As in business partner?"

"In every sense of the word. He has disappeared."

"When?"

"I last heard from him on the night the Burke woman was killed."

"There's a connection?"

"I believe so. But I don't believe he killed her. Dr. Osley saves lives; he doesn't take them."

"Who was blackmailing you?"

"Please, Mr. Deemer, I'm wet and cold, and I've had quite enough of this covert activity. You have appeared too often—at her apartment in disguise and still again at Renaissance Antiques—my credulity strains to imagine you an innocent bystander."

"I don't give a rat's ass about your credulity, Doctor. You invited yourself over here. If you have something to say, say it or get out."

"Very well. There's a war on. You've probably not seen all the combatants, but they've seen you, be sure of that. You've seen the dead, however. I heard you say so to Mr. Palomino, not gently. Your life is in danger."

"Is that what you came to tell me? I knew that."

"It's difficult to find a sound basis for communication with you. You do not inspire trust. You go about in disguise, you have no furniture, you leave a gun leaning against your wall. However, I will tell you what I want. I want to find Barnett. He was very upset by this business. He is not well. Perhaps he is dead. If you know anything, I will pay to hear it." His eyes pleaded with me.

"I don't know anything about Barnett Osley. If I did, I'd tell you for free. I don't want money."

"Then what do you want?"

"I want to know about Billie?"

"What do you want to know?"

"Did she literally come to you and say if you don't pay me money, I'll tell so-and-so such and such?"

"No, not to me and not directly. Her go-between spoke to Barnett, and he paid him to keep quiet."

"Go-between? What was his name?"

"I don't know that. Barnett was very upset. I asked him by what means he paid this go-between. He paid by check. I've looked for his checkbook—unsuccessfully."

"By check? Isn't that an unusual way to pay a blackmailer? He intended to deduct it from his income tax?"

Stretch shrugged, I guess in agreement.

"That's when Barnett vanished?"

"Yes."

"Why was Billie blackmailing Barnett in the first place?" I asked, but Stretch just shook his head. "That's the obvious question, isn't it?"

"Obvious, yes, but it's there that we confront a problem. I could tell you about our transgression—perhaps you'd even sympathize with our side of the story—but to what end should I explain? If you don't know already, it would not be in my interest to tell you. Perhaps you are an incipient blackmailer. You're clearly associated with blackmailers."

"I don't believe that Billie was one."

"Then I'm sorry to tell you differently. The go-between has been traced directly to her. Besides, didn't she die a blackmailer's death?"

"Traced by whom?"

"By my friends."

"Like who?"

He shook his head.

"This conversation's not getting us very far," I said, trying to think.

He was thinking. I let him do it without interruption. "Barnett Osley is a great healer. Under different circumstances he would be celebrated, not excoriated. I want to find and protect him. That's my only purpose."

"I'm not threatening him."

"If you have the photographs—the ones Palomino asked you about—then you represent a very great threat indeed. To me, as well, and to others far less civilized in their approach to getting what they want."

"Like who? Like Harry Pine?"

"Mr. Deemer, I have ten thousand dollars. Not on me, of course, but I can have it in your hands within the hour. That's all I have without selling my home."

"Billie used those photographs to blackmail you—is that what you're saying?"

"Basically, yes."

"Then you've already seen them?"

"No. I merely heard about them. I believe they might bring a cease-fire to the war they have started before Barnett becomes a casualty. If you try to use them in any other way, you will most certainly become one yourself."

"So Leon told me."

"Sage advice from an unlikely source."

"Then why shouldn't I take them to the police? After all, I'm innocent. You're not. When the partners of innocent people disappear, innocent people call the cops."

"Do you mean you have them?" He leaned forward, eyes glistening; then he covered his obvious excitement and leaned back in my Morris chair. His toes barely touched the ground.

Jellyroll had been staring into the old man's eyes. Dr. Harvey Keene smiled sadly at him, then began to stroke his head.

"I have them," I said. My thinking, if that's the word, ran thus: I was going to turn them over to Cobb anyway, maybe tonight, so why not try to learn something from little Dr. Keene before I gave up the photographs? I desperately didn't want Billie to have died a blackmailer. "But I don't want money."

"What, then?" he asked suspiciously.

"Who's Harry Pine?"

"Harry Pine is a very old friend of ours, Barnett's and mine. He is like a son to us."

"Was he part of your transgression?"

"I've yet to see a single photograph."

"I don't have them here."

"What!"

"Don't you think it's occurred to me that Billie was killed over them? I don't leave things like that lying around."

"Where are they?"

"In a safe place. If anything happens to me, they go straight to the police."

He sighed deeply.

"Suppose," I continued, "I tell you about them."

". . . Okay."

"Renaissance Antiques. They were all photos of the store and its staff. Jones, Ricardo, Frederick and Leon Palomino. Then there was you—making a phone call from the street."

"Yes, what else?"

"Nothing."

"Nothing? You're lying."

How did he know? I decided not to tell him about the Family Snaps to protect Billie's mother's privacy and peace of mind.

"What about the home?" he demanded.

"What home?"

"A nursing home, Mr. Deemer!" he snarled.

"Bright Bay Nursing Home?"

"Yes!"

"What do you have to do with—?"

"I own it. In partnership with Barnett Osley. There are innocent, helpless people living there, and we are helping them! They should be protected!"

"I—I don't mean to jeopardize it."

"But you are! If you don't give me the photographs, you are!"

"Do you know that Billie's mother lives at Bright Bay?" I asked simply. And I decided to go a step further. "Her real name is Beemon. She was married to a dead pilot named Danny Beemon."

Stretch responded as if I'd whipped him across the face with a wet towel, but he quickly recovered, and his face went blank. "Danny Beemon? I never heard of him."

"Come on, Dr. Keene, you about fell out of the chair."

He stood up. "You're right. I knew Danny Beemon. In fact, we were very close. But he was killed. Mr. Deemer, please don't mention that name to anyone. If you do, innocent people will suffer."

"I don't understand."

"I'm going now. Do you intend to stop me?"

"No, of course not. But what about the photographs?"

"Yes, the photographs. . . . I'll be back in touch with you about that."

"Back in touch? Christ, that's why you came!"

"Good-bye, Mr. Deemer." He headed for the door. Jellyroll followed. He turned and petted Jellyroll on the side. Dr. Keene's face was gray. He stared at me as if he were collecting his thoughts before speaking, but he didn't speak. He gathered his rain gear from the hook and fumbled with the locks. I made no move to help. Jellyroll sniffed his shoes. He finally got the dead bolts synchronized, the door open. He said, "If Barnett Osley should—" But he never finished the sentence. He left, letting my door fall shut. I quickly bolted it.

Thinking hard, I made myself a mean cup of coffee and sat down at my desk in the tiny maid's quarters adjacent to the kitchen. Jellyroll joined me. He curled up at my feet under the desk as if things were routine. What was Billie involved in? What had she involved me in?

"Who's this asshole we been seein' in the Con Ed suit?"

"Name's Artie Deemer."

"Got any clout?"

"He's got a dog."

"Take him out."

"The Glacier?"

"Yeah, send in the Glacier. Might as well take out the dog, too."

The coffee was making me half bilious. I had an idea, but it was utterly baseless. The phone interrupted me. It was Shelly, Jellyroll's agent:

"What, Artie, what? You don't return your phone messages now days? I been talking to your machine since noon. What, you looking for a new agent behind my back?"

"I've been . . . busy."

"Busy?"

"Yeah, Shelly, sometimes I'm busy."

"Okay, okay, so you're busy. You're fucking Lee Iacocca. Listen, Artie, they *want* him!"

"Who?"

"Who? Those Dracula idiots. It's all set. You sitting down? I got ten thousand for three weeks, ten thousand a week each week thereafter, plus all expenses in fucking Samoa! I told him you wouldn't allow Jellyroll in the baggage compartment, you know what he says? He says, hell, buy that dog a seat. Ha! We got them by the short hairs. The airline tried to give me a ration of shit about dogs on the plane until I mentioned what dog we're talking about. The R-r-ruff Dog! No problem, pleasure to serve him.''

''When?''

''Your phone must be on the fritz. I tell you we're gonna make maybe twenty-five grand and you say *when* like I just told you you gotta be in court on a bigamy rap. *When?* Saturday. Monday at the latest.''

''Can we put them off awhile?''

''Are you *nuts?* Look, let me speak to Jellyroll. Get some rational response here.''

''I can't leave just now, Shelly.''

''*What?*''

''I just can't.''

''Then stay. Send Jellyroll. You go later.''

''That won't work.''

''Why not!''

''He pines when I'm not there.''

''Fuck! I forgot. . . . Artie this is a bad career move. Ba-ad. They're gonna start sayin' the dog's a genius, but the handler's unstable. . . . Look, is it the woman?''

''Yeah. The woman.''

''Okay. I can understand that. Grief. Grief's a terrible thing. But think of this: Samoa is the best place in the whole fucking world to recover from emotional grief. Why do you think Gauguin went there? And Artie—do you know what they wear under those grass skirts?''

For a long time I sat and stared dully into what appeared to be an oil slick undulating over the surface of my coffee. Then the phone rang again. This time it was Sybel. I started to tell her about Leon, Stretch, and the Glacier, but she interrupted me before I could even say the word blackmail.

''Can you meet me? It's very important.''

"Where are you? Why don't you come over here?"

"No, meet me. Please."

"What's wrong?"

"Nothing. Can you meet me?"

"Where?"

"Columbus Circle. In front of the old Coliseum."

CHAPTER

THIRTEEN

THAT, CLEARLY, WAS THE VOICE OF A WOMAN IN TROUBLE, tight and husky, with panic in the upper register, as if a gun were pressed to her larynx. So what was I to do? Join her? That would be dull witted—to wait outside the Coliseum until whoever had her got me too. Just stand there like a chump in the rain. Even if I wanted to go, which I did not, I couldn't stride blithely out the front door as if off to meet Billie for a Buster Keaton movie at the Metro, not while a glacier encroached on the neighborhood. Maybe this was the setup—force Sybel to call me out and let the Glacier pulverize us both at once, along with the Coliseum if it got in the way.

About a year ago, after an unusually sordid incident, the tenants kicked in to hire a night guard for the lobby. Knowing I had nothing else to do, they badgered me to head the hiring committee. I hired Blue. Blue wants to be black. He's a young white sax player who longs to have been born in a Memphis ghetto because of what that would do for his technique. "Hey, Blue—" I called in a loud whisper from the first landing on the back fire stairs. Blue cautiously stuck his head around the corner.

"Whatchu doin' up there, Artie?" Blue wore a rumpled tan uniform with an officer's-style cap several sizes too small, and he carried a nightstick that I occasionally caught him "playing" as if it were a soprano sax. "They pay me to nose out suspicious persons and pound 'em into submission. You about the most suspicious person I seen since the pimp in 8E. Remember that dude?"

"Transitional neighborhood."

"Don't I know it, me bein' on the cutting edge of law enforcement."

I tossed him a tape cassette. "Julius Hemphill," I said.

"Thanks. Hey, this ain't a bribe? I'm clean. I'm Elliot Ness. I'm—"

"I'm expecting a cab. It should stop right in front. When it does, tap on the wall so I'll know, then go out and open the door for me."

"Gracious living, huh?"

"Right."

Blue went off to watch the door. My stomach snarled belligerently. I had forgotten to eat. Nothing but coffee and the rum from Dibbs. I was beginning to feel dizzy, but when Blue tapped on the wall, my head cleared, and I walked briskly out the door and straight into the cab. "Thanks, Blue." If I never come back, please walk Jellyroll every now and then. I told the driver south on Eleventh, then east on Fifty-eighth. I would approach from the rear, where I'd have a decent view of the sidewalk in front of the Coliseum. If things looked nasty, I could then retreat the same way I came. As we pulled away, I looked for the Glacier, but he was either well concealed behind a building—anything smaller would have left elbows sticking out—or he was waiting for me at Columbus Circle.

Though the big marquee still stood, the Coliseum was dark and doomed, all the action having moved to the Jacob Javits Center. The Coliseum would soon come down, and another smoked-glass tower, a giant oil filter, would ascend over Columbus Circle, further enriching the rich. I got out a block west of the Circle as a loose crowd emerged from the subway. I melted into it, fooling killers in the jam-up way I fooled them in my Con Ed suit. The International Bath & Hot Tub Expo had been the Coliseum's swan song. Big red letters on the marquee claimed it would run through January 15. I hung back, searching for a killer in a black leather raincoat, a silenced .22 in his gloved hand. A bag lady sang the national anthem with her hand over her heart. Another explored the rubbish for returnables, the trickle-down theory at work.

I looked under umbrellas for Sybel. I had decided they didn't mean to murder me. Decided. Based on years of experience with the psychopathic personality. Otherwise I wouldn't have attended this meeting. I wasn't that far gone. I was there to meet the participants, another level of participants, for what I could learn from them about Billie—I was *that* far gone.

I walked across the front of the hulking building under the Bath & Hot Tub sign and looked under other umbrellas. Just keep going north, I told myself, to Vermont. I started back the other way.

"You Deemer?"

I spun.

"Deemer or not?" He was a chesty man, mid-forties, with a round face and stiff, curly hair. He wore a sharp leather cowboy jacket and pointed snakeskin boots.

"Who's asking?"

"Just get in the car. It's raining. I don't wanna ruin the jacket." He pointed at a big black limo with deeply tinted windows, the kind of car hoods and stars travel in—the same kind of car Billie photographed from her studio window. Before she was murdered.

"Forget it. I'm not getting in any cars." I backed away. Pedestrians, happy couples, flowed around us. "I'm here to meet Sybel, and if I don't start seeing her, I'm gonna start yelling cop.''

"Artie—"

I spun toward the voice and took a couple of side steps to keep Tex in view. The back window of the car was down, and Sybel's face was framed in it. Her expression was grim. "Please, Artie. Get in."

The back door opened. No light came on. Sybel slid over, and I got in. Something was wrong with her, something in the way she moved.

"Have they hurt you?" I asked.

She shook her head. Then I saw what caused her awkwardness. Her ankles were chained together. A length of chain was wrapped tightly twice around her ankles, cinched in between and padlocked.

"Hey," I demanded, "take these chains off her."

Tex got in the front, shut the door, and didn't even turn to look at his cargo in the back. The driver merged with the Columbus Circle traffic and headed east on Central Park South. The windows were so dark I could barely see the lights outside.

I shoved the brown leather shoulder in front and said, "Hey, why have you got her chained?"

"Just sit back, shut up, and enjoy the ride. This is a Lincoln." He still didn't turn around.

I shoved his shoulder again and repeated my question.

"She's chained so she can't run away, at least not real fast. You can run away, but if you do, she winds up in a lotta different cans of cat food."

Sybel took my hand and squeezed it. To say shut up? Her hand burned, and there were tears, or the traces of them, on her cheeks. She seemed to be breathing heavily. I was having some trouble breathing myself.

Was this it? Was this the last ride you learn about from gangster movies? It had all the earmarks of the genre. Then why was I going quietly? Sybel, too; she sat there. Because we didn't believe it? Maybe the bogs of North

Jersey were fertilized by moldering disbelievers. Well, damn it, I would fight like a wounded wolverine. I longed to live, longed to attend the Bath & Hot Tub Expo, wherever it might be today. Tinted hotels and dressy tourists passed on the right. I had an ice pick in my jacket pocket, a Zinfandel cork guarding the point. I put my hand in there with it, and for future reference I picked a spot two inches up from Tex's collar.

"They made me call you," Sybel whispered hoarsely.

"I know," I said, thinking of other ways to kill Tex.

"Hey, shut up back there," he said.

"I don't think so, Tex."

He turned to face me over the seat back.

I said, "If you plan to kill us, it won't make any difference if we talk, and if you don't, you're not likely to change your mind because we do."

He grinned at me. "Yeah, you got a point there." He looked to the driver. "Four-eyes has a point there, don't he, Dickie?" The driver giggled. Tex faced front again. We passed the Plaza and continued east on Fifty-ninth Street. That was inconclusive.

Sybel sat stiff and rigid, frozen in her seat. I wondered what kind of night she'd had. At the stoplight on Park, I came up with an idea, but I held it back until my sluggish brain could go at it from different, thoughtful perspectives. When we turned south on Second Avenue, I decided to tell him, the ice pick being the only active alternative.

"Hey, Tex—" I poked his shoulder again. Glaring this time, he turned to me. His face was big and round, with mountainous jaw muscles that flexed rapidly. "I want to tell you about my arrangement with Ralph." I could feel Sybel looking at me.

"Oh, yeah? Who's Ralph?"

"Old friend of mine. We go back a long way. Our *grand*parents were pals. Ralph's a very dependable guy. He has a set of the photographs. See, our arrangement is this: if I don't call him every twelve hours and say—in code—that I'm fine, no problems, then he marches the photos straight to the cops. Detective Cobb. He'd like to meet you. He loves the rodeo.''

"Well, now that's some arrangement you got with—what's his name?—Ralph. Ain't that a sharp arrangement, Dickie?'' Dickie giggled again. "I tell you what, four-eyes. Nobody's gonna kill you, not unless you call me Tex again. Anyhow, I think it's great to have old pals like this guy Ralph. All my old pals are dead.'' He turned to the windshield and giggled. Dickie joined him. I decided if we left Manhattan, while on the bridge or in the tunnel, then that's when I'd do it, a short, sharp thrust.

Dickie pulled up to the curb and stopped in front of a movie theater at Fifty-first on Second. Tex turned and showed me his clenched fist. I was impressed. Then I understood that he meant to give me something. Why didn't he just say so? I put my palm under his fist, and he dropped a key into it. I set about unlocking Sybel's ankles. She rubbed them when they were free.

I considered closing the lock on the last link of chain and lashing Tex across the face with it when he opened the door on my side, but I left chain and lock on the floor and got out. Sybel slid across the seat, and I helped her out. Dickie drove away. Tex said, "Come on,'' and led us toward the box office. From a poster, Clint Eastwood pointed a .357 Magnum at our heads. Tex opened a glass door to the left of the ticket window and led us down a bright hallway to a bank of elevators. Only then did I begin to feel that this trip wasn't our last, at least not yet. We stepped out of the elevator on the twenty-third floor.

We approached a darkened office suite beyond glass doors with big teak handles and teak letters that said "Olsen & Olsen.'' Tex unlocked the doors, and lights came on automatically. He pointed at a wooden door marked private and said, "Wait in there."

It was one of those corner offices where the corporate heavies command panoramic views, this of the Queensboro Bridge. In the corner, where the two glass walls met, there was a sectional sofa that curved around a low-slung glass coffee table. Sybel and I sat—sagged—on the sofa. In the other corner was the seat of power, a sprawling teak desk about the size of a snooker table with a high-back leather chair behind it and two chairs in front where the supplicants could be made to feel appropriately dwarfed, but dwarfed was a hell of a lot better than dead.

"I think we're all right, Sybel. This is the kind of place you go to get your taxes done."

"I thought we were dead."

"How long have they had you?"

"Since about dark. That bastard leered at me for about five hours, told dirty jokes to that fool Dickie. Look, I'm about to fall apart. You're going to have to handle this."

"Don't worry." Sure, I'll handle it. No problem.

"Do you have any cigarettes?"

"No."

"I want one. Bad."

He was a pudgy, balding man, perhaps sixty years old, with a big toothy grin. The door seemed to open for him automatically. "Evenin', folks. Good of you to stop by on such short notice. Who's for a drink?" We stared stupidly at our host with the happy grin. It actually glistened. "No takers on the drinks?" He wore old chinos, scuffed Topsiders with no socks, a red knit shirt with an alligator, and a two-thousand-dollar Rolex on his stout wrist. "Couple of light hitters, huh, Chucky?" I hadn't seen Tex come in, but there he stood with his back to the door. He agreed we were sure a couple of light hitters.

"Can I have a cigarette?"

"Chucky, give the lady a smoke. Give her the whole pack." Tex walked across the room, which took a while, laid his pack of Luckies on the coffee table and resumed his post at the door. Sybel fumbled one from the pack, and our host lit it for her with a silver Zippo. He placed the lighter on the table beside the cigarettes. When I saw the name engraved on that lighter in big block letters, my heart began to pound, and the mad adrenaline jumped: Maj. Harry Pine.

"You're Harry Pine?" I blurted out.

"All my life. Chucky, could I have a bourbon like I like it?" Pine sat on the sofa around the bend from us, and Chucky put the drink on the glass table before him. "You've heard of me?"

"No," I said.

"Come on, Arthur, you damn near dropped outta that sofa."

"No, I didn't."

"Sure you did. Let's ask Sybel. Sybel, did he or did he not damn near drop—"

"I heard of you."

He grinned at me. "What'd you hear?"

"About the war," I ventured.

"You know about that? That was before your time."

"They have books."

"History books? It's hard to think of your life in history books. Anyway, I thought everybody forgot that war. WW II."

"Not everybody. My father was killed in a Mustang."

"KIA?"

"No. An accident. After V-E Day."

"Oh. That's tough. Sybel, I hear you're a lez-bean."

Sybel blinked.

"Exactly what is it you do down at the antique store, Sybel?"

"I keep track of the stock."

"Fill orders?"

"That—sometimes I buy."

"Sounds like a demanding position."

"Not very."

"Now don't you hide your light under a bucket. Lotta objects in there. I've seen them. Must be demanding for one person to keep track of all those objects."

"I'm unusually bright for a lez-bean."

"Ha! I like a lez-bean with a sense of humor. . . . Tell me, Sybel, did the Palomino brothers ever discuss blackmail with you?"

"Blackmail? No."

"What about Jones?"

"No."

"Never? Hell, let's not limit things. Extortion, grift, anything like that, around the water cooler, on coffee breaks. You take coffee breaks?"

"Not with them."

"You ever overhear them talking blackmail, extortion, or grift?"

"No."

"What about you, Arthur?"

"What?"

"Blackmail. Anybody ever discuss it with you?"

"No."

He was stronger than I at first thought. That was muscle under the reptile shirt, aging muscle but far from flab. His face didn't move much. At times it seemed lifeless, neutral, and at others merely still, but his eyes and voice were sharp and full of life.

"But me and Chucky, we've been seeing you every time we turn around. We never laid eyes on you before the, uh, trouble started. Before somebody tried to shake down two very dear friends of mine. Then we start seeing Arthur Deemer."

"Artie. Who are these friends?"

"Drs. Harvey Keene and Barnett Osley. Brilliant men. Humanitarians. Only great men I ever knew. I don't like to see them upset by any greedy fucking grifters." His eyes hardened. "I'd go out of my way to hurt those grifters. So would Chucky."

Yes, but what about the photographs? I'd already shot off my mouth about the photographs. When would that come back to haunt us? "I don't exactly know what a grifter is, but I'm fairly certain I'm not one," I said.

"The three of us, we ought to be able to strike a bargain. Ideals are nice, but you almost need a war for ideals to be the basis of loyalty. In peacetime, money's far more stable. Let's say I wanted you to work for me, Arthur. Would I need to negotiate with some present employer?"

"I'm self-employed."

"Yeah? At what?"

"May I have that drink now?"

"Sure may. Sybel?"

"Okay."

"What'll it be?"

"What you're having," Sybel said.

Fiddling with a drink would give me a little thinking time. "I'm an animal trainer," I said.

"Yeah? Elephants, like that?"

"Smaller."

"Like the R-r-ruff Dog?" He grinned at me, a kind of southern-boy charming smile, but I didn't ask how he knew. I grinned back at him. "That's some dog, the R-r-ruff Dog. He must do all right."

"It comes and goes."

"Got to make it when he's hot, huh?"

"Right."

"How hot is he? Ballpark."

"About a grand a week, average. I don't need money."

"You live off your dog?"

"Yes."

"Well, I'm glad to hear that. I don't trust poor people. I was a poor person once, and you sure couldn't trust me. That's why I pay my people well. You don't have much of an employment record, Arthur. I did some research. What have you been doing with yourself?''

"Odds and ends, nothing serious."

"I see. This and that. Make ends meet. What about this Billie Burke person?''

"She's dead."

"I know that. I read the paper. How well did you know her?''

"Quite well."

"Lovers?"

"Yes."

"How about you, Sybel? You know her well?''

"Quite well."

"You mean—?''

"Yes," said Sybel.

"She sort of swung both ways, you mean?''

"If you want to put it like that," said Sybel.

"Well, no matter. I'm a liberal sort of fellow despite my agedness. I don't much care who fucks who or by what means, but this Billie Burke, she's a very shadowy figure. Just take the name, for instance. Billie Burke. You know who that was? Glinda the Good. *Wizard of Oz*. Remember that? What was her real name? Your Billie.''

"That was her real name. But now she's dead."

"That's because she was a grifter," he said. "I mean, I didn't kill her. In my view, it was a falling out among thieves. Happens a lot. But what about those photographs? Chucky says you have 'em.''

"Yes."

"Where'd you get them?"

"From her."

"How's your drinks?"

"Fine."

"Want Chucky to freshen them up some?" He had just delivered them; we hadn't touched them yet. "This is very confusing to me. Arthur, you must have been working Glinda's grift. How else would you have the pictures?''

"They came in the mail. After she died." We had entered the mine field. I took a stout gulp of Harry Pine's old bourbon. Stay calm. That might spell the difference.

"Note?" he asked casually.

"What do you mean?"

"I mean a note. These pictures just arrive in the mail, no note. That's sort of odd."

"Yes, I thought so."

"I'll bet you did. Shadowy figure, this Glinda. Did you see the pictures, Sybel?"

"I showed them to her."

"Now, Arthur, just because you two shared the same lover, that doesn't mean you should answer for Sybel."

"Artie showed them to me." She too had a big drink. Was I taking care of things or fitting us out for an oil drum? Sybel was asking the same question, I suspect.

"Very confusing. Now before I get hopelessly befuddled—some pictures in the mail from your murdered grifter lover—you better tell me what was in those pictures."

"People. I don't know them. Except you."

"Me?"

"And Harvey Keene."

"You know Harvey, huh?"

"We met earlier this evening. He wanted to know about Barnett Osley. He said Osley disappeared."

"Yes, he has. Who else is in the pictures?"

"The Palominos, Jones, Ricardo."

"Renaissance Antiques?"

"Yes."

"No note?"

"No," I insisted.

"Note says, 'One of these suckers killed me.' Now there would be a piece of what law-enforcement folks would term hard evidence. Otherwise what have we got? Portraits and a legal business. What does it mean? Nothing. You see how I'm confused?"

I certainly did. So did Sybel. But neither of us spoke.

"I must be going simple in my dotage. Why did you tell Chucky you had a fancy arrangement with a guy named Roy for pictures that don't mean shit?"

"Ralph."

"Ralph. How come, Arthur?"

"Billie was killed. I thought I should take precautions before I took them to the police."

"Prudent. Sybel, what do you think of Jones?"

"He gives me the creeps."

"Creeps. I know what you mean. Cold sort of fellow?" Sybel nodded.

So did Pine. "What do you think of Jones, Arthur?"

"I don't know him."

"Now that's bullshit. Chucky saw you talking to Jones at the store. Chucky asked Jones who you were. Seth Klimple from Sausalito. You're a pretty shadowy kind of fellow yourself, Arthur."

"Renaissance Antiques appears in the photographs. I wanted to have a look for myself—before I took them to the police."

"I wouldn't bother the police, what with this crack business. They have their hands full. See, I own Renaissance Antiques, and Sybel, you're due for a loyalty raise. Chucky, go get me a thousand bucks." Chucky left. "Now let's talk a little about this agreement you got with Roy."

"Ralph."

Chucky returned with a fistful of banded bills and placed them on the glass before Sybel, then took his place as sentry at the door.

"You have a set of photographs. So does this fellow Roy. If you don't call in every twenty-four hours, he takes them to the cops. That about it?"

"Twelve."

"What?"

"Twelve hours, but never at the same time."

"Variable call ins, huh?"

"Certain times are automatic alarms even if I say I'm all right."

"Like now would be such a time, right?"

"Right."

"Thought so. Chucky, go get another thousand bucks." Chucky left. "Sometimes in the world of business you hire folks not so much for their skills but for their unique placement. You folks are uniquely placed. It's not as clear as I'd like it to be how you got there, but that's where you are."

Chucky laid new twenties in hundred-dollar wrappers on the table beside the first stack of bills.

"What if we don't want the work?" I asked, reasonably.

"Not everyone has a rich dog, Arthur. Take Sybel here. A working woman. A child to support. How is little Lisa? But to answer your question directly, you are either part of the solution or you are part of the problem. And I won't let an agreement with an asshole named Roy stand in my way if you turn out to be a problem worth solving."

"Okay, that's fine," snapped Sybel. "Then let's cut this good-old-boy bullshit. It's beginning to make me nauseous."

"Damn! I love tough women. Okay, Sybel, plain talk. Somebody's played hell with my business. All my holdings are getting fucked. It looks right now like Glinda's behind it. But she's dead. Who's still alive? Here I am, an old codger, I should be shootin' shuffleboard in St. Pete Beach, but instead I got people askin' me the tough questions. I got to have answers quick. You're gonna help or I drop both your asses out my airplane over the Gulf Stream." He looked from Sybel to me. His face was fixed, neutral, but his eyes scared me. Then suddenly they changed—warmed, sparkled—and he smiled. "I still do a little flying every now and then, an aging aviator. Right there's your first week's pay apiece. You get what you pay for in loyalty. I pay cash. However, if you'd prefer to be on a real payroll, receive medical and dental bennies, participate in the stock-option plan, that can be arranged too. Where are you from, Sybel? I got an ear for accents, and I hear some Florida in yours. I'm from Florida, born and raised. Where's home, Sybel? Sarasota?''

"Wisconsin."

"A Florida girl. I knew it. I'll bet you were chief cheerleader for the Seminoles of FSU."

"Just because I'm forced to work for you, do I have to hear your bullshit chatter?" asked Sybel.

"Chucky, go get me another thousand bucks."

"I brought another round just in case," Chucky said. He took a fat stack of money from his cowboy coat and gave it to Pine, who used it to double Sybel's stack.

"Now I pay you enough to listen to my bullshit chatter. Chucky went to FSU."

"Isn't that most fascinating," said Sybel. "Was he a cheerleader?"

"Chucky was on the marksmanship team. What was your weapon, Chucky?"

"Grenade launcher."

"I'm glad we had this chat," said Pine, "but back to business for a minute. You folks just go right on doing what you do. Only now you report back to me. Somebody comes to see you, I'd like to know. It's your job to tell me. G'head, take your money." We did so. "Good. Just one more thing. The pictures. I'll be needing them. Tonight. Negatives, too. Course I got no way of knowing how many sets you got—in addition to Roy's—but hell, in business you got to have trust."

Dickie driving, Tex riding shotgun, we took the Park Drive north toward my neighborhood. Dickie needed no directions. No one spoke. Tex fiddled with the radio, constantly switching channels until he found something he liked, which he never did. I sat trying to foresee what it would mean to "work" for Pine, but I found Tex's channel hopping too annoying to think through. Sybel had gone home in a limo two thousand richer. However, the job lacked security. Before I'd figured out anything, we arrived at my building. I got out, and Tex followed me to the front door.

"Where you going?"

"With you," he grinned.

"No, you aren't."

"Come on, don't be so unneighborly," he said, taking my arm the way the police do, but I jerked it away.

"I'm through being bullied by you, Tex. If you so much as set foot in the lobby, the deal's off and I take the photos straight to the cops."

"Don't even say that in fun."

"I'm serious. You're waiting here. I'll bring them down. I don't want you in my home. Take it or go back and tell Pine you dicked up the deal trying to be a tough guy."

Tex considered pushing the issue but decided not to. "Listen, four-eyes, you go ahead, but you better do everything just right or I'll turn ugly. Real ugly."

"Come on, Tex, in business you got to have trust."

I went up alone to get the photographs. I removed the Family Snaps and put the rest in an envelope. I took the negatives—minus the Family Snaps—from their hiding place in an empty Frusen Glädjé vanilla swiss almond container in the freezer, their natural habitat, and put them in the envelope. On the way out, Blue stopped me in the lobby.

He was crouching in the little alcove beside the entranceway and peering out the corner of the window, now welded shut against the members of the community. He beckoned me with his nightstick, and I joined him.

Tex was standing on the sidewalk near the fender of the car—and he was chatting with the Glacier. They were in this together. Pine's people. Throw in Dickie, who was leaning out the driver's window to listen, and that made a good ton on their side.

"See that huge black dude?" Blue asked. "I mean, how could you miss him. He's been hangin' aroun' ever since you left. He come in here and asked about you. I told him you moved to Pittsburgh. I'd go out there and beat him into submission, only I got on my new dress uniform."

"Thanks anyway."

Suddenly everything out there changed. Chucky tensed and stepped back a pace or two. Even through the welded window I could hear him say, "Beat it, nigger!"

The Glacier reached out, hooked his fingers in Tex's ruffled shirtfront, and parted it like a curtain, sending shrapnel buttons flying. A look of fierce outrage flashed over Tex's face, and he sent a pointed boot in an arc aimed at the Glacier's balls. It never landed. The Glacier caught the boot in his fist two inches from the target. He lifted Tex's leg skyward. Tex hopped twice for balance before the Glacier, in a movement full of terrible grace, blasted Tex flush in the face with a towering overhand right. We could hear the impact—like a well-hit line drive. He fell hard and lay motionless on the wet sidewalk except for his right foot, which twitched spasmodically. I clapped Blue on the back.

Showing more guts than brains, Dickie made to leap from the driver's seat to help his fallen fellow employee, but the Glacier kicked the car door shut on him. Dickie dropped into the flooded gutter and struggled to crawl under the car for refuge, but the Glacier dragged him out by the feet like a pair of dirty pajamas from beneath the bed, sort of squeezed him into a manageable ball, and flung him over the car into the street. I couldn't see him land, but it must have been rocky. Then the Glacier picked up his tiny umbrella, opened it against the drizzle, and strolled away as if he'd done nothing more strenuous than buy a lottery ticket.

"Jeez-zus!" said Blue.

Dickie got up first. He peeked cautiously over the hood to see if the ice had receded. He limped up on the sidewalk to tend to Tex, still supine. Dickie pulled Chucky up to a sitting position, but Chucky still had serious trouble with his head. He couldn't hold it up. It hung limply like Raggedy Ann's.

I went out. I had to sooner or later; best do it while Tex was on his ass. "Hey, what *happened?*" I asked. "Did you get mugged? Gee. This can be a tough neighborhood. You know what you should do when that happens? You should fake a fit."

Dickie, mouth agape, looked up at me. Tex tried, but he couldn't pull it off. Dickie was a skinny-faced little punk in his twenties with greasy black hair that now stood on end like the cartoon man with his finger in the light socket. His nose was skinned raw.

Tex was tough. His eyes were beginning to focus. Had the Glacier poleaxed me like that, brain death would have resulted. The fearful fist must have landed on Tex's forehead between his eyes. Ground zero was turning black even as I watched.

"Hey!" screamed Dickie in a voice laced with hysteria. "That nigger says he's your bodyguard!"

"Bodyguard?"

"That big nigger! You didn't see him?"

Bodyguard? Could he be? My lawyer never called to confirm. Of course he never calls to confirm. "Was this sort of a large fellow?" I queried.

"Large? . . . Large?" whispered Tex. "Did this asshole just say he was *sort of large?*"

"He was a Buick!" squeaked Dickie.

"Yes, that sounds like the fellow. He *used* to be my bodyguard, but I had to let him go. He was just too big to fit places. Well, here's the pictures Harry wanted." I dropped the envelope on Tex's thighs.

"We'll meet again," Tex threatened. "I promise you that." But Dickie largely carried him into the car.

"Nice to be working with you," I said, enjoying myself for the first time since daybreak. I could see, through the open side window, Tex's troubled head lolling on the seat back. I waved as they drove off.

"Hey," I called to the shiny, shadowy street. Blue watched from the window. "Hey, bodyguard."

"Over here."

Behind me! I spun. How'd he get behind me? He'd walked off in the opposite direction. What a bodyguard! He stood under his feminine umbrella and loomed over me, even though he was ten feet away. He was ebony black, like a West African. "I'm Artie Deemer."

"I'm Calabash. Bruce de lawyer say you need some watchin' over. Look like he's right."

We shook hands. I could have comfortably slept in his. "Did you say Calabash?"

"Dot's a fruit. My mom call me after de fruit of de same name."

"Welcome, Calabash. Come in."

"Rains a lot."

"Where are you from, Calabash?"

"Turks and Caicos. Bahama Islands. I fish. I'm a fisherman. But de fish left. Even de little ones. I'm up here doin' some library studyin'. Try to learn where de fish went."

"I see."

Blue met us in the lobby. "Blue, this is Calabash."

"Dot's a fruit."

"Well, you sure did Cala*bash* that dude!"

"Lotta bad men in dis worl'."

"Don' I know it," said Blue.

But I had to be sure. "Blue, can I use the phone in the basement?"

"Sure."

"Excuse me a moment, Calabash." I drove the service elevator to the laundry room and called Jerome's Billiard

Academy. After a long wait, my lawyer picked up. "Did you send me a bodyguard?"

"Didn't you order one?"

"Yeah, but you never called to confirm."

"Did you want a bodyguard or a phone call?"

"Losing, huh?"

"Never."

"What's he look like?"

"Well," said my lawyer, "I've seen smaller one-bedroom apartments."

I was *delighted* with my new bodyguard.

FOURTEEN

THE DEUCE. THAT'S WHAT THE JAZZMEN CALLED IT IN its heyday, this stretch of Forty-second Street near Eighth, before the clubs went under and society's fabric began to tear. Now dopers, dealers, and droolers patrol the Deuce with malice aforethought. Senseless violence hangs like fog in the lights. The aggrieved, sociopathic, and visibly insane pace aimlessly, propelled by the hope of someday kung-fu kicking the shit out of all the men and raping all the women. Sooner or later the city will *clean up Times Square,* and that will be worse. Some slippery pinstriper will suck up the air rights, and where there is so much worth preserving, refurbishing, he will choke the Deuce to death beneath a forty-story glass-and-aluminum testament to his dork. All hatless in the gray rain, a squad of Japanese tourists watched with impassive fascination as Western degenerates hawked their wares or themselves.

On the bright side, Calabash was back there somewhere, and that made my step lighter. An enormous body-guard does wonders for one's worldly confidence. I should have had a bodyguard during my formative years to beat back the malefactors, thimble riggers, footpads, nuns.

Should I father, I'll equip, thanks to Jellyroll, my offspring with bodyguards from birth, make their lives rich in the absence of cold fear. Calabash grew up in Queens, but after his own formative years, his family moved against the traffic back to Turks and Caicos in the remote southern Bahamas by way of the Berry Islands and Upper Bogue, Eleuthera. His father is presently head of the Grand Turk Town Council. "What my Daddy wants me to learn," said Calabash last night, "is if dis is a permanent kind o' ting— dis absence of fish—or is nature jus' shufflin' her feet gettin' comfortable again." Learning costs. I doubled his fee and offered him a room. Jellyroll would approve. We stopped at a Columbia bookstore on the way down to the Deuce and inquired after the ichthyology section.

I climbed a dingy flight of wooden stairs cut into the shadows between Souvlaki Heaven and a porno house now showing that old chestnut *Rump Humpers* ("No ifs or ands, just butts," said the poster) up to a heavily barricaded door. It was covered entirely, fattened like an old kiosk, with Eighth Air Force decals and squadron emblems, British rondels, and a spattering of Luftwaffe insignia. I knocked.

A burly white-haired man looked at me through the chained crack.

"Artie Deemer to see Buzz. He said to come anytime."

"Oh, sure. You're the writer." He shut the door to unchain it and offered me a friendly hand when he reopened it. "I'm Buzz." He was a little paunchy, and his jowls were going to flesh, but I could visualize him at twenty in a wartime photograph, one of those credulous 1940s faces, keen eyed, American, grinning from the cockpit of his Mustang and having the time of his life. People don't look like that anymore.

Buzz's office was wider than a bowling lane, but not by much. If the porn house had stolen two-thirds of his room, Souvlaki Heaven had taken command of the airspace. It reeked of roast lamb and gyro sauce. The cloying smell had infused the fiber of everything in this room—filing cabinets piled to the ceiling with books, yellowing newspapers and magazines nearing spontaneous combustion, the skeleton of a red Oriental rug, maybe even Buzz himself. He left a redolent swirl of gyro sauce in his wake as he ushered me in.

"Pardon our appearance," he said. "We're computerizing."

"Ha!" said a fat woman who sat at the other end of the room behind a typing stand. The loose flesh on her upper arms bounced against her sides.

Buzz grinned. "This is Bessie," he said, "the heart—and heartthrob—of this whole outfit. Bessie, this is Artie. He's writing a book about us heroes. It's Bessie here who looked up Danny Beemon for you."

"Thank you, Bessie."

There were two other men in the room. They had been sitting on the threadbare brocade settee and had stood up when I entered, partly out of courtesy, partly because the door would have hit them in the knees if they had remained seated.

"These are my guests, Artie. This is Rainer Hochheim." He was the short round one with happily twitching bushy brows. "Rainer here flew with Adolf Galland at the end. Jets. Uh, do you know Galland, Artie?"

"Me-262s," I said.

"Oh, good. You know. Some writers don't know anything. It's hard to talk to them."

I knew. I grew up on the books. I read Adolf Galland's book. He describes the jet pilots who flew under his command at the very end, when the war was lost. Rainer had been one of *them*, the first jet pilots in the world, the last gasp of the once great Luftwaffe. This was Jerry, the Hun in the sun, rounder now, softer and stiffer. Some forty-five years ago he was a teenager climbing into the cockpit of the first jet and firing up those fearful Junkers turbines. But by 1945 the Luftwaffe didn't have enough fuel for test flights. Rainer and his colleagues learned to fly the jet on the way to combat the daily skyful of Allied bombers with fighter escort. The temperamental machine often blew itself to bits inexplicably.

"Rainer don't speak a great deal of English," said Buzz. "Say, you don't speak German, do you?"

"No, I'm sorry."

"This is Kenny Brewster," Buzz said, his hand on the shoulder of the man who stood beside Rainer. "They used to call him Hawk on account of that's what he was. We still call him Hawk."

The physical opposite of Rainer, Hawk was tall, well over six feet, and wiry in a western sort of way. We shook hands, then sat down, Hawk and Rainer side by side on the couch, Buzz and I in desk chairs at either end. The narrow room prohibited a circle of seats.

"The Hawk smoked Rainer's 262 over Wetzlar on Thanksgiving Day, 1944. Hawk's modest. He says it was just a lucky shot—full deflection, Rainer movin' about seven hundred plus. But Rainer says—least as near as we can make out—that it was a brilliant piece of flyin' by the Hawk. See, Artie, this is their reunion. Reunions between friends and foes alike. We arrange 'em." It was then that I noticed Buzz had no left hand. He pointed at me and mimed scribbling motions on his stump and said, *"Das Book,"* for Rainer's benefit. He seemed to get it, bobbing his brows in the affirmative.

Suddenly I felt guilty about the lie. These men were genuine. I was not. I thought about my father. Had he survived, he might have attended a reunion here. I might have accompanied him, my small hand enfolded in his large one as we climbed the stairs to this wonderful smelly firetrap.

"How's for a cigar, Artie? Rainer brought 'em from Berlin. Havanas."

"Yes, yes," said Rainer, who with a smile offered me

the box of serious cigars. I took one, and Rainer lit it with
a battered Zippo.

"How's about a cigar, Bessie?"

"How's about a gas mask?"

"Would you rather I didn't smoke this, Bessie?" I
asked.

"Now see, Buzz, this is a gentleman. You could take a
lesson from him."

"I'll watch his every move," Buzz grinned.

"I knew Danny Beemon," said Hawk. "He was my
first commanding officer. I'll bet Rainer heard of him."
He turned to Rainer and said, "Danny Beemon," in a
loud voice to crack the language barrier.

"Yes, yes. Hot," he said and shook his fingers as if
they were wet. "Hot like my friend Hawk."

Even the enemy knew Danny Beemon's name. That
happened on occasion, but only with the very best. Ironically, the fighter pilots on opposite sides had more in
common with each other than with the civilians they fought
for. They subscribed to the same code of professional con-
duct, they dressed the same, their faces even looked the
same in the old photographs, as if their features were
formed not by national gene pools but by the airplanes
they flew.

"Naw," said Hawk. "Beemon was way out of my
league. I ain't just being modest. Danny was born to it.
You could tell."

"How?" I asked.

"Well, you just could, I don't know. By the way he
flew. I don't know how to explain it without getting all
weird, like religious. . . . Ninety-nine percent of the guys
had to *learn* to fly fighters. Right, Buzz?"

"I sure did."

"Me too. One percent didn't need to learn. They were
born knowing. They were natural." Hawk mimed a dive
for Rainer—feet on the rudder pedals, left hand on the
throttle and pitch selector, he shoved the stick forward

with his right and translated loudly: *"Das Natural."* Rainer understood the maneuver if not the word.

"Here's his file." Bessie drew it out of her desk, and Buzz went to get it, a soiled manila envelope full of answers. My heart was beating fast. I extinguished my cigar before it turned me green.

Buzz put on the half glasses that hung from a cord around his neck. Hawk and Rainer sat cross-legged and watched him. The file contained several typed sheets, a sheaf of news clippings, and the cover from *Life,* July 18, 1944. Buzz said, "Bessie copied the file for you."

"You mean I can take it with me?"

"Sure." Buzz read. "Right. . . . Right."

"What?"

"They dragged him home to do a morale tour."

"Yeah, kicking and screaming," said Hawk. "But you could see it coming. He was just too handsome to stay."

"I don't understand," I said.

"See, Artie, once a hotshot got some ink, well, his flyin' days were numbered. Especially if he looked like Danny Beemon. Too valuable to the brass hats to risk flying anymore. You sort of become this living advertisement for the war effort. One day you're flying the best airplane in the world with the best friends you'll ever know. *You* got no morale problem. But the next day you're flyin' home to tour airplane factories and shake hands with local politicians who don't know shit—pardon me, Bessie—about how you been spending your youth and who don't care long as they get their pictures in the paper with their arm around your shoulders. Maybe Hawk had the same experience."

"Nope. Only time being homely ever paid off."

"One time on a train this senator asked me—he was just trying to make conversation, the jerk—he asked me, 'Have you ever soloed?' Hell, I was a fighter pilot. They only *got* one seat!" Then Buzz showed me a sere yellow newspaper clipping. It was unmistakably Danny Beemon.

He stood stage center at curtain call in a tailored dress uniform, the breast covered with decorations. Bob Hope waved and smiled at the audience on Beemon's right. Lana Turner was on his left, her arm entwined in his. Behind Lana, Bob, and Danny, a long line of high-kicking chorus girls showed their stocking seams. "That don't look so tough to take, does it?" asked Buzz, passing the clipping to Rainer and Hawk.

"What happened to Beemon after the war?" I asked.

"Got killed testing jets," said Buzz, searching the file for confirmation.

"Lot of guys bought it that way," Hawk added.

"No," said Bessie. "It says in there he got terrible burned but he didn't die."

"Oh, yeah, here it is . . . 'Burns over seventy percent of his body, . . . critical condition.' Yeah, I guess."

"But there's the other article." Bessie waddled over to show us. She reached around Buzz's neck to flip through the file. She removed a long clipping and skimmed it. "Remember that British doctor McIndoe?"

"Plastic surgeon."

"I think he sort of invented it, or perfected it, back when so many of the RAF boys were getting disfigured in 1940. Here it is—this is the end of Danny Beemon: 'The C-47 was en route from Muroc AFB to the new McIndoe Burn Center in Miami when it went missing over the Gulf of Mexico. Search planes have been recalled. The airplane has been officially declared lost. Among the dead is Maj. Danny Beemon, the famous ace who was severely burned after his jet crashed in the California desert." Her task complete, she returned to her desk.

"Boy," said Hawk, "I bet D.B. sure hated dying as a passenger in a C-47."

"Yeah," Buzz agreed.

Rainer nodded solemnly. We sat in silence.

"I'd say one of the big reasons I'm alive today is the

stuff Danny taught me,'' Hawk said. "Me and Harry Pine got there together. He was our first CO.''

"Harry Pine," I blurted out. "Did you say Harry Pine?''

"You heard of Harry Pine, right, Buzz?''

"Sure. Met him once in London.''

"I wasn't in his league, either,'' Hawk said. "Well, hell, you're writing a book, maybe you'd like to hear a true story about Harry Pine and Danny Beemon?''

"Sure.''

"Witnessed this myself. Never forget it. Me and Harry were new, only Harry was one of those natural-born stick-and-rudder guys, and Danny saw it right away. You could tell by the way they looked at each other. So Danny—this was our first real mission—Danny put Harry Pine on his wing to get to know him. We escorted B-17s to Emden, then we broke off and went down on the deck to shoot up this Jerry airfield on the way home. Rainer's boys were getting on to that tactic by then, and they ringed their airfields with light and medium flak guns. We lost some of the best people that way. Only hope was to come in low—I mean *low*—so the flak guns couldn't bear so well. Jerry got on to that trick, too, and started mounting their guns on towers so they could fire down on us as we came in low. Harry Pine went in on his first run. I was to follow while other guys shot up the towers. Pine took a round through the canopy—big cannon shell passed right in front of his eyes and out the other side. If that had happened to me, I'd have crashed and burned right there. Harry just lost a little altitude, but his prop ticked the runway. Destroyed it, of course; destroyed the engine, too. Somehow he coaxed the P-47 up to bail-out altitude. You know, Buzz, those were great planes, but they glided like pianos. I don't know how he did it. He bails out and comes down in an alfalfa field not a half mile from the airfield we're still shooting up. You could see Jerry going after him. Trucks, cars, motorcycles, bicycles, converging on this kid standing in the field like a scarecrow. They *want* him. We made two firing passes at Jerry, and they kind of lost interest in capturing Harry—least till his friends went away. Then Danny Beemon comes on the horn and says in this quiet voice—I mean, this voice is so calm it seems like he's bored—he says, 'Cover me. I'm gonna pick that boy up.' "

"Great!" said Buzz.

"Pick him up? I didn't even know what he meant till I see him swing upwind in a landing approach. He *lands* in that alfalfa field smooth as if he did it every day. Pine jumped up on the wing as Danny turns back for takeoff, then we see Pine climb into Danny's cockpit. They couldn't even close the canopy it's so crowded. They got to know each other, all right. They flew all the way back to England like that. On the way Danny comes back on the horn, in that same bored voice says, 'Any of you guys endanger government property like that, you'll be peein' in the snow in Goose Bay, Labrador.' You should have seen the ground crews when two guys climb out of the 47, after they made a perfect landing. Harry Pine was the only man I ever met who could hold a candle to Danny Beemon for plain flying ability." Hawk leaned forward, elbows on his knees, and thought about his youth.

"Do you think we could see Harry Pine's file?" I asked.

"Sure thing." Bessie went to get it.

"Funny thing," said Buzz, "there was this other writer in here asking about Harry Pine."

"There was? When?"

"Yeah, he was stone ignorant, never even heard of a P-51."

"When?"

"I don't remember any writer," said Bessie, opening and closing file cabinets.

"I don't know you were here. It was a weekend or a holiday. About a year ago maybe. He called for an appointment, that's why I came in. I can't remember his name for nothing."

"Do you remember what he looked like?" I asked.

"Sort of. Skinny guy, dark hair. Tough talking for a little writer. Mustache, big droopy one."

"I can't find it," said Bessie. "Harry Pine is gone. Have you been fooling with my files, Buzz?"

"No, sir."

"Well, then Harry Pine is gone."

When Calabash and I returned to my place, it was barely noon. There was a message waiting for me on my phone machine: "What say, lover man. Cobb here. I thought you might want to know somebody claimed her body. Her uncle. California swish name of Gordon Jainways. He's in the book, 22 Perry Street. You keep in touch now, lover man."

Was that Cobb's version of a kindness?

I sat on the floor beside the bed and tried to think about connections. Jellyroll came over and nuzzled me in the ear, as he does when he wants to be brushed. I brushed him for a while. He loves it; he throws back his head and works his jaws in ecstasy.

I looked up Gordon Jainways in the telephone book.

CHAPTER
FIFTEEN

I ASSUMED HE'D TURN ME DOWN, A STRANGER WANTING
to talk about his murdered niece. Instead, he invited me
to his home. Twenty-two Perry Street, near Bleecker, was
one of a row of perfect four-story brownstones from the
years before all those wars, when civility counted for
something. This was the kind of home that would brighten
up one's world view just to live there for a few years. The
rain had stopped and birds trilled from sidewalk elms as I
rang the bell.

Gordon Jainways was in his late sixties, dapper, tweedy,
with a paisley tie tucked beneath his vest. He didn't smile,
but his handshake felt like a welcome. He led me down a
hallway paneled in oiled cherry wood that exuded its own
glow like a living thing and into what would have been the
drawing room originally. I stopped short.

"I'm a puppeteer, Mr. Deemer."

The room was filled with creatures. They hung on the
walls, stood on stands and on their own legs. Sometimes
there was only a head, often the entire animal, always
perfectly naturalistic. I approached. There were two hundred of them, maybe more, birds, reptiles, mammals, even

marsupials, animals from all zones of nature. Their diversity, from tropical forests to frozen tundra, and their colors were dizzying. I wanted to reach out and touch a speckled fawn, but I resisted.

"I saw your name at the morgue, Mr. Deemer. You identified her body."

The animals unnerved me. As a kid I fantasized a life with animals. Before I slept, they gathered in my room, an aggregation of species just like this one, all eyes on me; and on those nights the world seemed safe and sound. I sat down in an armchair and looked into an ocelot's eyes.

"I'm going to take her back to California, unless you can tell me why she should be buried here."

"No."

"Has my work upset you in some way?"

"No. It's exquisite. But it reminds me of when—never mind, pardon me."

He watched with kindly, credulous eyes while I collected myself.

"Mr. Deemer, what exactly is your interest in this?"

I told him I wasn't exactly certain, but that I had loved his niece and that I called him to learn something about Billie's past. I told him I didn't think I even knew her real name.

"It was Eleanor, after her mother."

I tried it out in my head, and the sound made me sad. A polar bear cub eyed me from the fireplace. I passed Jainways the envelope holding the Family Snaps.

Wordlessly, he looked at each, then up at me. I thought for an instant that he had a flash of gold in his iris, but he did not. It was only a trick of light, or a longing. "Where did you get these pictures?"

"Billie left them. . . . In my apartment."

"I took them," said Gordon Jainways. "This Christmas puppy—I gave it to her."

"Petey," I said. "Your sister told me his name. She is

your sister, isn't she, the lady at Bright Bay Nursing Home?''

He nodded.

''And she was married to Danny Beemon, Billie's father?''

He nodded again, but suddenly tears clouded his eyes.

''Your photos seem to show a happy family.''

''Shattered,'' he said.

''By Danny Beemon's death?''

''By airplanes. . . . Did she tell you about her baby brother?''

I shook my head. She told me nothing.

''He was called Gordon, after me. But he was dead by his eighteenth month. . . . I believe that Danny Beemon killed Gordon in a drunken rage.''

I didn't speak. Gordon Jainways looked away, into the midst of his animals, but his eyes were fixed on something I couldn't see.

''In 1952 Billie was five. Danny Beemon was a test pilot; the great war ace was doing the thing he was born to do, and my sister was happy, even though they lived in a shack on the high desert of California. A dreadful place called Muroc Air Force Base. All the best pilots were there. For them, Muroc was a dream come true—the best fighter planes in the world at their disposal and no supervision. When D.B. was happy, his charm was like a movie star's. People orbited about him, but he wasn't happy for long. During a single week, in separate accidents, the entire group of test pilots, except Danny, were killed. Burned beyond recognition. But that's not what made Danny Beemon sad. He was used to his friends' immolation. What made him sad was that the Air Force grounded him for publicity reasons. If an unknown boy gets burned up in a crash, that's too bad, a telegram to loved ones, but if a famous war ace gets fried, that's bad PR. The military mind blanches at that.''

''But I heard he crashed in a jet test.''

"He did. But first he was grounded. There's much in between. Do you want a drink?"

"Yes."

He poured us bourbon. "D.B. couldn't live life on the ground. He began to drink heavily and mix it with amphetamines, yet they stayed on in that foul desert because Danny hoped his flight status would change, and he'd be ready. It didn't, and the hero, the Ace of Aces, became a figure of pity on the flight line. Drunk, he once told me that even his flyboy chums started to avoid him, as if grounded were a disease you could catch. Well, tough shit, in my view," Jainways snarled. "I have little patience left for these military freaks. He could have flown for any commercial airline in the world, but airliners weren't good enough for him. He had my sister and her son and daughter to love him, but that wasn't good enough either." He paused. "I'm still angry, thirty-five years later. Billie told me all about the . . . accident. She had been standing at the bottom of the stairs. 'Like Dolly's neck,' she said, shaking Raggedy Ann's floppy head. I took Billie back to San Francisco at her mother's request. One night, I took her to see *The Wizard of Oz*."

There was her name. Glinda the Good. I felt like crying. Billie Burke.

" 'Are you a good witch or a bad witch?' She came to ask it of everyone. Every event in her world was caused by one witch or the other. My shrink friend, who owns this house, would call that magical thinking, and he says it's often seen in injured children. Meanwhile, my sister pulled strings and got D.B. reassigned to flight test."

"What strings?"

"Tight strings, Pentagon strings. You see, I'm the last son in a long line of military men—a Jainways died with McClellan's men at Malvern Hill, 1862, and my father was also killed in battle—but I am a puppeteer."

"General Jainways was your father?"

"Oh? You've heard of him? Are you a student of war?"

Legend had it that General Jainways, beleaguered with his men in the jungles of Burma and out of ammunition, ordered the company to hurl its own shit at the charging Japanese, who finally overran the defenders at the loss of some face.

"If your sister had that influence all along, why did she wait until then to use it?"

"I don't know. I've asked myself the question. In any case, D.B. crashed fifteen seconds into his first flight. Something broke. His face looked like a puddle of glue. They spent the next six months in a world of pus, until the final airplane got him."

"What happened to Eleanor?"

"Which one?"

"Both."

"Billie came to live with me. I haven't seen her in ten years. We had a falling out—about Danny Beemon. She seemed to have forgotten everything. For some reason, I took it upon myself to remind her. She hated me for it. I thought one day we'd make up, but . . . ."

I swallowed a sob. "What about your sister?"

"Little by little she lost her mind. Lately she's been saying that Danny B. is alive. One big happy family."

"How lately did she start saying that?"

"Why do you ask?"

"Just curious."

"Curious, Mr. Deemer?"

I nodded.

"About a year ago," he said, watching me closely.

The doorbell chimed, and he excused himself.

His animals stared at me as a group, three-dimensional memories. A great deal had happened "about a year ago."

Gordon Jainways returned and pulled the sliding door closed behind him. "There is a man named Watson at my door. He is an agent of the FBI. He wants to ask me questions about my niece. Why the FBI?"

"I don't know."

"I don't believe you, and I don't believe you are just curious. You'd better leave by the back way." He motioned me into the adjoining living room, a sublime wooden place with fifteen-foot-high ceilings. "That door will lead you to the garden. There's a path to the street on the west side of the building. Mr. Deemer, why are you paying for my sister's care at Bright Bay? Elwood Dibbs told me so this morning."

"Because Billie used to own the R-r-ruff Dog, but she gave him to me."

"Oh, my, Billie owned the R-r-ruff Dog. . . ."

As I left the house, I slipped on a wet flagstone and fell painfully on my hand. The rain had returned, hard and steady.

She was waiting for me in her original spot on the fire stairs. She wore a tight sweater and skirt, and her black hair was frizzed. There was trouble on her face. I quickly placed us behind double locked doors.

"The fridge!" Sybel hissed. "Now it's at Renaissance!"

"Is Freddy—?"

"Yes! I went to work like nothing happened, just like that bastard Pine said to do. I was alone all day—" She took a gasping breath. "I decided to look around. There's a temperature-controlled vault on the top floor—Artie, his face is fire-engine red!"

I hugged her. She trembled like a cold little girl at the beach. Somebody had moved Freddy in his Hotpoint crypt. Why? I wondered what you'd use for a job like that. A dolly? Why move him at all? To dispose of him? Or was it a setup? Pine setting up Jones? Jones Pine? Neither? I suddenly felt exhilarated and clear. Now it would blow up in their faces. Not only that—I could cause it to blow. Just tell the cops, anonymously. Now I had some power. That seemed so clear to me then, and I loved it.

Sybel sat in the Morris chair and hugged her stockinged shins. Jellyroll looked questioningly into my eyes—like a Jainways animal. I hugged him, and he licked my chin. Billie used to roller-skate everywhere she went. The image floated across my memory. Summer, Billie would wear shiny white shorts, and she would undulate her hips to slow herself down on the incline between West End and Riverside.

"What's the matter with you?" Sybel wanted to know.

"Me? Nothing."

"You had a funny look on your face."

"Naw," I said convincingly. It had suddenly dawned on me that I didn't *want* to make that call to Cobb, but at first I didn't know why. Cobb would take it away, that was why. This whole business—my life since Billie died—would come to an end without me. I'd be merely an observer, absent at the end.

Sybel watched me with unmasked suspicion. "You're obsessed."

"Obsessed?"

"It's written all over you. Billie has you by the balls. You're like her puppet."

"Billie's dead."

"Not for you." She headed for the door.

"Where are you going?"

"To the cops. Why didn't I go there in the first place?"

I stopped her. She gritted her teeth and slugged me in the shoulder. That seemed the rhythm of our relationship. I stop her from walking out on me, she clouts me for it. Jellyroll watched, distressed.

"Listen," I said, "we can't just tell the cops straight out. We've been withholding evidence in a capital crime!"

"You sure you're not a lawyer?"

"If Cobb chose to press it, we could land in jail."

"That's a lot better than a Frigidaire."

"I have to take Jellyroll to work."

"When? *Now?*"

"There's been trouble on the set. I've got to go. Come with me. Calabash'll be behind us. Then we'll come back here and call the police, but first we'll figure out a story. Please."

Sybel paused, then nodded. "Do you think she had all this planned?"

CHAPTER

SIXTEEN

NEW YORK CABDRIVERS REACT TO DOGS IN STRANGE, often voluble ways. In the home cultures of some cabbies dogs are food, not fares, and the sociological implications of a ride to work always make me nervous. Nothing in New York is simple. Maybe nothing anywhere is simple, but I've been here too long to know. Since they're prohibited from public transport, there's no other way to move a dog around the city. The rain didn't help. That made us considerably less desirable. However, a cab turned the corner and stopped before we'd been standing two minutes. Then he spotted Jellyroll, screwed up his face with repugnance, and waved us away from the door handle as if a dog on the floor of a car, a dented and swaying pollutant that didn't even belong to him, represented an affront to his sainted mother. Why didn't he see the dog when he stopped for us? It happens that way all the time. Is he half blind? Or did he figure we'd just leave the dog on the corner and get into his piece of shit wreckage, probably Mafia owned? On any other night, comfortable in my natural stance as keen yet invisible observer, I might have mused on the complexity of social interaction when so many cultures try to live together, but tonight it made me late, tense, and intolerant. That was no state to be in when one had to collide with Stockman Billingsly, as soon I must. Then there were no more cabs.

I glimpsed a flash of Calabash back there doing his job with the usual easy competence. I motioned for him to join us. Enough of this covert bodyguarding. The time for subtlety had passed. Now was the time to call in the fire-power for all to see, everyone, Pine, Jones, Cobb, Palomino, Stockman Billingsly. Let them imagine the cost in casualties and property damages to fuck with us. I pictured with a chill of pleasure Calabash and me wearing crossed bandoliers, festooned with lethal devices, kicking in the studio doors, leveling our flamethrowers at their hearts and saying, "Okay, fuckers, you're on Jellyroll's time now," and then Jellyroll himself would enter snarling, pulling a wagon loaded up with extra parabellum ammo.

Jellyroll was delighted with all the company, now that things seemed reasonably normal. We were off to work.

A Checker lurched to a stop. The driver, a bald black man, slid across the seat and rolled down the passenger window. "Hey, buddy, ain't that the R-r-ruff Dog?"

"Yes, indeed."

"Well, *get in.* The R-r-ruff Dog. Boy. You know who else I had the other day? I had *John Forsythe.*"

"Dey make TV *here?*" Calabash asked as we strolled into the studio. His innocent enthusiasm made me feel protective of him, my bodyguard. Sometimes I get sick of irony.

The "plot" was typical of the R-r-ruff mind. Jellyroll, wagging his tail with expectancy, approaches a bowl of ordinary dog food (It says "Ordinary Dog Food" on the bowl), sniffs it, and his tail drops dejectedly. Ordinary Dog Food. Then he lies down beside the bowl and puts his head between his paws. . . . His "Owner" enters, sees his dog's dejection, and says, "You want the Full Flavor Dog Food, don't you, R-r-ruff?" Jellyroll leaps up and barks. The Owner gives him a bowl of R-r-ruff, which he devours gleefully. Stupid, but no problem. Then, however, comes the reason we all were here for a makeup.

Jellyroll and his Owner cuddle and nuzzle lovingly after dinner, thus overcoming the audience with cuteness, moving them to purchase whole hillocks of R-r-ruff. Stockman Billingsly played the owner. There was a different "plot" about every six months, all brimming with cuteness. The present one should have taken about two hours' shooting. This was the second day. The problem was simple. Billingsly was a sour old sot who hated my dog, this job, and his own life. Jellyroll recognized his hatred and wouldn't cuddle convincingly, wouldn't nuzzle at all. He was probably frightened for his life. Jellyroll loves to please; it's easy to teach him things. In return for care and affection he has agreed to make me rich. But I couldn't make him nuzzle Stockman Billingsly.

The mood was instantly apparent. Long faces everywhere. Director, camera people—with a twinge of longing I saw Phyllis—agency people, the client, even the people in the booth, looked like shipwreck victims just before the shock set in. There he was stage center on the shitty kitchen set in skeletal light complaining to two young assistant stage managers assigned to take his heat and nod politely. Somehow, even through all that light in his face, Billingsly spied me. He made a big show of drawing forth his three-pound pocket watch and putting on hideous black framed reading glasses that sat on his face like a pair of handcuffs. "Finally," he said stentoriously, "I have plans for August." He looked at the ASMs and laughed like an old rogue of a charming kidder, and kept on laughing until he forced the ASMs to join him. Pretty soon he'd start referring to Jellyroll as the "cur." But tonight would be different, I told myself. Tonight I would murder him.

The director, a gifted stage director and a kind of friend of mine, came over to head off trouble. Kevin Malquist—he even had a director's name—smiled at me and shook hands. "Like a duck's back, Artie. Just like a duck's back."

"Sure, Kevin, no problem." I introduced Sybel and Calabash and asked Kevin if they could watch. He welcomed them affably and set up two folding chairs behind the center camera, from which Phyllis rolled her eyes at me. Calabash was awed. Jellyroll happily greeted all his friends on the way to stage center—and Stockman Billingsly. If a dog can be said to turn on his heel, that's what Jellyroll did. "Stay," I told him.

"Can we get started?" Billingsly wanted to know.

The stage manager called places, and I took Jellyroll to his entrance. The stage manager called quiet, and Kevin called action. It went beautifully—until the nuzzling part. "Cut." We tried it again. No nuzzling whatsoever. Cowering. He began to turn upstage toward me for some reassurance. "Cut. Let's take five, ladies and gentlemen."

Kevin took me aside. "Artie, isn't there *any*thing you can do? You agree that this isn't working?"

"Sure."

"Look at those guys over there—" The agency people and the product people hunkered in the corner, whispering encouragement to one another. "They're going to start dropping dead one by one, the overweight alcoholics first. I've got to do something, Artie, fast."

"He has to make up to Jellyroll, obviously. He has to pretend to like him. Then we can only hope Jellyroll buys it."

"There's nothing *you* can do? I'd be better if there was something you could do."

"I'm sorry, Kevin."

"I'd hate to think, Artie, that you'd leave my ass out on a limb just to make the old guy look bad."

"I wouldn't, Kev."

"So what does he have to do?"

"Ruffle his ears, smile, the usual."

Stockman Billingsly was a pioneer in the days of live TV. He appeared in all those weepy drama specials like "Omnibus," which I remember as a vaguely depressing blur of gray flickers when I was about ten. His claim to enduring fame is "Dad's Home!" He played Dad in a family of nitwits meant to personify basic American values without making viewers feel inferior. Neither Dad nor Mom had any genitals. The sons arrived in cereal boxes; just add baking soda to see your boys grow into men.

Kevin called me onto the set. The lights burned the back of my neck. "Artie, show Stockman what you were showing me about dog handling. That was very interesting. Show him how you ruffle his ears. Know what I mean, Artie?" Kevin pleaded.

I demonstrated how to pet a dog.

"Will he bite?"

"Of course he won't bite."

"Now maybe there's something in that, Stockman," said Kevin, trying another tack. "Maybe Jellyroll feels that you're frightened of him. If you would—"

"Excuse me, young Mr. Malquist, but you seem to imply that this is my problem when we both know it's the cur's problem."

"If you call him cur one—"

"Pardon me, Stockman—" Kevin smiled as he grabbed me around the shoulders and led me away from the set. His smile vanished. "I'm asking you, Artie, I'm asking you face-to-face. Give me a break here. I want to wrap this up. I got a rehearsal tonight. I'm doing *Danton's Death* at the fucking Public, and I don't want to show up a wreck. Now please," he hissed through his teeth.

"I'm sorry, Kevin, I've been upset lately."

"I know. I'm sorry too."

"But he's got to make up to that dog." I looked over at the money folks to see who had died. Nobody yet.

"Affection, that's what we're talking about, right? Maybe I can get him to do an improv." Kevin hurried back to the hot lights. I followed slowly.

I told Jellyroll to sit, which he did, and Billingsly reached out to pet his head, only he held his other hand— balled in a fist—cocked and ready to punch Jellyroll should he bite the hand that petted him. Three-year-old children in the park toddle over to pull his hair and the mothers show no concern at all that their children might get mauled after one look at Jellyroll's smiling countenance. Now he sat staring at this cocked fist and began to pant. He looked back over his shoulder at me with an expression that asked, "Just what is it you want from me?"

"I think you have to seem a tad warmer, Stockman. Try kneeling down to his level."

"Kneeling?"

"Sure, try it."

He kneeled. You could hear the poor bastard's knees click all the way to Queens. But he kept his fist cocked! Jellyroll turned away.

"I'm sorry, but this is unacceptable. Mr. Fleckton, are you out there?"

"Right here, Stockman." Fleckton was the account exec, who I believed cultivated consciously his obsequious exterior to mask a heart like a crushed beer can.

"I'm sorry, Mr. Fleckton, but this cur is impossible to work with. I've been in this business for forty years."

"But Stockman, that's our spokesdog."

Now we were down to it. It was that simple, and that's what stuck in Billingsly's craw. The *dog* was irreplaceable. Momentarily I felt sorry for the sad old man. But I didn't want to temper my anger with sadness, so I pinched it off.

"Then I think you should consider finding a competent handler, I really do, Mr. Fleckton. Okay, let's run it—"

And he charged to his place. Maybe Jellyroll thought Billingsly was charging him, maybe he was more generally confused, but he stepped directly in front of the charging has-been. Billingsly tripped over Jellyroll and would have fallen had he not caught himself on the phony breakfast nook, which cracked sharply and hung at a crazy angle. He stood still and collected himself. Then he drew back his boot to kick my dog—

"Halt, motherfucker!" It was me. I was pointing at his heart with my index finger. Every mouth in the room gaped open, and I heard on the fringes of my awareness a collective gasp.

"What! How dare you—?"

"You were about to kick my dog!"

"How dare—I was not! My shin—I injured my shin! I was rubbing it!"

"Bullshit!"

"Artie, drop it."

"I'll sue you, Deemer! Barbarian! I'll sue you for damages!"

"Damages? Damages!" I bellowed. "You haven't seen damages yet, you wooden fuck! I'll show you damages—" And I moved on him. Did I really intend to hurt Stockman Billingsly? Kevin, face contorted, moved to shield my victim, Jellyroll bolted, the camera people seemed to converge on me, but I only took a step and a half before being enfolded in black tree trunks. Calabash carried me away, my shoes two feet off the ground, and before he put me down, he said quietly in my ear, "Good ting you got a bodyguard—you a very hostile fellow."

"That's all for tonight," I heard Kevin announce. Then, pointing to Fleckton he said, "I'll meet you gentlemen in the conference room on three."

"Kevin," I said as he approached, "he was going to kick Jellyroll."

"That's not how it looked to me." He walked away.

Phyllis gently took my forearm and led me into the hall

near the restrooms. "Artie," she said, "you're having some kind of crisis here. You're in some kind of a rage. Are you in therapy?"

"I was—"

"Get back. I have names if you don't. After that you need someone else to love. I'll call you." She patted my shoulder and returned to the studio. People glanced my way as they buttoned their raincoats at the street door. They looked at me as if I had been fiddling with myself on the IRT, that mixture of revulsion and fear.

"I guess people in the arts," said Sybel, "tend to be a little high-strung."

"The Theater of Cruelty."

Sybel seemed more concerned than revulsed or frightened. I thought she'd walk out on me again.

Jellyroll sat down at my knees and looked up. "Are you in therapy?" his eyes seemed to ask.

He must have been watching my building. Sybel, Calabash, Jellyroll, and I weren't inside five minutes when the phone rang. "You watchin' it?" he asked.

Leon Palomino. They *all* had my number. "Watching what?"

"The news. Go turn it on."

We stood around in a clot, watching. Sybel caught on first and gasped.

Renaissance Antiques was engulfed in flame. "LIVE" said a sign at the bottom of the screen. The roof caved in with an enormous cough, and the flickering red reflected on our faces in the darkened bedroom. Fire-fighting equipment covered Eleventh Street. From the Broadway side, pumpers arced jets of water, hundreds of gallons a minute, but the fire didn't seem to blink. "No, we can't rule out arson at this time," intoned the chief.

"Did you do that?"

"What, you think I'm callin' for you to admire another guy's torch job? Look, I've been doin' some thinking about the night Billie and my brother got killed. Maybe you want to hear what I saw the next night. Maybe you want to pass it on to Pine, maybe not, I don't know.''

"What?''

"Not on the phone. I got two tickets to the Mets. Me and Freddy were hopin' to attend, but hell, he can't make it. Gooden's pitching.''

"What time?''

"One-thirty start, but let's get there for BP. I'll leave your ticket at the booth, third-base line, under the name Dog Walker.'' He was giggling when he hung up.

I told Sybel and Calabash.

"Jesus,'' said Sybel, "you didn't accept!''

"No, I just said that. We're off the hook,'' I said. "We don't even need to tip them off!''

"What?''

"They're going to *find* Freddy in that fire!'' What a beautiful prospect that seemed to me. I was so far gone that the exquisite irony—Freddy found in Billie's refrigerator after a conflagration in the building she'd been spying on—made me giggle, a lot like Leon's giggle. "We're in the clear!'' Events had leapfrogged over us and our photographs. We are obsolete and, therefore, my logic went, safe from the cops and crazies.

Sybel considered Freddy. "Do you think there would be anything left of him?''

"Refrigerators don't burn up. That's the beauty of it,'' I enthused. "This writer friend of mine keeps all his originals in the fridge. We never even *heard* of any photos or any note from Billie. Nothing. Innocent bystanders.''

"I'm going home,'' Sybel said. "Will you watch me home, Calabash?''

"Be my pleasure.''

"They're going to question you about the fire, Sybel.''

"No kidding.''

"But you're an innocent bystander employee. You didn't see a thing. No corpse in the vault, as far as you know."

'Will you shut up!"

"Yes."

"What about that poor Stockman Billingsly?"

"Huh?"

"He's going to lose his job, isn't he?"

CHAPTER

SEVENTEEN

CALABASH WAS UP EARLY, SITTING IN MY MORRIS CHAIR, loading guns, examining chambers, peering into barrels. Jellyroll lay across his feet. Every now and then Calabash would raise one foot playfully, then the other, causing Jellyroll's body to rollercoaster. He wagged his tail after each trip and growled for the next. Ignore the munitions and this would have seemed a sweet domestic moment. I pretended not to notice when, as we left to walk Jellyroll, Calabash stuck a gun into his waistband and covered it with rain gear.

The rain had slowed the city. Pedestrians had given up. That head-down urban gait had devolved to a primitive, melancholy plod. Even the Jersey car commuters had lost all hope, sitting in five-mile lines, indifference and lassitude painted on their faces. Riverside Park at a glance could pass for a rice paddy in Laos. Jellyroll loves to wade.

Calabash clutched my forearm and I froze. "Look at dat!"

A decapitated chicken, wings unfolded, lay at our feet in the mud. A penny had been placed on its breast, and the carcass was surrounded by candle nubs. Propitiatory rites. I had seen this before.

"Dey got dat here?"

"Everything." My bodyguard had gone rigid on me. "You're, uh, familiar with voodoo?"

"It runs in my family."

Rivulets of rainwater had separated the feathers on the chicken's breast, leaving channels of pink flesh, and Calabash seemed to be sinking into a private funk.

A wan, emaciated wino sat in the rain on a nearby bench. His clothes were saturated. He held the bare metal skeleton of an umbrella over his head, and in a chilling squawk he sang, "No, no, they can't take that away from me."

I bought a *Post* from Akmed's newsstand on Broadway. ARSON, in filthy two-inch type. Calabash and I hunkered under the awning to read while Akmed crouched to cuddle Jellyroll. This was a daily ritual, Jellyroll licking Akmed's face, whining with affection, while Akmed mutters sweet nothings in an ancient language. Too bad he had no English; Akmed would be a natural for Stockman B.'s spot. Two gas cans were discovered on the scene, "typical in cases of arson by amateurs," said an FDNY spokesman. But there was no mention of poor Freddy. At least a day of cooling, I proclaimed to Calabash, would be needed before they could search the debris. "How do you know dat?" he asked. Years of experience on the arson squad in major metropolitan areas. Besides, the headlines would have been different. FRIED FROZEN . . . CORPSE IN THE CRISPER. The *Post* would have had a field day. On the way home, Jellyroll did his business in the gutter and I picked it up with the *Post*, a perfect mating of tool to task.

Like Queequeg, Calabash sat in my Morris chair, brooding on the implications of that sacrificial chicken. When with distracted strokes he began to clean his guns, I went into the bedroom to call Sybel. No answer. Nothing to do but wait.

I tried to listen. I chose Ben Webster and Art Tatum, Red Callender on bass, Bill Douglass on drums, for their sumptuous, lucid tones. That's what I needed, lucidity. Sumptuousness would be a bonus. Jellyroll sighed, stretched, and flopped across Calabash's feet. I heard "All the Things You Are" and "Where or When," but I couldn't concentrate.

The air reeked of gun oil, but that's not what blocked concentration. It was Billie, haunting me. I saw her in that sweet organdie dress at the foot of the stairs as her infant brother bounced down them. "Like Dolly's neck." The stairs had a red runner, and the banister was white. There was a wood-framed mirror on the wall at the first landing where Billie stood, where Gordon died, and a half-round table beneath the mirror. The image was clear and sharp, but the setting was incongruous for a desert air-base cabin—too frilly, too suburban colonial. Then I realized that out of my own youth I had called up the set from "Dad's Home!," Stockman Billingsly's paean to domesticity. Billie—young Billie—in that setting, her brother dead at her feet, made me feel like breaking something. I phoned Buzz at the Big Eighth.

They hadn't found Harry Pine's file despite their top-to-bottom search. Bessie, however, remembered one thing. Harry Pine's last address. Moxie, Florida. "Bessie only remembered," said Buzz, "because the name's odd. Moxie." I looked it up in the atlas. Moxie was a couple of bean fields on Route 441, running east-west between West Palm Beach and Belle Glade on the shore of Lake Okeechobee. Near Lion Safari Land. Then I tried Sybel again. No answer.

I phoned Jellyroll's agent. "What a dog, what a dog," Shelly exclaimed before I stated my business. "I told them straight out. There will be a delay. Canine immunization. You know what they said? They said, 'You take all precautions with our star.' What a dog! I told them ten days.

How's that? Ten. You'll *definitely* be ready in ten days, Artie?''

"Right, Shelly." I was certain he had heard about last night's fracas. News travels fast around the small world that cared, at least enough to gossip, that the R-r-ruff Dog's owner was cracking up, and I wondered how Shelly would handle it. Discreetly, apparently. We chatted for a few minutes about Samoa. "Lotta fine twat in the tropical regions" was Shelly's view. Shelly was frightened for his livelihood.

"I'd like you to do me a personal favor, Shelly."

"You just name it, Artie boy."

"Do you know Stockman Billingsly?"

"The famous lush? Sure."

"I'd like you to help him out if you can."

"Stock-man Billings-ly," he said, pretending to write it down. "Check."

"Thanks, Shelly."

"No prob. Let me just say two words to you, Artie: *ten days.*"

"Right, Shelly." In ten days I could be awaiting trial. Or burial.

I tried Sybel again. No answer.

Then, before noon, I asked Calabash if he had ever seen the Mets play.

"I'll bring de heat."

"De what?"

"De gun."

"Oh."

"She's gettin' to dose reefy shores, don't you tink?"

Gary Carter swung in his distinctive fashion from inside the BP cage and drove two ropes over second base, then another deep to the opposite field, catchable, two strides in from the wall. I reminded myself that I wasn't there to study baseball. Before Carter's next swing, at a cue I didn't see given, the Mets jogged off the field, and the ground crew rolled out the tarp. Sheltering from the rain in the runway entrance to the third-base-line box seats, I scanned the spectators through binoculars. There weren't many. I saw no one I recognized—except Leon. Calabash jumped when a 747 from La Guardia cranked on full boost over left field. That goddam chicken!

Leon Palomino sat alone ten rows above the dugout. He was eating a hot dog. I pointed him out to Calabash, who found him with the binocs, then went to take a seat twenty rows behind him. It was too early and too wet for the ushers to care where we sat. Then I scanned the nearby seats in search of someone who seemed to be watching Leon, but I saw nothing suspect. Leon and I were probably the only suspects in Shea Stadium that day.

"Well, if it ain't Arthur Deemer, Mafia dog walker." He wore a big grin. Leon had no eyebrows, only singed follicles where eyebrows had been. His knife hand was heavily bandaged. He wore the same fatigue jacket as in the park and a green watch cap pulled down to where his eyebrows should have been.

"Artie," I said.

"You got it."

"How did you get my name?"

"I looked you up in *Who's Who in the Mob*. Sit down, check these seats, huh, have a frank."

"No franks. Aren't you a little nervous sitting here in the open today after burning down a half a city block yesterday?"

"Naw. How about these Mets?"

"Why did you burn down Renaissance?"

"The next night after Billie got greased, I sat in a parked car on Eleventh, waited to see what I'd see. You know what I saw? Jones and Ricardo. They wheeled this covered object about yea big"—he formed a half refrigerator-sized square with his arms—"out of Billie's studio building and across the street and into the Antiques. Next day I see you and you tell me you saw Freddy's body in that little ice-box. What would you a thought about that?''

"That they killed Freddy.''

"But I couldn't find either one, so I took out their building.''

I opened my umbrella and put half of it over Leon.

"That's okay. I don't give a shit.'' That much was abundantly clear.

"Who is Jones, anyway?''

"You don't know Jones, huh?''

"No.''

"That's odd, ain't it, you bein' in with Harold Pine so tight.''

"I'm not in with anybody. I'm just a guy who loved Billie and wants to know what happened to her.''

"Then it's a wonder you ain't been greased.''

"That occurred to me, yes.''

"Let 'em try.'' Leon grinned with a twinkle of delight in his naked eyes, and he flipped his jacket open for a moment. I saw a big black automatic in a holster duct taped to the inside of his jacket and the butt of another gun stuck down his waistband. "They greased Freddy, and so far I only got their building. We ain't *near* even yet.'' He wore combat boots, not the routine black leather combat boots but the jungle fighter's kind, with olive canvas cutouts like they wore along the DMZ in 1969. He was dressed for fantasy, but the guns were real, and so was his fire. He zipped up his jacket halfway.

"Why do you want to tell me anything at all?'' I asked.

"I'm leaving tonight. I want somebody to know what I saw. Hell, maybe they'll get me before I go. But they ain't ever gonna find poor Freddy, and I don't like it to end like that, Freddy bouncin' on the bottom of the sea with Jimmy Hoffa. . . . They ain't even going to play this fucking game. Look, I'll start at the beginning, okay?''

"Okay.''

"They sent us way the hell and gone into Dutchess County for a pickup, ancient clavichords or some shit."

"Who did?"

"Phone call at home from somebody I never heard of, says he's calling for Harry Pine. We get out where he said to go, end of a dirt road, wild forests, and I'm gettin' nervous. It just didn't feel kosher. I look over at Freddy, the fucking guy's driving like we got a load of nitroglycerin in the truck. Pine owns this psycho assistant who always wears a cowboy suit. Cute guy."

"Chucky," I said.

"Yeah, right. Artie, it ain't at all clear what you know and what you don't."

"Chucky tried to intimidate my bodyguard."

"You got a bodyguard?"

"A big one."

"What'd your bodyguard do?"

"Beat Chucky senseless."

"Aw right. Your bodyguard around now?"

"Yes."

"Armed?"

"Like a helicopter gunship."

"Good."

The stadium organist began to play "Singin' in the Rain."

"So Chucky's waitin' for us out there in front of this beat-to-shit cabin in the forest, and he's got four other psychos sittin' on the porch for show. Chucky, that phony smile, says we should have a beer, relax. So one psycho throws a Bud in the air, this other psycho whips out his Bulldog and blasts the Bud in half before it hits the ground. Two things: Me and Freddy, we're impressed, one, but two, we're also relieved. If these psychos meant to pop us, they wouldn't a treated us to a firearms demonstration. Then cowpoke Chucky tells us what he got us out there to hear. Somebody's blackmailing Harry Pine's friends, and it better not be us. Well, it wasn't us, but we both knew who it might have been.''

"Billie."

"Yep."

"Because you had told her something about the Antiques?"

"You name it, we told her. But then, see, I thought it was just me told her. Freddy thought it was just him, so neither of us said anything. We got back to Queens, we start makin' excuses to each other, things to do, get the trucks lubed. Christ. We both make a beeline for Billie's and show up on the stoop simultaneously. She'd been porking us both, and we'd both been singin' about what big-shot wiseguys we were. We about came to blows right there, Freddy and me. Big shots. That's all we ever wanted to be, but we fucked up again, just like school.''

"Exactly what had you told Billie?"

"About Harry Pine, about how we're his right and left nut respectively.''

"But what specifically?"

"About his airlines."

"His what?"

"You don't know about that?"

"No."

"You don't make much sense to me, Artie."

"Me, either."

"Yeah, well, I know that feeling."

The organist began to play ''Raindrops Keep Falling on My Head,'' and Leon listened.

"What a stupid fucking song."

"What kind of airlines?"

"It sure ain't Delta."

"It's illegal?"

"Yeah. Illegal."

"Mafia?"

"Sicilian International."

"Drugs?"

"You name it. Anything that'll fit in an airplane. Money, lot of the time."

"Money?"

"Say you got six million in twenties, you know, from all the pizza slices you sold. Harry Pine flies it to their bank in the Cayman Islands. People, too."

"What people?"

"Hotshot fugitives, crooked congressmen. I heard about this dictator. Crazy spic dictator, killed thousands. He's into the wiseguys for a couple mil, they want to protect their investment, so they get Pine to fly him out right under the noses of the Commie insurgents. Rumor has it they shot a hole in his favorite airplane, so he turns around and strafes the shit out a their positions while the dictator's screamin' at him, fucker can't believe he went back. Anyway, if it's big-time and you need some flyin' done, you call Harry Pine. You know what I told Billie? I told her I was his trusted copilot. The trucking business, that was just a front for my true life. Captain Leon Fucking Midnight at your service, ma'am."

"How do you know so much about Pine?"

"I told you. I wanted to be a big shot. Big shots *know*. Course only dumb fucks tell." He stopped and looked out across the covered field. "That's why Billie was such a big thing. Me with a woman like that. Educated, well-spoken, hell, an *artist*. Not to mention gorgeous. And she loved me. Wrong again." There was no anger in his voice when he spoke of Billie, only sadness.

"But why the store? Why did a man like him fool with the wholesale business?"

"He used it to launder his own money. After a flight somebody buys his whole stock, and now he's got legit bread."

The organist: "A Rainy Night in Georgia."

"So you confronted Billie?"

"Confronted? Yeah, that's what we did. Like we're joined at the hip. She laughed in our faces. Laughed. Like

167

we're a couple of clowns. Which we were. She ever do that to you? Laugh in your face?''

"No.''

"Well, you're lucky. Then she says: 'I've got Harry Pine right where I want him.' You believe that? We told her she must be hallucinating. You don't blackmail guys like that or anybody they know. You don't even *think* about it. But Billie says she has these photographs. She says if anything happens to her, these photographs will ruin Harry Pine. Ruin Harry Pine. You don't happen to have the photographs in question, right?''

"Right.''

"Yeah, that's what I thought. I hope that geek don't play any more rain songs.''

"So you and Freddy went to Billie's studio, drilled the lock, and ransacked the place.''

"That what you'd a done?''

"Yes.''

"We didn't find a thing but bums. We sat down in there and talked about doin' Billie. Borrow our friend's Mako and take her fishin', she's bait, but we were just jackin' off. Neither of us could a done it. Christ, I still love her a little. Freddy probably died lovin' her a little, even though she as good as greased him. So we decide to bounce her around some, throw a scare into her. We flip a coin to determine who's gonna do it. The other's gonna wait in the studio in case the bouncer learns where the pictures are hid, phone it back. I won the toss. I went to her place, but I couldn't beat her around. I was gonna fucking *plead* with her.'' He stopped abruptly.

"Well, what happened?''

"Nothing. She never answered her door.''

"Do you think she was dead by then?''

"Yeah. Or dying.''

"You went back to Acappella?''

"Where? Oh, yeah. By then Freddy was dead too. I didn't know it though. I started looking for him. I staked out Billie's apartment all the next day. That's where I saw you in your Con Ed suit. When I staked out the Antiques, I saw you again. I followed Sybel just to see what she was up to. She meets you at the library. That night I saw Jones and Ricardo wheel the object across Eleventh Street. You know what I thought it was? I thought they found the photographs. You know the rest. I saw you walkin' your dog— you told me what was in there. I greased their building. Here we are.''

I felt excited in a tingling, visceral way, as if it were a sunny day, bottom of the ninth, tied, bases loaded, two out, Darryl Strawberry stepping to the plate. It felt unified, at least this part of it. I understood the when and where and now the *why* of it. Pine's psychos threw a scare into Jones, and, just like the Palominos, Jones went straight to Billie. It surprised me to realize I was talking aloud; I thought I was thinking. ''Jones and Ricardo tied her up and tried to drown the photos out of her. Billie didn't tell, so they killed her. Then they went to the studio and found Freddy waiting. They killed him because he made a perfect scapegoat. 'Here's the blackmailers, Mr. Pine. They're dead.' ''

''Wait a minute,'' said Leon. ''How do you know she didn't tell?''

''What?''

''You said she didn't tell, so Jones killed her. How do you know she didn't tell?''

''Oh . . . well, I just assumed—''

''Yeah, you assumed because *you* got the photos yourself.''

''No—''

''Yes, you do, Artie. You're lyin', but I don't care. Those photos don't mean dick today.''

''I know.''

''So what did they show? Just for curiosity.''

I told him what the photos showed, but I didn't mention the Family Snaps. They were none of his business. They were mine. Besides, they didn't fit. They were part of another unity still unclear, perhaps never to be understood. But one thing was clear to me then—those family photographs constituted the most intimate statement Billie ever made to me.

"You mean she was bullshitting us totally? Those photos are a joke? I thought they'd show Harry's pals makin' a snuff film or something, wearing Nazi suits."

"I guess so," I said. "What about Harry Pine?"

"What about him?"

"You all flocked to Billie's."

"Yep."

"And he followed you?"

"I don't see the point otherwise. You been around long enough to pick up a tail yourself."

"I didn't see anyone."

"Course not. Could be usin' three or four psychos, but don't worry, Artie. You got two pals under my coat." I didn't like the way he grinned at me when he got to the part about the pals.

With a chill not due to the cold rain, it dawned on me that Leon was *hoping* for a shoot-out. "Leon," I said, "Mr. Jones still has a big problem."

"Right. Me."

"No, another one."

"What?"

A mean gusty wind whipped the center-field flags, first in one direction, then the opposite, with barely a pause in between. It felt sad to discuss such things in a ballpark, where reality should never intrude. "As of about four o'clock yesterday that refrigerator was inside the Antiques—and Freddy was still inside."

"What? How do you know?"

"Sybel saw him."

"Christ!"

"If they didn't move him between that time and the time you burned it down, then he's there right now."

He slid down in his seat petulantly, almost boyishly. "Fucking typical. I come along and burn up my own brother."

"If he was still in the icebox, I don't think he got burned up, . . . not entirely."

Leon slowly straightened and looked at me sideways as he did so. A light flickered in his eyes. I continued:

"The arson squad finds a corpse in a refrigerator in the ashes of a suspicious fire. That's a hard thing for the owners of the property to explain."

"Yeah . . . that's right. That would be their ass!" He grabbed my hand before I understood what he meant to do with it. He meant to shake it, delighted, exactly as if Strawberry had just homered to right to win the game.

"How many people know you torched the store?"

"Just you, pal."

"Then you don't need to worry. It's not in my best interest to tell things I shouldn't know in the first place. Just like the photographs. If you vanish, there will be no one to come looking for you. So don't do anything with those guns," I stressed, but he seemed not to be listening, staring out across the field. "Do you hear what I'm saying?"

"I hear you, Artie. . . . Great seats. Too bad they ain't gonna play."

"Leon—how do you know Billie was sleeping with Jones?"

"Huh?"

I repeated my question.

"She told Freddy and me she was, when we, uh, confronted her."

That was the part I didn't understand. Why tell? "What kind of person is Jones?"

"Freddy and me used to call him the Grave Robber. He's got fish eyes, nothing there. He likes little girls. I'd see him every now and then with a different little sweetie each time, about fifteen. Ricardo driving them around."

"What about Ricardo?"

"What is this? Know-your-enemy sort of thing?"

"I guess."

"You know what Ricardo does for a hobby? Raises fighting dogs. He was tellin' me once how you train the dogs to kill. Starve 'em one week, little puppies, beat shit out of them the next week. Dog gets hurt in the ring, can't fight no more, you know what he does with him? Ricardo thought this was real intelligent. He ties the hurt dog's front legs together and makes the healthy dogs tear him apart. Good practice, he said. I'd love to grease that motherfucker."

"You don't need to."

"You're right about that, Artie."

"Let me ask you one more question. Why do you think Billie taunted you like that? That doesn't seem like sound business. If you're blackmailing someone for money, why taunt those involved? Why even mention those photographs to you and Freddy, *or* to Jones?"

"Why? Because she was nuts, that's why."

The announcer told us that the game had been officially called. Leon shook his head. "Good luck, Artie." He got up to leave.

"Good luck, Leon."

"And good luck, Mets," he said with a wave at the field. Then, hands in his pockets, head down, he walked up the aisle and away. Shortly afterward I did the same, glad to have Calabash behind me. I walked through the runway and into the corridor, lined with refreshment and souvenir stands, that led to the exit ramp.

Calabash wasn't behind me; he was ahead of me. He stood by the men's room door, looming over the straggling diehard fans. With the tiniest movement of his head he nodded at the door. I went in.

I chose a urinal with a vacant one beside it. Calabash stepped up. I did not look at him, nor he at me. "You're bein' tailed," he said without moving his lips. I froze.

Was this it? Would my assassin pick Shea Stadium? In public? I'd rather it happened in my own home, John Coltrane in the background.

"You go out," said Calabash. "He'll pick you up, unless dey got a couple workin'. I gonna walk right behind him so you can view him. If you want the bastard cracked, you itch de crown of your head." Calabash walked out.

I was so far out there that little bits of reality, when they could reach me, left me reeling. The dirty tiles above the urinal, the spot of crust I had been watching when Calabash said, "If you want de bastard cracked . . . ," seemed to swell with meaning. All I had to do was scratch my head. That was obdurately real, just like the person following me. That hunk of dried something on the wall took on the image of death itself. I thought of Freddy's black face. Someone had written "fuck the circus" on the tile above the spot I stared at. I walked out the door, wondering what that meant.

Vendors were packing up their gear. I didn't look left or right until I'd passed through the turnstiles and onto the patio that fronted the parking lot on one side and the elevated walkway to the E train on the other. Then I stopped. I tried on a couple of Mets caps from a wet vendor who clearly wished I'd leave him alone. Careful not to touch the top of the cap once I put it on, I looked back to where Calabash towered over a short man in his mid-thirties, black hair. He wore a blue anorak. As I paid the vendor, I realized I recognized the man. From where? I looked back again. He had a dark Fu Manchu mustache. I didn't remember that, so I tried in two brief glances to picture the face without it. . . .

Jay Kiley! A playwright Billie and I met years ago at a party somewhere. I was being tailed by a *playwright?*

CHAPTER

EIGHTEEN

"HEY, ARTIE, WHAT SAY, DUDE? I THOUGHT THAT WAS you. I'd recognize that bald spot anywhere."

"Hi, Jay. Long time."

He looked deep into my eyes, his soulful act, and said, "What a tragedy about Billie, what a tragedy."

I nodded and resisted the temptation to scratch my bald spot vigorously. I saw a play of his once at some showcase house. All the women were cardboard, and all the men were him.

"Actually, I've been wanting to discuss that with you. Drink a beer, cry a little, know what I mean?"

I'd hang myself first.

"Actually, I wanted to talk a little business. Funny I should run into you like this. I wanted to talk about some photographs."

I didn't respond at all. Stone faced. He clearly sprung that on me to check my reaction. I gave him none.

"What photographs, Jay?"

"Billie's photographs."

"Billie took a lot of photographs."

"Yeah, but these are special."

"How so?"

"Come on, Artie, let's *talk.*"

I told him to meet me at the Liffey Pub in an hour.

Calabash was sitting at the bar by himself, and Kiley sat in a booth directly across the room. I had gone home and phoned Sybel, but there was still no reply. Phyllis had left a message on my machine. In her throaty voice she said she was wondering how I felt and invited me to call her when I could. I couldn't just then, but I wanted to.

I picked up a draft beer and sat in the booth across from Kiley. "So how you been, Artie?" His brow furrowed with concern for my well-being.

"What did you want to talk about, Jay?"

"Right down to business, huh? I never knew you were such a press-on sort of dude, Artie." He unzipped a leather portfolio that had been resting against his thigh and removed an eight-by-ten black-and-white. It was creased and dog-eared, the upper right corner gone. He dried the tabletop with a napkin and then put the photograph down before me. It was Harry Pine in front of Renaissance Antiques, back when there was such a place, taken with a long lens from the same elevated angle. Pine wore a dark knit shirt, light twill pants, and Topsiders, and he was doing nothing in particular, looking west on Eleventh. "Do you know this man?"

"No."

"You don't?"

"No."

"His name's Harry Pine. Billie gave me this picture, told me the dude's name and that he was a war hero. That's all she knew, but she offered to pay a hundred a day to find out more."

"When was this?"

"Let's see, this is May. . . . About a year ago. Strange, huh?"

"You tell me."

"Okay. I was between productions. I was up for a grant, but hell, that's all fag politics, so I took the gig. Jay Kiley, playwright-sleuth. I got my first lead from this old fart who runs a newsletter about old pilots." And then he stole Bessie's Harry Pine file from the file cabinet. He showed me photos of Harry Pine as a young pilot, the obligatory shot standing in front of his plane and alighting, big smile, after a successful mission. There were articles about him and a copy of *Stars and Stripes* from 1943. "They don't even look like the same guy, do they?"

He was right. The man of sixty-five photographed from Billie's studio bore no resemblance at all to the boy forty-five years before, the natural-born stick-and-rudder man.

"That made it tricky, but here was my next clue. I mean, this would make a *great* play." He showed me a faded newspaper photo with no accompanying article. Harry Pine posed in front of a ramshackle wooden building with a sign that said PALM COAST AVIATION. He tapped the sign with his fingernail and said, "This was in Moxie, Florida. Moxie, you believe that? Great details. I showed this stuff to Billie, and she said go. Gave me a check for five hundred dollars and said call me from Moxie. I start hanging around the jerkwater airport in Moxie. Check it out, Jay Kiley, ace. Can you imagine me at the controls, Artie?"

"No."

"Actually I thought I cut a dashing figure. Ronald Colmanesque. I took flying lessons. I mean I didn't get a license or anything. I split without paying—I was protecting Billie's investment. I figure that's the way to get the old geezers talking about Harry Pine. Become one of them. You know, Artie, everything's got groupies, everything. There's about twenty old geezers who did nothing but hang around Moxie Field every day. They'd show up about ten with their Igloo Coolers and drink beer under a banyan tree. I don't know, this would probably make a better movie. Your dog's agent, does he handle film scripts?"

"Nope."

"So once I got these guys talking, they never shut up. I told the geezers I was doing an article for *Esquire;* they started bringing me show-and-tell shit. This Harry Pine was a local legend back in the late fifties. And there was another guy, another hotshot ace from the war around back then. They called him D.B. I learn his name. It's Danny Beemon. So these geezers keep bringing me clippings from old papers, and I begin to piece together this incredible story. You want to hear it?"

"Sure," I said indifferently, and put my hands in my lap so he wouldn't see them tremble.

" 'You can't kill D.B.' That's what the old geezers used to tell me, and I'm telling you that up front because it's kind of key to the story. You can't kill D.B. Okay. It's 1967, a dark and stormy night. Just kidding. 1967. A plane crashes on takeoff from Moxie Field. This plane, a twin-engine something or other, was owned by Harry Pine's Palm Coast Aviation. But when cops and rescue units get to the crash site, they find no pilot. Vanished. You know what they *do* find? This is where it gets good. After they put out the fire, they find the airplane's filled to the roof with medical supplies."

"Medical supplies?"

"Yeah, and surgical supplies. They found an operating table, top-of-the-line stuff. About three-quarters of a million worth of stuff in 1967 dollars. Artie—" Kiley glanced from side to side as if someone might be listening—cheap theatrics. He lowered his voice. "The stuff was all stolen."

"Who filed the flight plan?"

"Oh, you're a quickie, you are, Artie. I'll get to that anon. What I'm telling you now took about two years to come out. Big investigation, widespread scandal. Entire Miami administration toppled as a result. FBI was involved in the case, FAA, you name it. Turns out two doctors were stealing the city hospitals blind. Of course you couldn't do that unless you had some officials in your pocket. The doctors did. They stole an estimated four million worth of medical gear.''

"What were their names?''

He gave me his between-you-and-me-sincerely look. "Harvey Keene and Barnett Osley. You know them?''

"No.''

"You don't know any of these people?''

"Not yet. What were they doing with all that stuff?''

"This is where it gets better. All this came out in the trial, see. These two doctors—they weren't in this racket for the loot. They were redistributing the equipment to small rural clinics throughout Florida. Guess who owned the clinics.''

"Keene and Osley.''

"Right, only these were free clinics. They had some state support, but the patients paid nothing. Keene and Osley were performing surgery at their little clinics. They were supposed to have performed organ transplants, shit that, say, New York General would have considered radical. They're doing it free of charge. That organ transplant business, that was never proved, but they were still doing some outside stuff. Here's where it gets even better. The trial becomes this media circus. Everybody's hysterical. You ought to read some of the news accounts—'' He reached back into his portfolio and thumbed around for an unbearably long time before he removed two photocopies of news articles. "Check it out.''

I read both as carefully as my excitement allowed, but they didn't need a close reading. They were not subtle. One called Keene and Osley a couple of Frankensteins, then went on to ask righteously, "How many died under their knives?'' The other took the opposite tack. It called them Robin Hoods and charged that they were being persecuted by the AMA for operating free of charge.

"These are two of the calmer ones. You ought to see the editorials. But you probably get the picture.''

I was beginning to get the picture.

"There were a couple other factors in this trial. One, they're fags. Two, the fags won't talk. Clearly, Keene and Osley couldn't have stolen all that shit without some heavy help. Stand-up guys, these fags. They won't even admit that they ever heard of Palm Coast Aviation or Harry Pine. 'How did the stuff you stole get on that airplane?' 'I don't know.' That's what cooked their goose. If they'd have talked, they'd have walked. They got sentenced to five years, reduced to two, and their licenses were permanently revoked."

"Who filed the flight plan?"

" 'You can't kill Danny Beemon.' According to the geezers, Danny Beemon walked away from fatal crashes all over the world. Then he disappears after the fiery crash of a plane full of stolen operating tables on the way to curing poor people. How's that to fuel the fires of legend? You know what those geezers told me half shit faced under the old banyan tree? They said, *'He'll be back,'* and they all nod sagely, like one day he'll fly in and make their lives beautiful or something."

"Where was Harry Pine during the trial?"

"Vanished. The night of the crash. Poof. Harry Pine and Danny Beemon, gone. 'Just like the old days,' the geezers said. I'll tell you, Moxie Field was a time warp. 1943. Stop the clock."

"So you came back and told Billie all about it?"

"Sure, that's why I went."

"You told her about Danny Beemon?"

"Just like I told you."

"What did she do?"

"Whoa, slow down, Artie. I thought you didn't know any of these dudes."

"I don't."

"Okay. What did Billie do? She dismissed me. She wrote me a check on the spot for five hundred, but it hurt my feelings, Artie. I had just done this bang-up job for her, risked ass flying, got prickly heat, now she's giving me the brush without telling me why I did it.''

"How did she react when you told her about—about Florida?''

"She dismissed me. I told you.''

"No, I mean personally." Why was I asking him? "What was her mood?''

"Oh. Excited. No, more. Vibrating. She could hardly hold her coffee cup. Look at it from my view for a minute. I didn't get the grant. Some twenty-year-old Yale prick got it. I happen to know he can't write squat. Plus my wife bolts with my life savings. Glum financial outlook. Stealing dinner from the Red Apple gets depressing after a while. Billie just gave me five hundred dollars to do a pretty mysterious job. Five bills, no problem, like it was the Con Ed bill. What would you have thought—if you didn't have a rich dog?''

"That there was real money nearby." That's what he wanted to hear. It was my pleasure to give it to him.

"Exactly! But where? I started thinking along these broad lines: if Pine's in New York, why not Keene and Osley? You know how I found out? The AMA. Keene and Osley still subscribe to the journal. Where is it sent? Staten Island. Bright Bay Nursing Home. Ever heard of it?''

"No.''

"No?''

"What did you do then?''

"When are you going to know something, Artie?''

"When you get to the punch line.''

"Okay. I went back to Billie, and I said, Gee this is quite some story, old pilots, the Robin Hood doctors, flaming crash, and now I find they all live in New York. I said, This sounds like a great story for *New York* magazine, did she mind if I wrote it? She wanted to know how much *New York* would pay. I told her about two grand. She wrote me a check. Bingo. You loved her, I loved her— God rest her soul—but, Artie, she was after bigger game.''

"Pine?"

"Yeah. But she wasn't ready to tell me anything. She said it was personal, nothing to do with money. I decided to test the water, see what was personal and what financial."

"What did you do?" I asked, because he wanted me to.

"I paid a visit to the good doctors out at their place. I told the manager I'd wait, sat down in the lobby and talked to the old geezers. I like old people. I don't want to be one, but I like them. Finally, Barnett Osley arrives, and we have our chat. I'm writing this article for *New York* magazine, and I'd like to talk to him about Florida. Then, when he put his dentures back, I asked if he could line up an interview with Harry Pine. The geezer about shit his chinos. He hems and haws, and you know what he says? He says, 'We wouldn't want to disturb Danny Beemon, would we?' And he's getting out his checkbook."

"Danny Beemon? You mean—?"

"Yep. Right there at Bright Bay resides D.B. *You can't kill Danny Beemon.* He's burned to a crisp, Artie, an invalid. This is a good part here. Osley, his hand shaking all over the check, says, How much would *New York* pay you for an article like that? I say, About five thousand dollars. Bingo."

It hit me physically, the realization. It drove me back in my seat. *That* was the blackmail! Osley went straight to Pine after Kiley shook him down, and that puts us to the evening of Billie's murder. The Palominos—and Jones— were summoned to the country, where Chucky told them that somebody was trying to blackmail Harry Pine's friends, and here was the blackmailer sitting across the table from me.

"What's wrong?"

"Nothing. Tell me, Jay, when did you talk to Barnett Osley?"

"When? . . . Last weekend. Saturday."

Billie died Sunday night.

"Have you told me everything now?"

"Huh? You all right?"

"Just fine. Is there anything else?"

"Hell, yes. There's the photographs."

"Exactly *what* photographs, Jay?"

He was growing exasperated, but that wouldn't be the half of it, because as I sat there looking into the bastard's face, I knew what I would do. I would call Harry Pine and sell out Jay Kiley, let the psychos use him for target practice. He was as good as dead, and that helped me relax enough to talk to him.

"Come on, Artie, the photographs Billie took. The photographs she got killed over! What do you *think?*"

They didn't make sense in this context. "Jay, how do you know about those photographs?"

"What? Billie told me, how else?"

"I don't see why she'd tell you about them. You said yourself she was very secretive about everything. Why would she tell you about the photographs?"

"Then you *have* them?"

"No, I told you, I never heard of them."

His shoulders sagged, his brow wrinkled. I thought he was going to cry. "I need those photographs, Artie."

"Yeah, do you? What do you plan to do with them?"

Jay Kiley was melting before my eyes. "Take them to Harry Pine."

"Good idea. Run your *New York* magazine scam?"

". . . Yes."

"Shrewd, Jay. I sure hope you locate them. Sounds like there's some fine money in it for you. Of course, it's a tad risky. You might end up like Freddy Palomino."

"Freddy Palomino? What is he, an actor?"

"You never heard of him? Well then, like Renaissance Antiques—ashes."

"What are you talking about?"

"Renaissance Antiques."

He looked at me blankly.

"Never heard of it, Jay?"

"No."

"Billie told you about the photos, but she never mentioned the Antiques?"

"Right, she never—"

"You're a liar. How do you know about the photographs?"

He collected himself and said, "Billie told me about them."

"Good-bye, Jay," I said with as much finality as I could fit into two words, and then I walked away from him. I set my untouched beer on the bar beside Calabash, who didn't even glance at me. "Follow the prick," I muttered to Calabash. Then I went home.

I greeted Jellyroll for all of thirty seconds and left him with a woebegone look on his face as I made for the phone. Danny Beemon was alive at Bright Bay. I called Gordon Jainways.

CHAPTER

NINETEEN

GORDON JAINWAYS SAT MOROSELY IN THE CAB IN THE depths of the Brooklyn-Battery Tunnel. "I hope he's dead," he said after I told him about events at Moxie Field. If I were him, I probably would have felt the same. I wanted him to be alive. "What are we going to do if he is there?" Gordon demanded with a glare.

"Do? I don't know. Talk to him."

"About what?"

We crossed the Narrows, and I looked north into the Upper Bay, but it was lost in the murk.

"What do you propose? Do you propose we barge in on him and peer into his burned face? 'Is that you under there, D.B.?' "

My proposal didn't seem quite that crass until he spelled it out. It was easily that crass. But I didn't care as long as he didn't try to thwart me.

Nothing had changed at Bright Bay. Probably nothing ever changed except the grinding turnover of residents. I peeked in. The lobby was full of old folks. I saw Gordon at the desk talking to the receptionist. He was to draw her away by asking for his sister, leaving the way clear for me to slip into the residence wing, but the lobby was too crowded.

The receptionist stood up and tinkled a little bell. "Dinner is served," she announced.

Obsessives need to remain flexible, ever ready to modify crass plans when an even crasser alternative arises. Perhaps the receptionist would leave her post; perhaps she would even join the others for dinner, leaving me to slip into the residence wing unseen by anyone. I waited five minutes, then reentered the lobby. It was empty. I could hear the clank of dishes and the mix of elderly voices from the rec room as I slipped through the double doors that separated the residence wing from the lobby. I ignored the sign that said PRIVATE in gilded letters. Red carpet runner and nondescript artwork, the hall extended deeper than I had imagined, then turned sharply to the right. I began to knock on doors. When no one answered, I opened the doors. None was locked. Each room was a simple single like a college-dorm room, personalized with sweet touches of home and heart, framed photos of loved ones, down comforters, toiletries and private objects, the mementos of long lives, the past fixed and the future predictable; but those poignant fragments didn't dissuade me. A woman approached, shuffling down the hall on her aluminum walker. I recognized her. Elwood Dibbs had put a flower in the top buttonhole of her sweater. What was her name? Dibbs had asked her about her feet. Mrs. Florian.

"How do you do?" I said.

"Good evening," she smiled, and continued her trek to the dining room. When she passed through the double doors and into the lobby, I continued my search. I knocked on number 10. No answer. I opened it. A Raggedy Ann doll sat propped against the pillow on the neatly made bed. I went inside. Her clothes, dresses mostly, were hung in perfect order in the doorless closet. They smelled gently of flowers. Jasmine?

Then I saw the framed photograph above the headboard.

A large photograph, perhaps fifteen by twenty, and slightly grainy for that reason, it showed Billie and her mother, the two Eleanors, in a room standing arm in arm, smiling. What room? I stepped closer. It was Billie's studio. Unmistakably. They looked happy together. When was this picture taken? I left before I started to cry. Never before last Sunday night had my life been so filled with intense and quickly changing emotion.

I opened six more doors, numbers 11 through 16, before I took a break, turned right, and walked to the end of the long hall. Two more double doors. I pushed them open, and the hallway changed completely. The floor inclined slightly, a rubber runner for traction, to still another set of double doors, but these were different. These were made of polished aluminum, with small glass ports reinforced with chicken wire between the panes. A janitor's bucket on wheels was propped against one door, holding it open. I looked in.

It was an operating room! Tanks of oxygen and other gases, a high aluminum table with a circle of powerful lights suspended from the ceiling above, machines with little green windows overlaid with red grid lines, many other gadgets and arcane apparatus, most of which appeared as hulking, vague shapes, since only one small fluorescent light was on—they were doing it *again!*

"Excuse me, sir—"

"Ha!"

He was a scrawny Hispanic guy about sixteen. He wore a white uniform and carried two spray bottles of cleaning fluid. "Oh, sorry, didn't mean to scare you."

"That's okay."

"I'm sorry, sir, but guests aren't allowed back here."

"I guess I'm lost. I'm looking for Danny Beemon."

"Beemon . . . Beemon?"

"He was burned a long time ago."

"Oh, sure. Ace."

"Ace?"

"He likes you to call him Ace. He's in seventeen."

"He is?"

"Back down the hall right where it turns left." He pointed.

I nearly ran.

Number 17. The door was closed. I knocked. No one answered, so I gently opened the door.

He sat in a wheelchair silhouetted against the dull light from the picture window. Head hanging, he seemed to be sleeping. Across the arms of the chair lay a metal dinner tray, but instead of food the tray contained pieces of a plastic airplane model, the fuselage already assembled. It was a Hawker Typhoon. Other plastic planes hung from the ceiling on nearly invisible monofilament strings, single-engine fighters, all of them, all meticulously painted, an instant frozen from a forty-year-old dogfight in miniature. His hand moved. He wasn't sleeping. He looked up at me—

His face was scarred and twisted. His upper lip was gone, or fused into the flesh above it, exposing teeth and gums. Except for a tiny tuft above his left ear, he had no hair, and his right ear was absent entirely. When I was a boy, an older neighbor taught me to assemble plastic models, airplanes, ships, cars, my interest following his. Barrett was his name. He's dead now. When Barrett's models broke or when he simply grew tired of them, he'd arrange them on the garage floor, squirt on lighter fluid, and set them on fire. We younger boys would gather to watch, say, the *Forrestal* burn while we imagined the real thing. "Neat," Barrett would say as the flames buckled the flight deck. I thought of Barrett and his sacrifices at that moment because when they were over, when only a puddle of charred plastic remained, it looked exactly like this man's face. The fingers of his right hand, which reached for his Typhoon, were fused into a claw. The hand stopped in mid-movement when he saw me.

"I—I beg your pardon. Wrong room." I closed the door

and stood trembling on the red carpet in the silent hallway. I don't know how long I stood before, mechanically, I began phase two of my plan. I really didn't have the stomach for it anymore, but we had come this far. . . . Could Gordon recognize *any*one under all that scar tissue, let alone a man he hadn't seen for decades?

I returned to one of the empty rooms I had already violated. Phase two depended on the phones. I hoped for private lines independent of the switchboard. The room I chose in a random fog had a phone with a number on the dial different from that of Bright Bay. It took ten rings or so before a woman answered, "Good evening, Bright Bay, may I help you?"

"Could I speak to Mr. Gordon Jainways? He's visiting Eleanor Burke."

"Oh, yes. I believe he's in the dining facility. Please hold."

Gordon answered in an voice filled with trepidation.

"I found him. I *found* him."

"Oh, yes, I see," said Gordon.

"Room 17. You go through the double doors to the right of the desk."

"Oh, yes, I see."

"Can you get away? Unseen?"

"Yes, that will be fine. Thank you for calling." He hung up, and I waited in the hall seemingly for a couple of days before Gordon pushed open the doors. He barely glanced at me.

"They've got an operating room!" I squeaked. "The end of the hall. Keene and Osley—they're doing it *again.*" But Gordon didn't respond to that news; he wouldn't even look at me. "Room 17 is this way—" And he fell in behind me as we marched off.

I knocked on number 17, then pushed the door open for Jainways. Gordon stiffened at the sight framed in the dreary harbor light. They stared at each other for a long time, me peeking in like a sick joke. Then Gordon said, "Good God, D.B., is that you?"

The burned man began to cry. Then I realized there was something behind me. Flowers. Jasmine? I spun. Face-to-face with Eleanor Burke, who said, "Excuse me, please," and stepped into the room. She said nothing more. She walked past her brother and knelt painfully down beside the wheelchair. She put her arms around his neck, and he, still sobbing, lowered his face into her jasmine-scented gray hair. All four of us held that tableau.

A hand grabbed my shirt collar and jerked me sharply away from the door, shoving me into the opposite wall. It was Elwood Dibbs, and his face was contorted with rage. I saw him take a wrinkled handful of Gordon's tweeds between the shoulder blades and yank him nearly off his feet, out the door. Dibbs closed it quietly, then turned on us. The tips of his ears glowed like embers.

"Get out!" He shot a finger at the double doors. We started walking that way like scolded boys caught at the bathhouse peep-hole.

"Listen for a moment, Mr. Dibbs—perhaps you're not aware of what just went on here. That's Danny Beemon. Eleanor Burke is his wife. Why didn't you tell me he was here?"

He shoved me from behind. "Get *out!* You, too!" And he shoved Gordon. "You have no idea, Mr. Deemer! No idea about anything, but if you have the slightest shred of decency, you'll leave all these people alone."

"Woody—"

"I want no explanations—I want you *out!* Mr. Deemer, you lied to me about the police. You didn't keep them away. You *brought* them!"

"What? What do you mean?" By that time he was marching us through the lobby.

"The FBI was here this morning to question Eleanor. They *told* her, Mr. Deemer. They just came out and told her her daughter was murdered."

"But how did I bring—?"

"Get out!" He threw us into the rain, where we stood for a time, trying to collect ourselves.

Finally, I turned to Jainways. "If the FBI is questioning Eleanor, then they must know—"

"Excuse me, Mr. Deemer, but I don't want to hear it. In fact, I've heard quite enough of you altogether. I'm going home, perhaps by ferry, perhaps by cab, but whatever my means, I want to travel without you. I don't want *any further contact* with you." Gordon Jainways turned and walked down the hill toward St. George Road and the ferry slip.

I put my face up to the slate clouds and let the raindrops slap my eyes.

CHAPTER

TWENTY

I USED FIDEL'S KEY ON THE SPIKED GATE GUARDING THE service entrance and took the stairs from the basement to the lobby, where Blue called to me.

"Hey, Artie—Julius Hemphill, the cat is beautiful. Thank you."

I waved on the way to the elevator. I didn't want to talk about the saxophone or about Julius Hemphill, beautiful as he is, but Blue called me again, offering me a white business envelope with my name penned on the front.

"Guy left this for you."

"What guy?"

" 'Bout thirty-five, little guy, mustache, black hair, no distinguishing marks."

"Thanks, Blue." Kiley.

Calabash stepped into the elevator behind me. He appeared from out of nowhere. There is nothing in my lobby, an expanse of marble floor. All the furniture had been stolen. There was nothing to hide behind. Where did he come from? He clutched my upper arms as the door slid closed.

"You ever do dat again, I leave your ass in de lurch. I

believed you were comin' back here after you leave de bar, but you don't. Dat's fuckin' stupid! You got a bodyguard, but you go off without tellin' him. Dey could have killed you— where would dat put me?''

I burst out crying like a child. I had had it, I could take no more reprimands. Shoulder-wrenching sobs.

"Hey, it ain't *dat* big a thing. I just tellin' you, dat's all."

But I couldn't stop. Calabash hugged me in giant arms and patted my back until we reached my floor. "I'm sorry," I managed.

"Dat's okay; no problem. What we need is a big rum swizzle like de tourists drink all day."

He made one. I had some rum and juices, and he put together something with the trade winds in it. I drank it in one gulp, then opened the envelope. Inside was a typed note:

I know who killed Billie. Call me. I'll be at the Place Pigalle Health Spa on West End until 11:00. Home after that. Call me. Maybe we can work out a deal.

He left both numbers. I showed Calabash the note, and as he read it, the rum struck.

"You goin' to call him?"

"Huh?"

"We got to phone Sybel."

"Yes. I think we need another round."

"No question about dat."

He made one while I tried Sybel again. *Still* no answer. I called the Place Pigalle, where the upwardly mobile keep their asses firm. What was Jay Kiley doing there? I could hear the receptionist paging him.

"I'm sorry, sir. Mr. Kiley isn't here."

I tried his home number, and his machine answered. I left no message. He knew who killed Billie. I wondered if he actually did or whether this was a cheap ploy to extract the photographs from me.

"I think this Kiley got Billie killed by trying to shake down a man named Barnett Osley," I told Calabash.

"What are you goin' to do about dat?"

"I don't know. Where did he go from the bar?"

"He went straight to de police station over on 100th Street."

"What? The police station?"

"Dat's where he went."

What did *that* mean?

Jellyroll walked over and sat down on that spot near the radiator where he used to pee on newspaper when he was a puppy. Jellyroll has extraordinary holding power, but when he sits on that spot and stares at me, I take him to be in distress.

Calabash and I walked east toward West End with Jellyroll. Dogs must go outside regardless of the operative level of insanity. Jellyroll peed in the gutter between two parked cars. Before he finished, another car, a green one, pulled up beside us and stopped as if to double-park. The interior light blinked on when the driver opened his door and stepped out. I saw his face over the roof because he had stopped directly under a street lamp. I recognized him. He propped the butt of his handgun on the roof and aimed at my chest. Calabash shoved me out of the line of fire. I flew into the rear of the parked car and bounced into the flooded gutter, so I didn't actually see the gun fired, but I heard it, and I saw shards of masonry fly from the hole in the building when the bullet struck—precisely where I had been standing. I grabbed a handful of flesh on the back of Jellyroll's neck and yanked him under me. I curled into a ball and didn't even realize I was lying in three inches of water.

Calabash dropped behind the other parked car and drew his big black automatic from his waistband, but he had no time to use it before the machine gun ended it all.

Every window in the green car disintegrated simultaneously, the side-view mirror cartwheeling in the air. I heard screams from somewhere. Neighbors in terror taking cover. The green car trembled and shuddered under the barrage, pieces flying. I never saw the effect of those bullets on the man, and for that I remain grateful, but I can extrapolate from his car.

The silence seemed ghostly after the cease-fire. Jellyroll struggled to stand, but I held him down.

"Hey, Artie," someone called.

I looked out from under a rear tire and saw Leon Palomino standing behind a red Japanese car across the street. He held his gun above his head with both hands like a guerrilla fighter posing for a publicity shot, smiling. It wasn't actually a machine gun but the next best thing, an M-16, that fearful weapon the Vietnam War made familiar. Then Leon laid the gun on the hood of the red car and said, "Hey, Artie, you take care now, huh?" He put his hands in the pockets of his fatigue jacket and walked west in no hurry. I never saw him again.

Screams from my neighbors. Faces appeared in windows. An incessant whine near my head. Why? Was someone hit? Was that the sound of dying? Was *I* screaming? No, it was the burglar alarm inside the green car, more holes than anything solid. Calabash walked around to see the body, but he didn't linger. I stood up, careful to keep the car between the body and myself. A fat rivulet of blood flowed from beneath the car and like a tributary joined the stream of gutter water. The next thing I remember was my living room and the strange absence of music. My eyes were blurry, but I saw that Calabash's forehead was bleeding. I clutched his cheeks in my hands to focus on the wound. It seemed to be a scratch, nothing more. Sirens wailed from all directions.

"Calabash!"

"What?"

"You've got to get out of here with your guns!" I handed him the key to Jerry's apartment. I have no view of 104th

Street from my apartment, but I didn't need one to know it was filling up with police cars. The streets of Beirut. "At the end of the hall. Apartment E. Hurry."

"I call you in ten minutes," he said, and left.

Jellyroll's body trembled and shook. I sat on the floor and stroked his back, told him lies like "It's okay, boy." He buried his head in my armpit. I don't know how long I did that before they pounded on my door as if with battering rams.

"Police! Open up!"

I peeped out the view hole. They *did* have a battering ram. It was a squat cylinder of steel with pipelike handles. I saw Cobb and Loccatuchi and a hall full of uniforms. They were all wearing bullet-proof vests like fencer's plastrons. Every man had his gun drawn; two carried shotguns and one a sledgehammer, probably used in conjunction with the battering ram. All that battle gear notwithstanding, it was the looks on their faces—determined, tense, and dangerous—that frightened me.

Careful to keep my hands in full view, I opened the door. They poured in on me. Two uniforms wedged themselves in the doorway shoulder to shoulder in their haste, but their comrades dislodged them from behind. The flood of armed officers drove me into the living room. The jig was definitely up. Cobb grabbed me by the shoulders, spun me around, and shoved me against my own wall. He kicked my legs apart and frisked me with, I thought, undue roughness. Then he yanked my arms behind me and handcuffed them there. Only then did the troops holster their guns. Mutilated corpses and automatic weapons fire in residential neighborhoods make the NYPD edgy.

"Now it's your ass, lover man," said Cobb as he squeezed the cuffs tightly against my wrist bones.

"Fuck me!" someone said. "That looks like the R-r-ruff Dog!"

"That *is* the R-r-ruff Dog," said Loccatuchi.

Then the phalanx swept me into the hall, now full of my

neighbors. Mrs. Fishbein, her mouth agape. Fidel, looking grim. News crews shot blinding lights at me. A female reporter stuck a microphone in my face and asked for a statement, but Cobb knocked it out of her hands. Six cops and I crowded into the freight elevator, which Fidel drove to the lobby. I didn't see much point inet then in explaining that I was the intended victim, not the perpetrator.

Lined with blue-and-white squad cars, lights pulsing everywhere, 104th Street looked like a war zone. Two cars had been driven up onto the sidewalk, their headlights pointing into my lobby, where Blue narrated events he probably didn't witness to a clot of reporters. When they saw me in handcuffs, they bolted from Blue and charged, but a cordon of uniforms headed them off. Out on the street stringers and free-lancers stuck cameras in my face, flashbulbs popping. Cobb straight-armed them roughly aside with one big hand and dragged me along by the shirtfront with the other. I glimpsed two attendants in yellow foul-weather gear load the black rubber body bag into the rear of an EMS truck before Cobb shoved me into the backseat of a squad car. There was more blood on the pavement beside the riddled green car than I imagined a single human body could contain. The media were getting some great blood shots, film at eleven. Siren blaring, we sped east after Cobb, on the loud-hailer, bullied the curious out of our way.

"Who was that fucker, Deemer?"

"Ricardo."

"The other guy! The guy who shot Ricky?"

"Ricky?"

"Ricky Ricardo, asshole! Who shot him?"

"I don't know."

"You're in deep shit now."

CHAPTER

TWENTY-ONE

LOCCATUCHI TOLD ME THAT I HAD THE RIGHT TO REMAIN silent, but if I spoke, anything I said could and would be held against me, that I had the right to a lawyer, and if I couldn't afford one, the court would supply a freebie. I was soaking wet. Cobb ran all the lights en route to the 24th Precinct on 100th Street off Amsterdam. Uniformed police and overweight plainclothes cops scurried this way and that; squad cars and unmarked vehicles lurched to a stop in front as others squealed away. Cobb pulled me from the car by the handcuffs, and his colleagues stopped to watch—*me*. Why were they treating me like this? I was the intended victim. Cobb *knew* I wasn't the gunman. Up a flight of concrete stairs by the handcuffs and into the seedy squadroom. Cobb sat me down on a long wooden bench, the heavy oaken kind one used to find in railroad waiting rooms, and a cop in a white shirt with sour BO used his own set of handcuffs to lock my ankle to the bench leg, then went away, leaving me helpless. Cops dressed like civilians from all walks of life gathered around to view the prisoner. One, a black man who on the street

I would have taken for a fall-down wino, said, "This is the shooter, Sal?"

"Could be," said Loccatuchi.

"Did you read him?"

"Sure."

"He looks like a bad one, all right," said the wino.

"Break it up, guys," said Cobb, and the semicircle around me dispersed.

"You *know* I didn't do it!"

"Shut up, lover man. Whose desk is this?" Cobb wanted to know.

"Carmine's," said the wino. "Hey, Carmine, can Cobb use yer desk to write up Machine-Gun Kelly?"

"Just don't let him carve no dirty suggestions."

Cobb sat down at Carmine's desk, pulled out papers, and working like a card sharp, inserted carbons between each one.

"Cobb! There a Cobb here?" asked a man in dirty jeans and fatigue jacket from the doorway.

"Yeah, right here."

"The college boys are on the way. Just came over."

"Thanks," said Cobb, accelerating his paperwork, and the cop in jeans left.

What was going *on* here? "You know I didn't shoot Ricardo!"

"Name?"

"He was trying to kill me!"

"Just shut up or you'll find your ass strapped to a bed in Bellevue with a hole to piss through." He was writing furiously. *"Name!"*

"I demand to know the charges! What is this, South Africa!"

"Oh, hear that, Carmine?" asked the wino, cupping his hand behind his ear. "Political satire."

"Did he call us Nazis yet?" Carmine said.

"Soon."

I lowered my voice, volume not working so well, and

said, "Detective Cobb, I believe you know I did not shoot Ricky Ricardo."

"Oh? You're innocent?"

"No, I did some things—I'll be happy to tell you about them—but I didn't shoot anyone."

"I'd be happy to hear all about your exploits, but thanks to you, there ain't time."

"Why isn't there time?"

"Name, Deemer!"

"Arthur N. Deemer."

"What's the N. ?"

"Nathaniel."

"Address."

"Three Sixteen West 104th Street."

"Eyes."

"Green."

"Hair. What there is of it."

"Brown. I want a lawyer."

"It ain't lawyer time yet."

"Then I demand to know the charges," I said, this time a request, a plea.

"You want to know the charges? Sure. You ready? We got B and E, one count, no, two counts, we got obstruction of justice, conspiracy to obstruct justice, conspiracy to extortion, arson in the second degree, plus four, count 'em, four counts of homicide. Deep shit, like I told you."

"Homicide?"

"Frederick Palomino, Ricky Ricardo, Billie Burke—"

"You bastard!"

"Nazi!" said the wino.

"—and Jay Kiley."

"Jay Kiley is dead?"

"Yep." He pulled Kiley's typed note from his jacket pocket. "Recognize this?"

"Sure, but that doesn't mean—"

The room fell silent. Four young men in blue pin-striped suits walked in and planted themselves at the door.

"Ladies and gentlemen—" said Carmine. "The Four Freshmen—"

They surveyed the room with unmasked distaste, which the cops returned. In striking contrast to the cops, they were neat, clean, impeccably coiffured and blown dry, also younger. No cop in that room was under forty-five; the Freshmen were in their twenties. "That him?" asked one, approaching my bench for a look. The other three hung back as if they worried about soiling their Brooks Brothers.

"Who?" asked Cobb.

"Him."

"Oh, him. That's him, yes, sir."

"I want him downtown. *Now.*"

"Now?" said Cobb, suddenly a simpleton.

"You heard me."

"But sir," said Cobb, "we have certain formalities and procedures to which we must abide."

The boy glared at Cobb and tried to look mean. "Ten minutes," he dictated, turned and walked out. The other three Freshmen made an opening for the fourth, then backed out the door after him.

"Your old man still sniffing little girls' bicycle seats?" called Carmine. The chief Freshman popped back in, jaws clenched furiously. "Who said that?" he demanded, a history teacher who'd just been spitballed from behind.

"Barney Miller," said the wino.

One Police Plaza is an architectural incongruity in Chinatown. I didn't see much of it, however. Three uniformed cops led me, still tightly handcuffed, through an obscure back door into a room empty except for an airport-style metal detector. By then my clothes had nearly dried on my back, leaving me shivering with cold fear, and my shin, apparently due to a crack from the bumper on my flight into the gutter, throbbed so badly I limped. I was going to jail, limping, shivering. Who would take care of my dog? They twice ran me through the metal detector, and twice the alarm rang. They searched me again and ran me through. The alarm rang.

"Oh," said one cop, a young guy with rosy cheeks. "The handcuffs."

Was this jail? A large open room with a battleship-gray floor, three sets of cages. They rehandcuffed me in front. A black man in the blue uniform of the New York Department of Corrections—COs in jail-house parlance—led me to a lecternlike stand where he rolled my fingers and thumbs on an ink pad, then rolled each on a card. Fingerprinted. I always assumed I'd get through life without ever being fingerprinted for murder and arson. The fingerprinter handed me a paper towel, which did not remove the ink.

There were not three cages as I thought but one large L-shaped cage. The fingerprinter unlocked the door. I walked in. What choice had I? He slammed it shut behind me. The COs, I came to notice, never merely closed a door. They always slammed it. The slammer. About fifteen fellow arrestees sat on the floor or stood around, a nearly even mix of blacks, whites, and Hispanics. Everyone was handcuffed in front, and I was glad to see that. I had heard stories about jailhouse gang bangs. Easy, I counseled myself, this was not prison where they gang-bang the new guys with impunity. This was part of a process, a *legal* process, the end of which was a court appearance as stipulated by the Constitution. Besides, we were all handcuffed. Cobb knew I didn't kill anyone; he knew I didn't put the torch to the Antiques. This was all to intimidate me. Wasn't it? No D.A. would dare press those charges. They had no merit at all. Well, it was working. I was intimidated. It wouldn't take much of this to make me tell them who *did* burn down the building and who machine-gunned Ricardo. What else did I know that Cobb didn't? The photographs and the note from Billie.

And who were the Four Freshmen? What did they want from me?

I glanced up at my fellow arrestees, hard-looking fuckers who seemed right at home. They had segregated themselves into three islands. That troubled me, a jailhouse race war. I segregated myself into a gene pool of one, leaned against the grimy bars, and stared at my hands chained together in my lap. I was *in the system*. I have a phobia of bureaucrats. I feel like Joseph K., even going to the Motor Vehicles Department. I have no passport for that reason. And here I was, stakes elevated far beyond foreign travel, my person in the hands of hostile authority.

A lanky white guy with a roving right eye and tattoos of naked women on his twitching biceps sat down beside me. I ignored him. A black guy paced back and forth in front of us, jerking at his handcuffs. A hyperactive or a speed freak, he chanted, droned, "Fucking-BobbyfuckingBobbyfuckingBobby—" Then he arrived at the white guy's outstretched legs and stopped as if before the Continental Divide. He stared at the legs, but the white guy would not move them.

"I'm walkin' here, motherfucker."

"No, you ain't."

"I'm walkin' here, motherfucker."

"No, you ain't."

The breakdown of rational discourse, another of my phobias. When that happens, violence floods in to fill the vacuum. Fifteen minutes in the joint and I get killed in a racially motivated incident over some legs. I scurried away in search of a neutral corner and settled in midway between black and Hispanic headquarters. Both eyed me with cold indifference. Great. Indifference, that's all I could ask for.

"FuckingBobbyfuckingBobbyfucking—"

Then a tall, handsome black guy with a close-cropped beard approached. "Greetings," he said.

That sounded friendly enough, and I certainly wanted to avoid discourtesy. "Greetings," I returned.

"So you're some kind of white-collar felon? You in for Xeroxing?"

"No."

"Botherin' the little white girls?"

"No."

"What then? I mean, yer the only fucker in here wearin' Topsiders. You steal somebody's yacht boat?"

"Murder," I muttered.

"Murder?" he said loudly, and the jailhouse fell ominously silent. "How many?"

"Three. No, four."

"Four?"

"And a building."

"Them four, they just happen to be in the buildin' when you took it out?"

"No, they were separate."

He nodded, watched me. I tried for a psychopathic glint in my eye. The black guy returned to his colleagues to report. They glanced over their shoulders at me as he did so. Word spread to the Hispanic delegation, thence to the white one, while I tried to come off like the psycho with three names everyone thinks is just a quiet loner until he's arrested for serial murders throughout the Sunbelt. Don't fuck with that dude or he'll dismember your sister.

"Arthur Deemer."

"*Here,* right here!"

I leaped to the door on my tortured shin. Was this it? Was I out?

"Lawyer's here," said the obese CO, who with a key from a twenty-pound ring unlocked the door. What lawyer? I called no lawyer. The CO led me into an alcove off the holding pen. It was lined with tiny dark cages. He locked me in one and left. When he returned, my attorney was with him. My attorney wore a "Zig Zag Rolling Papers" T-shirt, black high tops with no socks, and he carried his cue case under his arm. It wasn't too late to pretend I'd never seen him before.

"How did you know I was here?"

"It was in *Variety.*"

"Calabash called you."

"Right."

"Can you get me out of here?"

"Looks doubtful for tonight."

"Aww—" *Don't cry. Serial killers never cry.* "Tomorrow?"

"Tomorrow looks good. They want to check your priors on the computer in Albany, but Albany's closed now. You have any priors?"

"Of course not."

"That's in your favor. What's this about all the slayings?"

"I think they're trying to scare me into talking."

"About what?"

"Other slayings."

"Don't tell these people anything without me present. These people are Nazis, Artie. They got places in this building that aren't even America anymore. As your attorney, I advise you to eschew those places." I looked into my attorney's eyes; they were abnormal.

"How the hell would you suggest I do that, Bruce? Straighten *up!*"

"It's crucial they understand you are not without legal representation. These people are brutes, Artie. They understand only naked power. If they suspect weakness, they'll rip you to shreds." Then suddenly he shouted, "Guard! Guard!"

"Bruce—"

Two fat COs with angry bloated faces appeared in the alcove.

"Bruce, don't—"

"Perhaps you tubs don't know who you have here. This man is Artie Deemer! This man has a famous dog."

"Shut up, asshole," said the fatter of the two COs.

"If you don't release my client hastily, I'll call in the world of *advertising!*" He turned to me. "I'll handle this, Artie. We'll discuss the fee when I have you out of here." Then, back to the COs, he said, "You—with the Uniroyal—release my client."

"That's all, asshole," said the CO, who put a whistle to his fleshy lips. The shrill blast blew me back against the rear wall of my cell and summoned a half-dozen other COs like guard dogs. They were clearly itching for action, flexing rubber cudgels.

I remained encaged as they bodily ejected my representation. "There isn't a nine-ball player for shit in the whole municipal system," I heard him bellow from beneath an igloo of blue uniforms.

A hostile CO grabbed my upper arm and ran me back to the holding pen.

The black guy slid down the wall and sat beside me. "Let me give you some free advice, sailor. Get yourself some different representation or you're gonna *fry.*"

"Arthur Deemer."

"Here, right here, sir."

Still another fat CO unlocked the door and led me down a hall and stood me before a wooden desk. There were four other arrestees in line ahead of me. By the time my turn came around, I had the idea. The black guy behind the desk gave you a manila envelope into which you emptied your pockets; then you removed your shoelaces and put them into the envelope with your pathetic belongings. But my shoelaces were not removable. I worried about that as my turn approached. Could unremovable shoelaces land a man in one of those rooms not in America anymore? I figured I was on thin ice with my COs, since they didn't get to cudgel my attorney senseless. . . . Or did they? After you had filled your envelope, you signed it, and then the black guy consulted a chart and called a number, like a bakery.

"Those permanent shoelaces?"

"Yes, sir."

"Okay, put him in seven."

Seven was a tiny cage with an updated bench bolted to the steel wall and a seatless toilet, used but unflushed for weeks. I was alone. You can't get gang-banged alone. Was this where I was to spend the night? Could I sleep? I longed to be unconscious while time passed. I sat in that dim cell and for the first time noticed the unrelenting din of the place, steel slamming steel, shouts, curses, nameless clanks, clatters, and crashes and from somewhere close by an unintelligible rap song from a cheap radio. Maybe later they'd tune in WKCR for the celebration of Duke Ellington's birthday. "Mood Indigo." Sleep would not be possible.

They brought in a young white boy I had not seen before, about twenty-one, his face covered with volcanic acne and fresh tears. They slammed the door behind him. The boy didn't register my presence but stood near the door, put his ravaged face in his hands, and sobbed. Even the back of his neck was aboil with pimples. "I ain't goin' back there! I *ain't!*"

"Where?" I asked.

"Home!"

"Take it easy. . . . Maybe they won't make you," I said, the Birdman of Alcatraz. I felt like holding the poor bastard, but I did nothing. I let him stand there in his laceless Nikes and weep. Suddenly he took two deep breaths like a swimmer about to plunge into cold water. He bent at the waist and ran into the steel wall. The top of his head bore the brunt of impact, and a new sound was swallowed up in the din, the sound of someone slapping a honeydew melon with his open hand. I couldn't believe what I'd just witnessed, but there he was, with his ruined complexion and ruined spirit, staggering around as if one leg were six inches shorter than the other. I reached out to grab him—he batted my hands away—and I saw that his pupils were rolled back, only the whites visible. Then he did it again. Bent and rammed the steel plate with the top of his head. This time he dropped flat and did not move.

"Guard!" I screamed. "Guard!" I went to the boy, but the CO at the door told me to get away from him. This was not real. I did not see this thing. Other COs arrived and looked at me with a mix of hostility and suspicion.

"No!" I squeaked. "He—he hit the wall with his head!"

Four of them picked up the boy lengthwise like a limp railroad tie and carried him away, his sad laceless shoes bouncing behind. I sat there for several hours and thought about that boy's life, of which I witnessed no more than three minutes, possibly the last three minutes.

"Everybody up. Yer movin' out!" One by one, the cells were emptied, and we were herded into another holding pen, about twenty of us. "Greetings," said the black guy. They prodded and shoved us into groups of four, and another CO produced chains about six feet long, each with four wrist cuffs implacably attached. They locked us to the chains and left us that way. The slightest movement jerked at one's neighbor. Given my neighbors, I squatted, unmoving, until they herded us by quartets onto a loading dock and into the back of a big van. All aboard, they slammed and locked the van doors. Everyone braced for movement, but none came. We waited. I stood at the rear of the dark, crowded van where the double doors met and tried to breathe fresh air. I thought about all that blood shining on my street.

Finally the engine started and we lurched away. Unable to see the turns from our windowless cage, we bounced around helplessly inside. A skinny Hispanic guy at the front of my chain (I was number three) began to twitch and tremble.

"He's a junkie, mon," said the man behind me. "Soon it get bad for heem."

"Chill out," a black man advised the junkie helpfully, and the junkie nodded about ten times and made to grasp the black man's hand, but it remained out of reach.

We arrived somewhere and stopped. We shuffled into position to alight, the grimmest cell being much preferable to this stifling van. But nothing happened. We waited, chains tinkling. Panic began to spread as the air thinned. I could hear us breathing. I sucked air through the tiny crack between the doors and feared someone would notice my access and take it away from me. Normal breaths no longer sufficed in the wet heat. The young junkie began to whimper, then to chatter in Spanish. I caught the word *muerto*. Two inmates at the front end of the van began to beat on the driver's steel partition. "Hey, we got a sick man here!" We fell silent awaiting help or at least an answer. None came. The junkie shook himself like a wet dog.

"Arthur Deemer."

"Here!"

They unlocked the junkie's wrist and my wrist. Mine got cuffed behind my back. We were on a loading dock identical to the last one. They led the inmates in one door, the junkie in another, and me in through a third, down a hall, and into an elevator. I was helpless, but still two COs, one black, one white, both fat, gripped my arms on either side. Was I leaving America, no passport necessary? They planted me in a room very different from those in which I'd languished thus far. There were no bars. Only the cyclone fence bolted over the window spoke of jail. I looked out on a sooty brick wall ten feet away, but I saw daylight. The night had ended. The room was gray and bare except for a metal table with four chairs. My shin throbbed. I pulled out one of the chairs and sat sideways on it to accommodate my handcuffs. More comfortable physically than I'd been since my arrest, I waited.

I recognized them immediately. The Four Freshmen, minus two. The spokesman was there. He looked like an investment banker arriving with an attaché full of insider information. He sat opposite me, opened the case, fastidiously arranged its contents, then got around to looking at me. "We've been looking forward to meeting you, Mr. Deemer. I'm Agent Watson and this is Agent Hargrove. You've been a very busy young man," said the condescending little prick as he removed Billie's photographs from his case and spread them out before me on the tabletop. Jones and Ricardo, Leon and his late brother, Harry Pine and Harvey Keene. I waited for the rest of them, for the Family Snaps, but he didn't produce them. Did that mean he didn't have them? I could see into his attaché—it was empty. When I fetched a set of photos for Chucky, I had removed the Family Snaps and hid each in separate record jackets along with Billie's ice-tray note. I own many records. "Do you recognize these?" Watson asked.

"Of course. You got them from my apartment?"

"Hidden beneath your refrigerator," he said, and it was clear he thought himself pretty clever.

"I suppose you had a search warrant."

"Unnecessary under the circumstances. There was a note, Mr. Deemer, from Billie Burke that said"—he consulted a leather-bound black notebook—" 'I'm dead, darling, look in the ice tray—Acappella.' Did you acquire these photographs from that ice tray?"

"Yes." How did he know what the note said?

"And where is that note now?"

"I lost it." This was the man who told Eleanor Beemon that her daughter was dead. I'd take my chances with Cobb any day. Besides, if I told him that the note was hidden in Cleanhead Vincent's Greatest Hits, he'd likely search the other jackets and find the Family Snaps. I still viewed them as a thing between Billie and me. I wondered if he knew about Danny Beemon at Bright Bay.

"You lost it? Is that what you just said?"

"That's it."

He glared at me, but by then I'd been glared at—and shot at—by tougher. Where was Cobb?

"I have a right to a lawyer. Do you deny me that right?"

"Do you know this man?" He pointed a squeaky-clean finger at Harry Pine's chest.

"We've met."

"Is it not true that Harry Pine paid you to report to him?"

Sybel! How else could he know that? "Yes. But there has been nothing to report."

"Nothing to report? His building was burned to the ground. His employee was found dead in the same icebox from which you got these photographs. Still another of his employees was shot to pieces outside your door. Nothing to report?"

"Why don't you ask him? You know I didn't do any of those things. You're denying me my civil right to an attorney. Is that your intention?"

"I heard about your attorney. He sounds almost as responsible as yourself." He gestured dismissively over his shoulder at Hargrove, who left. "All right, Mr. Deemer, I haven't the time or the inclination to play with you. You are in trouble, serious trouble, and you have only one alternative—that is to cooperate with me."

Hargrove ushered Sybel into the gray room. They had her hands cuffed together in front. Her face was pale and drawn, her black hair oily and disheveled. Our eyes met. She seemed too exhausted for surprise as she sat at the head of the table and folded her chained hands. Jailhouse grime was lodged beneath her fingernails. What had she told them?

"Sybel, did they allow you to phone a lawyer?" I asked.

She shook her head wearily. "They kept me in a cell for two days. They had me strip searched."

"We were looking for that note," said Watson smugly. I didn't get it. Why would he do a thing as stupid as hold Sybel incommunicado for nearly twenty-four hours? Even

Bruce could get his whole case tossed out on the basis of that kind of disregard for procedure. Was I overestimating the power of our Constitution? Or underestimating Watson?

"I told them how you got the photographs, Artie." Then she seemed for the first time to see that those very photos were spread out on the table.

Watson consulted his notebook. "At 11:07 P.M. Thursday, Leon Palomino informed you by phone that he had touched off the fire which destroyed the building at number 89 West Eleventh Street known as Renaissance Antiques. I believe you were present during that time, Miss Black. That makes you both accessories after the fact to arson in the first degree."

"Come on, Watson," I said. "You know it can't be first-degree arson if the building is not inhabited."

He looked at me with a smirk. "A jailhouse lawyer. Well, that will stand you in good stead if you choose not to cooperate with me. What else have we?" Back to his book. "Destruction of evidence in a capital crime, withholding evidence in a capital crime. I have two eyewitnesses who heard the gunman after he killed Richard Ricardo call you by name."

Sybel's mouth gaped open. She had been in jail when that went down.

"The gunman said, 'Now you take care, Artie,' at which point he walked away. Who was that man, Mr. Deemer?"

"I don't know."

"It was Leon Palomino, wasn't it?"

"Perhaps you haven't been in the line of fire of a machine gun lately. Details blur."

"Hardly sounds like a detail to me. 'Now you take care, *Artie.*' I want Leon Palomino!"

"I'm not hiding him."

"Did you or did you not meet Leon Palomino at Yankee Stadium?"

"No, I did not."

"Mr. Deemer, I told you time is short. And if I were you, Miss Black, I would not place my fate in the hands of a man as reckless as Mr. Deemer." Back to me: "My men saw you at Yankee Stadium with Leon Palomino."

"No, they didn't, they saw me at Shea Stadium."

Watson looked back at Hargrove, who nodded slightly. "Shea Stadium, that's what I said. What did he tell you during that meeting?"

"That he saw Jones and Ricardo wheel the refrigerator across Eleventh and into Renaissance Antiques." I waited for him to follow up on that, but he did not.

"What did he tell you about Harry Pine?"

"That someone was trying to extort money from Pine's friends. Jay Kiley." He didn't care about that, either, or at least he pretended not to care.

"Let's get back to that note from Miss Burke, shall we? Where is it?"

"I lost it."

He shook his head sadly as if at our impending fate, then looked at Sybel: "Mr. Deemer thinks I can't make these charges stick because of certain technicalities. But what he doesn't recognize—what you *should* recognize— is that I don't care about making them stick. I can, and shall, make your lives miserable for a long time to come without making anything stick. I'll request at your arraignment that bail be disallowed because your freedom might subvert my ongoing investigation at a crucial stage and could defeat the ends of justice. All the lawyers in New York, Miss Black, won't keep you out of the Women's House of Detention for a couple of weeks. And you, Mr. Deemer, will be arraigned and sent directly to Rikers Island."

"Don't do that to us," Sybel said.

"You have a daughter, don't you, Miss Black?"

"Yes."

"Staying, I believe, with your mother in New Jersey."

"Yes."

"I want nothing more than to reunite you with her, but I'm in the midst of a very serious investigation, and the small people will be sacrificed if they don't cooperate. You are either part of the solution or part of the problem."

"What do we have to do?" Sybel asked in a small voice.

"Give me that note."

"Artie lost it. He told me the night after I gave it to him."

"I see. If I had more time, I'd send you both back to jail until such time as you recalled where you lost it, but I don't." He paused theatrically before his captive audience, then said, "I'm after Harry Pine. If you help me get him, you will leave this building in about half an hour, and I will protect you from any harm that might come as a result. You may think I'm uninterested in the murder of Billie Burke, but you would be wrong. I want to use suspicion of murder as probable cause for arrest, and that's where you come in. I want you to tell Harry Pine about how you came to acquire those photographs, including the part about Miss Burke's note, and then I want you to offer them for sale. If he buys, we have probable cause. You will be wearing a recording device and transmitter when you make Pine the offer, and you will be under surveillance the entire time. I can guarantee your personal safety. My men are not like the NYPD. We get the job done."

What? Sell the photos to Pine? Pine *already had* the photos. I glanced at Sybel, but she avoided my eyes.

"Is something wrong, Mr. Deemer?"

"Yeah, these handcuffs hurt."

"So what do you say? Do you assist me, or do you return to jail? It's your choice."

CHAPTER

TWENTY-TWO

"THAT HORRIBLE MATRON," SNARLED SYBEL. "SHE TAPED the damn thing to my nipple." Sybel clutched her sweater at the side of her breast and yanked. Tape ripped.

We sat savoring the outdoors on a bench graffitied with Chinese characters and English obscenities in Columbus Square, a concrete pocket park behind the Criminal Court Building from which five minutes earlier we had been released, with strings attached. Technicians had taped listening devices to our bare chests. I had envisioned space-age whizbang microchips straight out of "Mission Impossible," but these were nothing more than small tape recorders. Watson buzzed about nervously re-explaining what the technicians had already told us, belaboring the obvious: flip the switch to ON when we were going in for the setup, otherwise leave it OFF to conserve the batteries; and the setup had to happen *today*. The technicians kept referring to us as CIs, and when I asked my technician what that meant, he thought I was kidding and giggled. As Watson opened the last door, he came on all avuncular and trustworthy. "Don't worry," he said. "My people will monitor you every step of the way."

"Do you have any money?" Sybel asked me.

"Yes." Watson had returned my envelope full of personal belongings.

"Will you buy me a pack of cigarettes?"

I bought cigarettes and two cups of stagnant coffee from a Chinese lunch counter on the corner of Bayard and Mulberry, and the cashier wished me a nice day in a thick accent. I asked him the time. Nine-thirty A.M. Saturday. Billie died last Sunday night. I wanted time to stop while I slept for about three days, no thinking, worrying, or scheming, but first I wanted to sit on the Chinese bench beneath the lovely English plane tree and drink coffee, never mind the slack drizzle, with Sybel, the only other person in the world who shared my experience, if not my obsession. Kids played stickball on the wet cobblestones.

"I can't go back in there, Artie. Whatever happens, I can't go back in that cell."

"Maybe we can think of something," I said, but I doubted it, feeling my body sliding toward lassitude, my brain close behind. Energy and hope waned together. What could we do? Certainly not visit Pine wearing wires and offer to sell him incriminating evidence we had already sold him.

Sybel said, "I've been thinking about—" And she pointed to the place beneath her right breast where her wire was taped. She pulled me close to her mouth and whispered the rest, her lips brushing my ear. She asked me why we should trust the on/off switches. What if they were phonies? What if Watson, even now, was listening in?

"Excuse me, Sybel. I'll get us some more coffee—" Next door to the Chinese luncheonette was a Chinese Crazy Eddie's where I bought two of the cheapest and tiniest radios ever made in Taiwan. I tuned both to the all-news station—"Give us twenty-two minutes, we'll give you the world"—gave one to Sybel, and as surreptitiously as possible, we tucked them beneath our shirts next to

Watson's ear. Hell, this was *thinking*. Maybe there was still hope.

"Can I take about six showers at your place before— whatever."

"Seven," I said.

"Do you have cab fare?"

"Yes. Can you carry me to the curb?"

We didn't need to travel any further than the curb. A cab was waiting. We named our destination and headed north toward Canal. Sleep gripped me by the shoulders and gently drew me back in the seat.

"Jesus!" Sybel said.

"Wha—?"

"Look who's driving!"

Cobb! He wore a Mets cap, and phony black hair spilled out from behind. "We need to have a little sit-down, you and me, but you got so-called agents hanging off you like warts, so we got to take unusual steps."

"Why can't you just leave us alone!" Sybel squealed, and struck the door panel with a soft fist.

"I'm sorry, Sybel, but those are my murders, and I want 'em," said Cobb.

"Do you know they held her incommunicado for twenty-four hours?" I demanded, but my fist was soft, too.

"Of course I know. Things are way out of hand. That's why we need to have this sit-down. Sybel, I didn't have anything to do with the way you were treated inside. I tried to stop it."

"You failed," she said.

Cobb, playing cabbie to the hilt, laid on the horn when the bakery truck in front lagged at the light. "By the way, lover man, Sal Loccatuchi went up and walked your dog last night."

"He did?"

"Billie's killer's gonna walk, and that offends my professional pride. Cops got professional pride just like anybody else. Hey, what's that noise?" Cobb pivoted in his seat, and I showed him our broadcast system. He grinned at Sybel and me in turn. "Smart. Smart but not necessary. They don't work."

"They don't?"

"Nope. My guys set them up. They'll record about twenty seconds, then drop dead. Mysteriously. That's how far out of hand things are."

"So you and the FBI are playing a game of steal the bacon, and we're the bacon."

"Steal the bacon. Yeah, I remember that. . . . Those fucking college boys don't care about Billie's murder. They think they got a shot at the wiseguys, get promoted off the street, as if they ever been *on* the street. The street is mine. The college boys think Pine's gonna turn over as easy as Jay Kiley did. A child could see that ain't about to work."

"Kiley was working for the FBI?"

"Yep. Do you folks know what went down in Moxie, Florida?"

"I do. Sybel doesn't, because she was in jail having her civil rights denied."

"The college boys get word that Kiley's down in Moxie asking a lot of questions about Harry Pine, and they lean on him. It comes out Kiley's working for one Billie Burke. But she gets killed. That's where you come stumbling in. When Sybel told them about the photos, they sent Kiley out to Shea to buy them from you, then make Kiley use them to set Harry Pine up, get it? But you told Kiley to fuck himself."

"You mean Kiley was wearing one of these wires when he met with me?"

"Sure. You dicked up their plan—until Ricky Ricardo gets whacked in front of your place. Then they got an excuse to lean on you directly, make *you* set up Pine. Get a stupid idea and stick with it no matter what, even if it means stepping all over my murder case with their Bass-fucking Weejuns."

"What happened to Jay?"

"Died naked in the steam room of an ass shop called Place Pigalle Health Spa. That ring a bell?"

"Yes."

"Did you talk to him after you got his note?"

"I tried, but he didn't answer." Because he was already dead? "What happened to him?"

"Well, somebody sat down beside him on the bench and popped him with a syringe full of air. Embolism." Cobb snapped his fingers to signal the suddenness of Jay Kiley's end. "A syringe, lover man. That ring a bell?"

"Doctors?"

"Yeah, I'd say so. Doctors. Kiley used the Moxie dirt to blackmail the doctors, while Billie used it to blackmail Harry Pine. That about the size of it?"

"I don't know."

"You *don't?* I think you do."

"What exactly is supposed to happen after we set up Harry Pine with the photos?"

"The college boys start waving murder charges in Pine's face. Billie's, Kiley's, Palomino's, they don't care which. By the way, we found that poor fucking Palomino in the fridge." He fixed me in the rearview mirror, but I said nothing. "The college boys think just lay a few half-assed murder charges on Pine he'll sing like Perry Como about his wiseguy bosses. Get Mr. Big or some shit. Here's Pine, a big war hero, ace of aces, he's gonna fall apart in front of some college boys with their dorks caught in their zippers? Right. Am I going too fast for you, lover man? You happen to know Pine's a big Mafia pilot?"

"Yes."

"Pretty knowledgeable guy."

"Sybel doesn't know about that, because she was being held—"

"Yeah, yeah, I know—"

"Let me ask you something," said Sybel. "Suppose you're Harry Pine and we come to you and offer to sell

218

photographs that could implicate you in several murders—what would you do?''

"I might chuck you out my airplane over the ocean."

Then Sybel made a frightening point that had not occurred to me. Perhaps Watson's plan was not all that half-assed when viewed from a twisted pragmatic perspective. Our murders would be a big boon to Watson's case. He would then have real charges to press against Pine, at the same time ridding himself of the threat to his case caused by this wanton violation of our civil rights. "How do we know that isn't your idea, as well?" Sybel finished.

"Because you're not going to *sell* him anything. I'm going to give you a big bone to throw to Pine. See, Pine's got some problems I mean to exploit. There's a drug war brewing between the wiseguys and the spics. Used to be the wiseguys ran that show, but now the Colombian gentlemen are getting too big for their sombreros, and the wiseguys are getting edgy. How's that Pine's problem? Because he's got two Colombian rats in his organization. No, one Colombian rat, now Ricky Ricardo got capped."

"Jones?"

"Yeah, Jones. I want you—wearing my wire—to go tell Pine about Jones. Tell him you overheard the college boys talking about it before they released you. That's how I got it, the fuckups. He's going to have to get rid of Jones. Then I get rid of him."

This was growing Byzantine.

Cobb dangled two tape recorders, identical to those taped to our nipples, over the backseat. "You wear these, forget the photos, tell Pine about Jones the rat. That's all there is to it. Except for Billie's note. You give me that and I'll get her killer."

"We want two things in return," I said.

"Yeah, what?"

"I want you to leave Leon Palomino alone. That's one."

"Why's that, lover man? Because he saved your life gunning Ricardo?"

"No. . . . Let's just say he's a nice guy."

"Right, he's a prince, but it might be tough for me to protect him. Since the college boys put a tap on your phone, they know he burned down the store and about your meeting at Shea. They set up to arrest him there, college-boy dragnet, only Palomino beat the shit out of three so-called agents and escaped." Cobb giggled almost boyishly.

"Leave Sybel out of this entirely. That's two."

"What are you, some kind of hero?" she asked.

"There's no need for you to go to Pine," I said to her. Then to Cobb I said, "Sybel's going home to her daughter or there's no deal."

"Jeeze, lover man, you really got me this time."

Sure. I really had him. I leaned back in the seat. Sybel took my hand in hers. "What's a CI?" I asked him.

"A CI? That's what you are. A confidential informant."

Artie Deemer, CI, RIP.

CHAPTER

TWENTY-THREE

EVEN BEFORE I OPENED MY APARTMENT DOOR I KNEW Jellyroll was gone. A dog's consistency ingrains itself in one's consciousness like a familiar piece of music. Note follows note with a predictability that speaks of safety at anchor in a stormy world. He should have responded to the sound of my key in the lock with a single bark; then I should have heard him run headlong at the door, skid to a stop, toenails clattering on the hardwood foyer floor. When I opened the door, he should have jumped at my face, attempting to lick it in midair. I would have ruffled his ears to elicit his smile, roughhouse for a while. A dog's greeting is a gift of nature.

"What is it?" said Sybel.

"Jellyroll's gone."

"How do you—? Calabash—maybe Calabash has him out for a walk?"

"No. There's his leash, on the hook." Weariness vanished. Death by natural causes? Sensing death's approach, dogs sometimes slink off to die alone. I tore my closets apart, I ripped the spread from my bed to look beneath it,

I searched every dog-sized crevice in the place. He was gone. "Someone took him," I said.

"Why?"

"Coercion."

"But that doesn't make sense."

"Why not?"

"If you want to coerce somebody by kidnapping his dog, you tell him you have the dog. Nobody even mentioned Jellyroll."

I wasn't interested in sense. "No, Cobb mentioned him. He said Loccatuchi came to walk him. If they hurt him—" Could I kill? Yes. Cops? "Well, it won't work! I don't do shit till I get my dog back. If they hurt him, they're *dead!* Cobb, Watson, both, I don't give a fuck!" Yes, I could kill, I could slaughter entire families in their sleep.

"Artie—"

Here in my dogless home, exhaustion and grief, lumped as one, went to fuel rage. I shredded my shirt to get at the dead device taped to my chest. I barely noticed the pain of hair torn out. I hurled it overhand at the floor, and when it stopped bouncing, I stomped it to a powder. Then I went for Cobb's devices, which I'd thrown onto the dining-room table before my mad search for Jellyroll's body, and they would have suffered the same mashing had Sybel not snatched them up and held them behind her back.

"No, Artie, I won't let you! . . . These things might save our lives—"

I'm not given to the spontaneous act. In fact, I tend to rehearse everything—action, speech, even thought—two or three times, knock off the rough edges, polish, then do nothing. I turned and made straight for Jerry's shotgun in the bedroom closet. I flipped dirty clothes and unused sports paraphernalia out between my legs until I found the gun. I liked its feel, its heft and balance. It felt like a friend. What did I intend to do with it just then? Pump some shells through the mechanism, lend a little palpability to my revenge fantasy? I don't know. To Sybel, there was nothing inexplicable about that gun in my hands. Sybel knew it was meant for her—exactly as I would had I seen me from her perspective. I don't remember hearing her scream or perceiving her there on the floor near the door, curled in a tight ball. Yet I heard the key in the lock—I was at that moment selectively alert enough to hear the footfalls of roaches under the stove had I listened for them. It's clear to me now how Sybel might have thought I was drawing a bead on her, but I wasn't. I was aiming at the door jamb. Send in the dog killers, I'll cut them in two and—Calabash!

It was not a pretty sight, the pile of friends on my foyer floor. Calabash had thrown himself atop Sybel to shield her from the terrible blast. They were both shouting for their lives, but I didn't grasp the words. The sight was enough. It made me sick. Literally. The shotgun dropped from my arms. Sybel and Calabash were untangling themselves as I made for the john.

When was the last time I'd eaten a square meal? I even turned down that frank at Shea. When was that? I retched and heaved without satisfying result until strained muscles gripped my chest from either side like strong fingers. Then I lay for a while on the tiles, and that felt cool and sweet like a happy childhood. But Jellyroll was still gone, and there wasn't a goddam thing I could do about it.

Sybel lay sprawled on the carpet on her back when I emerged. She rolled a sweating water glass full of what looked like bourbon back and forth over her forehead. Calabash was on the phone. "I'm sorry," I said dimly.

"He just called," Sybel said without looking at me.

"Who?"

"Pine."

Calabash was passing the receiver to me and saying, "Dey musta come while I was off after dat crazy attorney you got."

"What?" I took the phone—tapped.

"Hey, Arthur, doesn't do a man's business standing in

the community a bit of good when his employees get themselves arrested.''

"Do you have my dog?"

"You ought to get that dog out of town more often. He's having a ball. Out on the runway right now chasing sticks with Chucky."

"If you hurt that dog, I'll sell you out to the FBI and the NYPD, and if that doesn't work, I'll kill you myself."

But Pine just chuckled. "Okay, Arthur, fair enough, but I need a little employee incentive, and he's it."

"Incentive for what?" Watson was hearing this. What did that mean for Jellyroll? Would it jeopardize or save him?

"We need to sit down, drink a beer, and figure out where our mutual interests lie. I got a few questions; you name a price for the answers."

"Then Jellyroll and I walk away?"

"Sure, but one thing, Arthur—don't let my affable exterior mislead you. I'm in deep shit. I got feds, cops, and Boombotts coming at me everywhere but up. I'm a desperate old man, Arthur, and I don't want you showing up here wearing wires and other such devices, not Cobb's, not Watson's, not nobody's. That clear?"

"Yes." Boombotts?

"And by the way, they had a tap on your phone. My people cleaned it up."

Oh. . . . "Where do you want me to go?"

"There's a Checker waiting out in front right now. You just get in, leaving the driving to us. *Now.* By the way, Arthur, you should have told me you wanted a bodyguard. That's covered in my employee benefit program." He hung up.

"I've got to go." I related the conversation.

Sybel was leaning against the wall. She had put her drink aside. "He knew about these tape recorders?"

"*Both* sets."

"How?"

"I don't know."

Calabash left the room with a somber look on his face. Sybel was putting on her jacket.

"What are you doing?"

"Putting on my jacket."

"Why?"

"Why? Because we're all going together."

"No—you don't need— Why would you do a thing like that?"

"Because I have a feeling you'll be safer in a crowd."

Calabash returned with a battered canvas gym bag full of heavy objects. "Dey ain't seen de mean side to Calabash yet."

On instinct I put the Family Snaps and Billie's note in an envelope, which I hid in the torn lining of my rain gear. Then we left, the three of us, together.

There was indeed a Checker cab waiting curbside. Dickie, hair slicked back and greased down, sat behind the wheel with the engine running. Sybel and I got in back, Calabash in front beside Dickie, who cowered, remembering the ease with which Calabash had chucked him like a volleyball.

"Hey," said Dickie bravely, "I didn't hear nothin' about *all* youse. It was supposed to be just him—I got to clear it with Pine—" A radio was mounted where the fare meter should have been, and Dickie reached for it. Calabash got there first. A wrench, a twist, a final yank, and Calabash had extracted the radio; he rolled down the window and dropped it in the street.

"Hey, pal, take it easy, see, I just drive, I—"

"Den do it. Drive," said Calabash in a menacing whisper.

Dickie drove. I watched to see who would follow. The law-enforcement combatants. I detected no one, but they had to be there somewhere.

Calabash reached into his gym bag to remove a big black

automatic that he cocked noisily and stuck into Dickie's ear. "You know what I do if tings feel funny when we get dere? De teeniest ting don't look just so, you know what I do?"

Poor Dickie began to shake.

"I ask myself where's dat skinny kid wid de shiny hair? Den I shoot your brain out on your shirt."

CHAPTER

TWENTY-FOUR

THIS TRIP HAD BEEN PLANNED, ORCHESTRATED, AND CHOreographed. Tensely, Dickie drove us up the Henry Hudson and across the George Washington Bridge, then north on Route 17, surely one of the tackiest strips on the Eastern Seaboard, also one of the most congested. That was part of the choreography—use the congestion. Dickie bobbed and weaved. Suddenly I noticed we were not the only Checker cab in North Jersey. There was another in front, identical to the one behind. The three began to exchange places randomly as opportunity allowed, a kind of automotive shell game, three-car monte. Without notice or signal, Dickie swerved into the Parkway Diner; one Checker followed, while the other continued north.

"We change cars here," said Dickie, driving through the parking lot, and behind the building where a big blue Buick waited with driver. The second Checker parked beside us between two hulking dumpsters.

"You drive," said Calabash.

"No, this other guy drives. That's how Pine's got it set up—"

"*You* drive."

We got out of the Checker and headed for the Buick, but its driver, a bullnecked fellow, alighted and said to Dickie, "Hey, what the fuck you doin' with this *crowd?*"

It was a short punch, no more than ten inches from start to finish. The bullnecked guy's head snapped back, ending further debate. His knees buckled, and he dropped in a quivering heap. De mean side of Calabash. "You drive," he repeated, and Dickie offered no argument. The other Checker driver never even got out of his car. I wouldn't have either.

After some tricky jinks and turns, we picked up the Thruway at Suffern, but we didn't stay on it long. We took the scenic route to the southern Catskills, and it was somewhere near Saugerties, on an empty country road, that we turned off to the airfield.

EAST COAST AVIATION, said the sign in faded red letters nailed to a telephone pole, flooded corn and stunted alfalfa fields on either side, the mountains up ahead. I squeezed Sybel's hand across the seat and wondered if she questioned her own sanity for making the trip. Dickie began to prattle about his limited sphere of responsibility, a driver nothing more, a service employee not privy to the decision-making process of his betters. Then Calabash asked, "How many men dey got out here?"

"Jeeze, I don't know. . . . Pine and Bert. Bert's his mechanic. It's like an airport. People come. Go. Jones came last night. Chucky."

Jones? Jones was here? . . . What did that mean?

"Dey armed?"

"Armed? Jeeze, I don't know. *Every*body's armed now days. I mean, this ain't no *am*bush. I mean, if Pine wanted you popped, he ain't gonna drive you way the fuck and gone out to his own property to—"

There it was. The airstrip.

"Slow down," Calabash ordered, taking a hand grenade from his gym bag.

"Aw, Jeeze—"

Calabash explained the process to Dickie. When Calabash called for a halt, Dickie would get out of the car and walk beside it as Calabash drove the rest of the way. Then Dickie was to serve as a shield behind whom we would walk slowly, directly to Jellyroll. Any divergence from that plan and "I blow you up."

The puddled road curved around the end of the grassy strip lined with single-engine airplanes tied down against the cold, gusty wind. There were two buildings, a low-slung cement one not much bigger than a mobile home topped by a control tower made of girders like a fire observation tower, but shorter, with a glass-enclosed crow's nest; nearby there was a large metal hangar painted powder blue. Red letters along the eaves said EAST COAST AVIATION. As we approached the hangar, Calabash ordered Dickie out, and we covered the last hundred yards at the pace of his stiff walk. There was no one about, but then this was no weather for recreational flying. We stopped in front of the hangar. The door was open, and inside was a huge black twin-engine airplane. It seemed familiar, but I couldn't make out its lines. Two men were up on the wing, poking at the starboard engine. They looked up when we arrived. One of them was Harry Pine.

When I stepped out of the car behind Dickie, Jellyroll sprinted from the hangar with a single bark, his tail spinning circles as he ran. He leaped at my face, and I crouched down, a lump in my throat, to ruffle his ears. I picked him up and squeezed him. He was fine; somebody had even brushed his coat. He greeted Sybel and Calabash in turn.

"Thank God," muttered Dickie.

Harry Pine climbed down from the wing and strode out to greet us. All smiles and glad hands. He looked not a day over fifty. I had to remind myself that if he were, say, twenty in 1944, he had to be at least sixty now. The muscles of his arms and shoulders bulged beneath his blue knit shirt. His walk was brisk and his handshake firm.

"You got an airplane dog here, Arthur. I can't hardly keep him out of 'em. Sybel, always a pleasure to see you. Hope your jailhouse experience wasn't too scarring. Bunch of Nazis. You must be the bodyguard."

Calabash put the hand grenade into his pants pocket and shook hands with Harry Pine. "Calabash is de name."

"Calabash. Well, I heard a lotta fine things about you. Looks like you're pretty well armed there, Calabash."

"Dat's true."

"Well, you won't be needing firepower today, but if you're ever looking for steady work, you know where to come. Let's go into the hangar, get out of the rain, have a drink, and I'll show you my pride and joy."

His pride and joy was a Martin B-26 Marauder, a fearful medium bomber that made its appearance about 1943. It was fast, maneuverable but dangerous. I had never seen one in the flesh, but I had seen pictures and read books. Short wings made the B-26 difficult to land. If your landing speed dropped a tick below 170 miles per hour, she stalled and dropped with the aerodynamics of a calliope. Pilots nicknamed her the Widow Maker. Her long flatblack nose stretched out over our heads. Her fuselage bore no numbers or identifying marks.

"Hey, Bert," Pine called up to the man who stood atop the enormous engine nacelle, "come on down, meet my friends and have a bracer."

The hangar was spotless, cleaner than my kitchen floor. A spare engine was mounted on a wheeled rack. It looked mean.

"Is that the original R-2800?" I asked.

"Whoa, Arthur, you know about the R-2800? You hear that, Bert? Arthur knows what he's looking at."

Bert, a tall, gawky fellow who looked as if he just stepped off the *Grapes of Wrath* set, appraised me critically, wiped his hands on a spotless rag. "He's kinda young, ain't he?"

"They got books, Bert."

Pine poured bourbon neat into five unmatched mugs and passed them around. "Yeah, Arthur, we got two originals in her right now. Two thousand hp on either side." He poured water from a cooler into a sixth mug and put it down for Jellyroll, who lapped up half of it. We stood under the looming black wing and drank our bourbon. Pine explained in loving technical detail the modifications he'd made to his "Bird"—expanded tankage that increased her range to something over three thousand miles, new propellers with finer pitch control, and fuel injection. "Bert here keeps her in the air. Bert's a genius."

"Yeah, well," said Bert, Adam's apple churning modestly, "there ain't many of these birds around no more."

"Like to see her inside? I had to make a few modifications, but I left the cockpit just like she was. Come on."

"I'll wait here," said Sybel.

"Aw, come on, Sybel. Let an old flyboy impress a pretty lady with his macho machine." Pine smiled and ducked beneath the belly of his black pride and joy. He opened a round hatch and pulled down a stepladder made from aluminum piping.

I wanted to see inside. So did Jellyroll. He bounded to the foot of the little ladder, and Pine hoisted him aboard. "Ladies first—after the dogs." Sybel climbed aboard and disappeared inside the dark hull. I followed, and Pine motioned for Calabash to follow me.

"After you," Calabash said to him.

"Sure, Calabash. You ever need work—" Pine climbed in, then Calabash.

It took a moment for our eyes to adjust to the gloom. We stood on the flight deck aft of the pilot's compartment, where the navigator and the flight engineer might have sat forty years ago. Six airline seats, three on either side in tight rows, had been added, but that was the only visible compromise to amenity. The compartment was unpaneled. The thin alloy outer skin curved around the spars and ribs. You could even see the rivet heads.

"Listen to this music," said Pine with boyish delight. He went forward, ducked through the open hatch, and sat in the pilot's seat. I leaned over his shoulder to watch him fire up the big radial engines. The port propeller turned slowly two or three revolutions before it exploded into a blur. Needles jumped behind tiny glass dials, oil and manifold pressure, fuel pressure, temperature, other identifiable indicators. The right engine roared to life with an angry spit of blue flame. The airplane shook and vibrated, and Jellyroll seemed to love it. "Come on, sit down," Pine shouted at me. I sat in the copilot's seat on the right side. That put Pine and me shoulder to shoulder. Then he tapped my knee and pointed out the left-hand side of the windscreen.

A black car had pulled up beside the Buick that brought us. Four men in suits got out simultaneously and stood beside the open doors in the rain. They watched us. I couldn't see their expressions clearly, but I wouldn't have called them friendly.

"Who are they?"

"Boombotts," he shouted.

"What is this Boombotts?" I shouted back.

"Hoods, wiseguys, La Cosa Nostra, no sense of humor. I don't want to talk to them right now." Harry Pine pushed both throttles forward—and we began to roll.

"Hey!" Calabash demanded, leaning into the pilot's compartment. "What's dis?"

"Take it easy, Calabash. We're just taxiing out to the other end of the runway where we can chat in peace. Got Boombotts to port."

"Boombotts?"

Pine taxied past their car, and they watched without moving a muscle until Pine—intentionally, I thought—kicked the tail around ninety degrees, brushing the Boombotts with the prop wash, a blast of dust, debris, and hot air that must have been moving about two hundred miles an hour when it hit them. There was no mirror on my side, but Pine was looking in his and grinning like Peck's Bad Boy.

"You don't fly this thing off of this airstrip, do you?" I ventured tentatively.

"Of course. Where do you think I fly it from?"

"But it's so *short,*" I shouted.

"Short. Yes, it is." He giggled and pulled on a Mets cap that had been hanging on a hook with the radio headphones.

"Wait—you're not—"

"Sit down back there, buckle up."

He *was.*

Both engines screamed, but Pine kept the brakes full on. RPMs climbed steadily. The airplane churned and bucked to go. The tail seemed to rear in frustration. Pine popped the brakes and shoved the throttle full forward; Bert's props at maximum pitch ate through the wet air. The acceleration jerked me against the bucket-seat back.

Trees! A mature forest ahead! Now I could distinguish oaks from elms, too close, white knuckles. Everything changed. We were airborne and over the treetops. Pine gently drew the wheel toward his belly, and daylight turned to darkness and turbulence, rain. But then we burst into sunlight, the first I had seen in weeks, still climbing.

"Yep. It's short, all right." Pine grinned at me as he pulled on a pair of sunglasses.

CHAPTER
TWENTY-FIVE

WE FLEW DUE NORTH BY THE COMPASS FOR SEVERAL MIN-
utes, which Pine measured on his weighty Rolex, then
turned westerly for about five minutes. The sky was co-
balt, deep purple at the outer reaches, and the tops of the
low, dirty clouds billowed white pillars that rose five thousand feet above us. I was frightened, but that was nothing
new, a given like a head cold; yet sitting there beside Harry
Pine in this vibrating—living—relic, I felt something else
rare to reclusive temperaments like mine, something like
exhilaration. I didn't ponder the landing to come—a short,
forest-ringed field, limited visibility, aboard an unforgiv-
ing killer. Or perhaps I did, and those facts only contrib-
uted to my exhilaration.

I thought about my father in a kind of evocative, detail-
less way; since I never saw him, that was typically the
way I thought about him. The airplane summoned him up,
the olive drab, the dials and flickering needles, the monotone roar of the engines, Harry Pine himself. Airplane
things, airplane smells of oil, paint, and other liquids in
unique combination, airplane views of earth and sky—
these were the final things my father experienced. I glanced

at Harry Pine. He flew with his fingertips and toes, he activated things, deactivated others, rolled trim wheels, adjusted and anticipated with practiced, economical movements. This is what he was born to, said the Hawk. Pine grinned at me and said, "We're gonna buzz some Boombotts."

"Huh?"

"Sure, liven up their day. See, this is the Italian Alps, the area down there. More Boombotts than hemlocks, the dumb fucks. They come up for the weekends with their wives and mistresses and psychos, leave the cars running just in case." He turned in his seat and shouted, "Hey, you folks back there—you're just gonna have to take your seats. You got this airplane all out of trim."

Sybel and Calabash settled into the seats along the port side. Jellyroll flopped in the narrow aisle, never taking his eyes off me. Is this all right, his eyes asked me. How would I know?

Pine edged the wheel forward—instant acceleration—and we nosed back into the dirty, turbulent clouds. I searched the olive instrument panel for the air-speed indicator. I couldn't even see the engine, whose propeller tips arced two feet from my right ear. Pine dove calmly on instruments. Sybel shouted something in a tight, throaty voice. Raindrops, one by one, materialized on the windscreen, to be sucked away in the rush of air. They fascinated me. . . . But what if this murk held, opaquely, right down to the granite mountaintops? I'd read the books. These conditions killed. The pilot grows confused in the absence of ground orientation, fucks up, stalls, spins in, dies. Film at eleven. Yet Pine was not confused. I looked at him, his profile—I really didn't want to see the cliffside prior to impact—long, straight nose and brow, cool, keen eyes moving in counterclockwise circles over his instruments. This man was not the sort to fly us into a mountain; despite white knuckles and stiff legs, I *knew* he wouldn't do that. He was talking to me. What was he saying?

"Huh!"

"Casa Palermo."

"Casa Wha—!"

"Casa Palermo. That's the name of the place we're gonna beat up—" He flipped the sunglasses up on his forehead.

Then the dive steepened. Forty-five degrees, easy, screaming down through visibility like that in a cup of two-day-old instant coffee. Then he began to show off—at least I think that's what he was doing. He plucked a Baby Ruth bar from his shirt pocket, bit the wrapper, and casually munched, flying one-handed. He passed half to me, but my fingers wouldn't hold on. It bounced off my knee and fell to the floor. "You don't like Baby Ruth, Arthur? There—" he said flatly as we punched through the bottom of the rain clouds in direct line with the Casa Palermo. I saw several buildings, twin swimming pools, a city block's worth of tangent tennis courts.

We went in at umbrella level. . . . What sort of person sits around a swimming pool on chaise longues in weather like this? We were low enough to see their heads flash toward the onrushing typhoon. Maybe 450 miles per hour. Screaming. I saw them panic and dive beneath their seats or bolt in terror, slipping, sliding on the wet deck like Keystone Kops. Mortality on the wing. The crazy *casa* vanishing beneath the black nose.

Pine giggled. "Boombotts don't grasp subtlety." The skin at the corner of his eye crinkled and danced.

We climbed back into and above the boiling rain clouds, up into clarity seldom seen from the ground. Pine pulled on the shades.

"Where are we going?" I asked.

"Place called Dutch Frigate Shoals."

"Where's that?"

"Northeastern Bahamas."

"Bahamas? Bahama *Islands?*"

"That'll give us time for a nice long chat. We got all the amenities aboard—head, running water, movie."

"No. Take us back, *now.*"

"Well, the fact is you don't have a long list of options, Arthur. Sure, you could ask Calabash to wad me up like a ball of cellophane. Flimsy old codger like me wouldn't stand a chance against the likes of Calabash. Can you fly a B-26?"

I tried another approach. "If you plan to kill us, you better plan again. The FBI *wants* you to kill us so they have cause to swarm all over you."

"They're out of luck, Arthur. I don't often kill my employees. Bad on morale. However, I have a bone to pick with you on that score, the employee score. You failed to tell your old boss about Jones and the late Ricardo. Or maybe you didn't think it worth mentioning I had rats aboard?"

"How did you know about that?"

"More pressing question is how'd *you* know about that?"

"Cobb told me."

"Interesting. Why?"

"He and the FBI are stepping all over each other to get at you. I'm supposed to be bait."

"Gee."

"You know about that, too, don't you?"

"Actually, yes."

"Just like you knew about the wires."

"Yeah. What was Cobb's ploy supposed to be?"

"I tell you Jones is working for the Colombians. Then, when you kill him, they arrest you, using the tape as evidence."

"Not blindingly bright, but it doesn't matter much now. By the way, who gunned Ricardo?"

"I don't know."

"You were there, weren't you?"

"How do you know what the cops are doing?"

"I got employees on the force. Friend name of Sal Loccatuchi. That young man loves to fly. Can't get enough."

What would Cobb think about that, his own partner? That argues for remaining in one's Morris chair, where the corruption of the world at large is merely an abstraction, but I didn't go into that under the circumstances. "What do you need us for?" I asked. "You knew about this from the beginning."

"Funny you should put it like that, Arthur. The beginning's why you're here. I know what the cops know, but thanks to you, that ain't a great deal. What I want to know is who in hell's this Billie Burke?"

I looked at him and he at me. The shades had closed his face. Eyeless, it had turned stony, impassive. What *did* he know about Billie? "She was Danny Beemon's daughter."

The take was almost comic. "Huh?"

I repeated the statement, and his face jumped to form a lot of little Os, his mouth, his brows—"Liar!" he screamed.

Awareness, like a film of mucus, slid up the back of my neck. I pulled the Family Snaps from their envelope inside my jacket. I showed them, shuffling slowly, one by one, Danny and Eleanor Beemon and young Eleanor with her puppy named Petey. "That's Billie Burke," I said.

He batted the photographs from my hands. "You *had* these? You fuck!" He choked, and that turned to violent coughing. The bottom dropped out. The right wing tripped over the left. The sky swirled and from behind, screams. Photographs fluttered weightless before our faces. Pine regained control, and the black plane flew level. The floating photos dropped around us.

His entire body, even his legs, trembled, and his face went ashen, the same colorlessness of death I had seen on Billie's face. His sunglasses hung at a bewildered angle by a single earpiece, and he brushed them away, sent them clattering down between the rudder pedals, with the back of his hand. Then a wave of crimson, like a wine spill on real linen, seeped up from under his collar, over his ears, and upward beneath his hairline; by the time it was done, even his bald crown blazed red. His head began to bob up and down as if that motion might throw off the red spill.

"It's you," I said. "You're Danny Beemon, aren't you."

He said nothing. He sat motionless behind the controls. But I didn't need confirmation or explanation—I had seen his face. Billie's father. It made sense that way, perversely. The red retreated, and the crazy head bobbing ceased. Quietly, Danny Beemon said, "Please pick up my pictures, Arthur."

I did so.

"Now leave them on your seat as you get the fuck out of my cockpit."

I did that, too. I climbed out through the cutaway bulkhead into the passenger compartment—

Jones. He sat in the first seat starboard side, and Chucky sat behind him. Where did they come from? I stopped, shocked, halfway through the bulkhead and stared stupidly at Jones. He averted his eyes, leaving his sharp beak in profile. He looked exactly like Ichabod Crane. Chucky shouted something at me, but I lost it in the engine noise, louder back here than in the cockpit.

Sweating deeply, I made my way to the third seat portside behind Sybel and Calabash. Jellyroll joined me. I stank sourly.

Sybel knelt on her seat and faced me, while Calabash crouched in the aisle beside me. "He's not Harry Pine. He's Danny Beemon," I said.

"Danny B—?" Sybel gasped. "Oh, Jesus."

"Where'd they come from?" I asked.

Calabash pointed at the solid bulkhead forming the aft end of our compartment. So the passenger list for this flight had all been planned, invitations issued simultaneously.

"Did you tell him about Jones?" Sybel asked. She seemed to be thinking, and I was grateful again for that.

"He knew," I said. "He's got Loccatuchi in his pocket."

"Where are we going?" Sybel wanted to know. "We seem to be going somewhere."

"The Bahamas."

"De Bahamas?"

"A place called Dutch Frigate Shoals."

Calabash shook his head.

"You've heard of it?"

"I heard of it, okay. Bod fockers. Dey don't allow no boats to land. Snapper fisherman I talk to was once sinkin' off de Shoals. Boat come roarin' out. De fisherman tink he bein' rescued, but he ain't. Dey towed his sinkin' boat 'bout five miles seaward and left 'im. He sunk, but he lived to tell de tale o' Dutch Frigate Shoals."

Great. Energy vanished. Nothing exhilarating back here, only sunless gloom, engine noise, Jones and Chucky. We would simply vanish from the face of the earth, Jellyroll, too, in the prime of his career. Calabash might get a few bod fockers—I might get a few myself—before they overwhelmed us, dumped our bodies well wrapped in anchor chains off the cliff-edge of the continental shelf.

"You don't know how to fly, do you?" Sybel ventured.

"I only read the books."

She turned and faced forward. Calabash returned to his seat. I stroked Jellyroll's head with phony reassurance.

Head framed in the sunlight, Danny Beemon turned and grinned the same affable grin at his captive crew. "Hey, Jonesey, come up with me," he said.

Jones didn't move. Until Chucky gave his seat a shove from behind. Jones climbed into the right-hand seat beside his boss. We watched silently. Then Chucky yelled something at me, but the noise garbled it.

"What do you want!"

"Four-eyes, tell that big fucker to put those guns away before they go off and hurt a white person!"

Calabash returned to crouch in the aisle beside me. "Since dere ain't much else to do, I might as well crush dat cowboy, don't you tink?"

"Might as well."

Calabash calmly turned and went for Chucky. Something exploded, and the sound, well above the pain threshold, slammed around the confined space. The airplane staggered, slewed, then fell. Sybel screamed. Jellyroll, with a clipped yelp, was thrown from my lap to the floor. For an instant, I thought Calabash had shot Chucky, but there he was, like the rest of us, screaming, and bouncing to and fro. The explosion had originated in the cockpit! Had Jones shot Beemon?

No. The airplane leveled off, and with it the engine noise; the monotone returned, and we welcomed it, hope for survival at least until we arrive at Dutch Frigate Shoals.

"Chucky," Beemon turned aft and called in a voice so calm it suggested boredom. Chucky picked himself up from under his seat and staggered forward. He leaned in to talk to the pilot, then began to yank at Jones's shoulder, but Jones fought him. . . . No. The difficulty in dislodging Jones arose from the inherent difficulty of lugging dead weight. Jones's head, eyes open, lolled in a way no living head could, a Raggedy Ann head, as Chucky pulled his upper body from the seat and dragged him by the armpits aft along the short aisle. A yellow plastic handle protruded from the center of his chest. Blood, still on the move, soaked his clothes all the way under his crotch. Numbly, we watched Chucky, averting his eyes from his load, open a hatch in the bulkhead, enter himself, then drag Jones through. His heels hooked on the bottom of the hatchway. Chucky reached an arm out the hatch and one by one lifted them in by the shoes. Did we *really* just see that?

Chucky returned and flopped in the portside seat. He was shaken, shoulders heaving for breath. When he caught it, he called forward, "Whenever you're ready, Chief—" Then he looked at me.

A loud rush of air and an ear-popping pressure change— the airplane trembled, then abruptly it was over, pressure and noise back to normal. I suddenly had to sleep. I didn't want to know what caused that change. I felt the edges of hysteria brush across my brain as a caution not to try to figure it out. Jones was just *back there,* where you don't want to go even for a visit, even to relieve this throbbing pressure from the bladder, back where they store the people with screwdrivers in their hearts. Just sleep. Windows would have helped, sunlight to cut the psychic darkness, the dream of blood-soaked crotches passing by, but there were no windows, a tube of prestressed aluminum, that was all, louder than the IRT express bearing us to an is- land full of bod fockers. Sleep will turn all that to a sunny beach. Suddenly that fucking Chucky was beside me, pok- ing me in the arm muscle, disturbing my sleep.

"What!"

"He say where we're going?"

"Dutch Frigate Shoals."

"Shit," muttered Chucky, standing, returning to his seat.

"Wait—what's going to happen when we get there?"

"He didn't tell you?"

"If he told me, I wouldn't be asking, would I!"

"You take a peek behind that bulkhead, four-eyes." He flopped in his seat and lit a cigarette. Sybel asked him for one. He complied. I didn't want to look back there, but I did. I twisted the recessed latch and punched the little door open. I waited, childhood night fears whirling before my eyes as they adjusted to the darkness. . . . There was a catwalk leading around them, not much more than a crawl space. A catwalk. Around the bombs. Six bombs, squat and black with little propellers on the nose, toggled to a strong tripod frame above the bomb-bay doors.

That was Jones's way out. . . . *We must be over the ocean*, I reasoned sluggishly. I was relieved. I felt a strange and giddy happiness. We weren't being delivered to our deaths on this Dutch Frigate Shoals. It was going to be them, not us! It felt like a gift.

CHAPTER

TWENTY-SIX

I CLIMBED INTO THE RIGHT-HAND SEAT. HE HAD TAPED the photographs of his family to the instrument panel, and now he was crying silently to himself. Like the copilot in the war movie, I looked away from him in deference to the sanction against masculine tears my generation inherited from his. I watched the ocean, on which the late afternoon sun shimmered in blinding contrast to black-and-white war movies.

A high-pitched whine made my ears itch. I followed the sound to its source, a thumb-round bullet hole in the side window inches from Beemon's temple.

"She wanted me to kill her, Arthur."

"You—? Did you?"

He nodded.

I'm uncertain what happened then. Did I fall asleep? Absurd. Yet day became night, and I missed the change. Her father killed her. When he said so with that short nod, I was squinting into the sun, but when my awareness returned, sea, sky, and horizon were gone, no stars or moon, blackness. The only light in our world glowed red for night vision behind the old-fashioned dials, and the red bled eerily through the photos taped over it. He was saying something, speaking to me as if it were unremarkable that day should vanish into night during a nod of the head.

Billie's "I'm dead" note was duct-taped above the compass and under the row of photographs. How did he get it? I hadn't given it to him. I had it hidden in the torn lining of my jacket. He pointed to the note, tapped it with his fingernail, and he said, "She knew what you'd do. She knew her man. The photographs, they're all about my life, but this note is all about you."

"What do you mean?" I asked as if I didn't know.

"My daughter set it up. The whole goddam thing. Somehow she learned I was alive, then she set it up so I'd kill her. But she had to have somebody to tell me who I'd killed or else her revenge wouldn't work. You with me, Arthur? You look a tad bilious. Think how I feel. You were the man for the job."

"I don't believe that," I lied, and D.B. laughed at me. This had been a family affair from the beginning, and I was nothing more than the gentleman caller.

"Acappella Productions," he was saying. "I looked it up. It means alone, without accompaniment, but you and I, we know she had a hell of a lot of accompaniment. Only we didn't know that's what we were."

"Tell me what happened."

"When? You mean the night she died?"

"Don't say it that way. She didn't just die, like from a stroke."

"I found her tied up in the tub. I went to her apartment because that's where all my employees flocked when I threw a scare into them, and I found her tied and gagged with her own panties. Jones did that, left her like that while he went looking for the photos. She looked at me standing over her and began to choke, so I removed the gag. She wasn't choking. She was laughing."

I pictured the scene played out against the night as if it

were the wide screen, Billie contorted, probably in pain, but laughing at her father.

"She said, 'You're dead, Pop.' Pop. She actually called me that. Course I missed the joke at that point. Right then I was thinking here's this grifter all tied up, helpless, but she's acting all out of character for a grifter caught in the act. Put yourself in my place, Arthur, what would you have done?"

"Hell, under the circumstances, I'd have drowned her. Only way to teach a grifter."

"I didn't intend to drown her, Arthur. I wanted to find out some things. How did she know about the doctors, the whole Florida business? What were these photographs she said would hang me? I had my life to protect, Arthur, so I ran some water in the tub. Put her face in it. . . . She drowned. I look back on it, I'm convinced that's the way she wanted it."

"Now you're batting a thousand," I spit, enraged at the scene I saw before me, Billie drowned, her hair undulating on the surface, her bound hands clenched into fists.

"What'd you say?"

"Two for two. You got *both* your kids!"

His head didn't turn; he flew his airplane. After a while, he said, "Here, you take over." He was climbing out of the cockpit.

"Are you nuts!"

"Just while I take a pee."

"It's on auto pilot, isn't it?"

"Auto pilot's in the shop." He turned and walked aft.

No, he wouldn't do that. It was on auto pilot. No! We were accelerating. I gripped the half wheel. No, we were *diving!* That meant the nose must come up—

Behind me, I heard Sybel shout and Beemon say, "No sweat, Arthur's at the controls."

I heaved back on the wheel. Things slowed down. That felt better, now I could think. . . . Why were the engines screaming as if in distress? The stall! I had read the books,

I knew the danger. When dick-up pilots raise the nose too high, the angle of attack grows so extreme that the wings lose all lift properties and they stall. Then the aircraft drops like a pool table. Get the nose down! The books say that surviving pilots fly with a light touch. They don't bend the wheel into a pretzel out of crippling terror. I eased the wheel forward and felt us edge over the top of the arc. . . . Why were we diving? How long does it take for a pee! I yanked the wheel into my stomach. Almost immediately my seat began to shudder. Now I'd done it, totally fucked the laminar flow. So I shoved the wheel forward again, but nothing happened except that the shudder grew more violent. We were finished. We would fall into a spin from which I could never recover. A seat cushion or a thermos bottle might float ashore in East Hampton, where a strolling yuppie might toe the jetsam curiously before moving on—

"Give it a little throttle," a calm voice advised. Beemon! He was back, and he was flying.

I was gasping for breath. My arms ached. "What did you do that for? Are you crazy!"

"Well, pard, the fact is I don't like your attitude. You come aboard my favorite airplane and tell me some pretty foul news only to go all righteous on me. You're nothing more than an outsider at the family fracas. Hell, you can't even fly my favorite airplane. That was a ham-handed piece of work, all that up and down. You don't even have any instincts. You about killed us in the time it takes a real pilot to spray one. You can't pretend to know a goddam thing about my life unless you got about five thousand hours in your book. So if you don't change that righteous attitude, I ain't inviting you along no more."

I understood. I nodded. "But there's another thing you don't seem to know," I said.

"I've had enough revelations for one flight."

"Eleanor lives at Bright Bay."

"Eleanor—?"

"Billie put her there. Knowingly." It was my job to tell. I didn't leave it unfinished, Billie.

He seemed smaller now, compressed into his seat. The Ace of Aces seemed to me a vulnerable little boy. I didn't want to pity him; I wanted my loathing untainted. Tears flooded the crow's feet at the corners of his eyes. I wondered if Billie would have felt gratified. "There it is," he said quietly.

It was land, reef tops on which stray mangrove roots have taken hold. One islet was about the size and shape of a bus roof, and five others, smaller, barely out of water, were strung along behind.

"Called Hen and Chickens Reef. Pretty slick piece of flying if you didn't notice due to all the emotional distractions. Dead on the landfall after thirteen hours over water at night."

I noticed.

"Now we bend east forty degrees. . . . Did you talk to Eleanor?"

"Yes."

"Was she—? How did she seem to you, Arthur?"

"She seemed—" I stopped. My impulse was to lie, to make her life sound better than it was. Why did I want to protect his feelings? What about my feelings? "Her mind is gone. She thinks Harry Pine is you."

CHAPTER

TWENTY-SEVEN

THE DYING DAWN FANNED THE EAST WITH STREAKS OF red, and an island began to form and grow on the horizon. D.B. sat straight in his seat, pulled on his shades, and said, "Dutch Frigate Shoals."

"Do you really mean to bomb it?"

"Sure."

This was it, the drug war. When Cobb told me about it, I hadn't expected to be in the vanguard of the air assault. "Who's down there?" I asked.

"A scumbag name of Jackie. That's the nerve center for all the dope boats bound for the East Coast. Jackie's an old fart, about my age. He used to be pals with all the scumbags. Papa Doc, Somoza, the Colonels. He and Klaus Barbie were buddies. No, I got no compunction about blowing Jackie to shit. I just hope he don't keep pets."

We passed low and less than a mile to the north of Dutch Frigate Shoals, crescent-shaped, like a waning moon. The southern hook was overgrown in scrub and mangrove, but all vegetation had been cut away in the north to accomodate human luxury. There was a sun-bleached airstrip, two planes parked on it, a white house with a pink roof from which radio antennae sprouted incongruously—like a black antique bomber in the blue tropical sky. And there was a long whitewashed dock to which a motor boat with a tuna tower was tied. Also crescent-shaped, the house curved around a blue tile swimming pool. The water shimmered invitingly. I saw no movement.

"This is what you do? Bomb villas for the Mafia?"

"Nope, this is my first. But don't get righteous again. You live off your dog. My daughter is the reason we're here."

"How?"

"Let's say you're my boss, Luigi Boombott, and you employ this asshole to do some flying for you. This pilot's been dependable up till now, but lately his entire holdings are falling apart on 'Eyewitness News.' His building gets torched, his employees shoot each other to pieces on a residential street. This guy's trouble, and why bother? Pilots come a dime a dozen. You could get an astronaut, if you wanted to hang around with one. Get *rid* of that asshole. And they would have, too, except I struck this deal with them."

"You blow up the competition and they don't kill you."

"Right. Except I have to vanish. We won't be able to play squash on Thursdays anymore."

"Where are you going?" I asked.

"Maybe I'll retire to St. Pete Beach, play shuffleboard and listen to the bugs get electrocuted. I'm feeling kind of old. You're looking a little aged yourself."

"I'm not used to nights like this."

"Well, it's almost over now. We'll just swing upsun to confuse the flak gunners. A flight through hot steel shards."

"You're kidding."

"Yeah, they're probably asleep with their dorks in hand. Jackie samples his wares. Arthur, how did my daughter know I'm alive?"

"I don't know, for sure."

"Do you have an idea?"

"I think Eleanor saw you. There's a photograph on her wall. It shows Billie and Eleanor together—in Billie's studio. She could have seen you the day it was taken. Your face is different, a lot of years have passed, but maybe there was something she recognized, your walk, a gesture. I don't know, but I bet that picture was taken about a year ago."

He sat silently, sadly, for a while before he pressed us into our seats with a cowboy bank turn to the right. I liked it. When we leveled off, D.B. straightened in his seat, pulled on his shades, and produced another Baby Ruth from his shirt pocket. He bit the wrapper off and broke the bar in half. We went in munching. The pink roof filled the windscreen. "We're operational, Arthur."

The roof vanished beneath our nose like a fantasy. Nothing happened. Was this all some kind of sick joke?

Explosions slewed the tail around.

We turned 180 degrees.

Jackie's house had become a hole. Not even a jagged piece of wall stood upright. Pink chunks were strewn all over the island and were sinking in the shallow sea. Some parts hadn't even come down yet. I saw a sectional sofa pirouetting lazily in the air. Little fires flickered in the hole, and only half of the pool remained in the earth; the rest was flickering down like blue tile confetti. Transfixed, I watched the boat roll onto its side like a bathtub toy, fill and sink in the transparent water.

"We'll strafe some."

"Huh?"

He pointed the black nose at the airplanes parked on a coral revetment covered with swimming pool parts and opened fire. The cannon, or whatever it was, slammed the bottom of my seat, and red baseballs arced out, seemingly in slow motion. The single-engine plane withered and collapsed like a silent comedy prop. The gun beneath my seat was so powerful its recoil caused the black bomber to slow noticeably. D.B. turned it on to the twin-engine airplane, and after no more than six whacks to my spine, the gas tanks exploded. A wing jinked high in the air, and a flaming ball that might have been an engine rolled into the water and steamed spectacularly.

D.B. stood the B-26 on its wing and we orbited the destruction. It was total. I sat in a puddle of sweat reminding myself that what I was seeing was heavily actual. It only looked like a war movie in living color. The cockpit reeked acridly of gunpowder.

"Too bad," he said. "That was a nice twin Beech. Did you see it?"

"Briefly."

He put us on a course due west, and in minutes we were flying over deep blue Gulf Stream water. Fly west from the Bahamas and you come upon the coast of Florida.

"You're going back, aren't you?" I asked, but I didn't need an answer.

"Harry and I, we had some good times out of Moxie Field, but you know, Arthur, we should never have survived the war. That was our big mistake. We were just too good to get killed in combat. Course we could have flown into a bridge like your old man did."

"What? How did you know that? I didn't tell you that!"

"They have books, Arthur. I looked it up. He was young."

"Twenty-one." I began to feel cold from the drying sweat and the devastation.

"What do you think we ought to do with these photographs, pard?"

"I don't know. They're yours. I guess this note is mine."

I knew somehow what he was going to do with them even before he slid open the little side window. Summer air entered with a roar. One by one, he pulled them off the instrument panel and fed them to the slipstream. The note alone remained taped in place. I peeled it off and handed it to him. After it was gone, he closed the window.

"Can I try it again?" I asked.

"What?"

"Flying."

"Sure. She's all yours."

I found the rudder pedals, then took the wheel in my fingertips.

"That's the way," he said. "The light touch." He sat back and folded his arms across his chest. "Why don't you gain some altitude? We don't need to horse around down here on the deck."

I eased back on the wheel, and the horizon slipped below the nose.

"Good. Give it some gas. Like a car going uphill."

I felt around for the throttles on the console between us. D.B. took my hand in his and brought it to the levers. We pushed them forward until the climb grew steady and powerful. I leveled off—deftly, I thought.

"Fine. Here, let me trim her up some. Shock waves from the bombs jacked the tail out of trim."

"Yeah," I agreed. Shock waves. "Can I try a turn?"

"She's all yours."

I needed help with the first several, but after that I felt comfortable and confident turning. I even flew a big figure eight. I don't know how long we turned and banked around towering cumulus chimneys, but soon I lost all sense of direction in my concentration on the light touch. D.B. tapped the compass and motioned for a turn to the east. The coast of Florida appeared first as a smudge on the horizon, then took form—a long yellow beach, white breakers, tall glass condos, and low, rich houses with familiar pink roofs. I took her all the way. The houses in the subdivisions grew squarer and poorer with more objects in the yards as we flew due west, until houses gave way entirely to agriculture on the banks of Lake Okeechobee.

"There's Moxie," D.B. said, pointing down at a short grassy airstrip. Planes were parked between the runway and endless bean fields. There was a miniature control tower with a limp orange windsock. "I better take her now."

I gave up the controls reluctantly.

D.B. said, "You're a natural, pard."

"Really?"

"You can always spot 'em."

Did he mean that? I wanted to know, but I couldn't think of a way to ask. "So this is it?" I said.

"What more do you want?"

What more did I want? I wanted something. I longed for something.

D.B. made a low, slow pass over Moxie Field. There were people on the ground. As one, they shaded their eyes and looked up at us. I could see them point and shout to others. D.B. gave them a long look at the black bomber before he stood it on its wing in a wild approach turn. When he leveled out, we were on the ground, in one brilliant, stomach-wrenching motion. He taxied to the white stucco control building and spun his airplane around in its own length, ready to go again.

A crowd was gathering.

"Give that dog of yours a pat for me, pard."

I wanted to say something.

He offered me his hand. I shook it. There was nothing more to say. I climbed out of the cockpit.

The passenger compartment reeked of vomit, and the passengers were pale. Chucky was acting desperate. He had the hatch open, but the little aluminum ladder made him wild. It wouldn't go down. He yanked and swore until Calabash grew impatient, placed his big black Ked between Chucky's shoulder blades, and expelled him through the hole. Jellyroll wagged his tail and circled the hatch anxiously. I told him, "Go," and he jumped into the grass.

254

His ears flying in the propwash, Jellyroll lifted his leg and peed on the landing gear. Calabash was next out. Sybel said something to me, but it was lost to the engine roar. She rolled her red, swollen eyes, smiled thinly, and climbed out the hatch.

I glanced forward at D.B. He turned in his seat to give me the thumbs-up sign. His face was smeared with tears. I dropped out of the black belly.

The heat clobbered me, an alien from a cold island, as if it were something solid and blunt. My knees collapsed, and I literally crawled aft under the tail toward my friends, who stood on the edge of the tarmac sizzling in the wavering heat. My dog sat panting in Calabash's shadow. We stood together and watched.

The snarl of the engines, the fine white dust set in motion by the whirling propellers combined with the breathless heat to blur the edges of reality. This was where Billie's death had led, and I wanted to see it crisply, precisely record its details for later when I could figure out what it meant. But things had no sharp edge; people looked ghostly in the white dust. They glanced at us as they pressed toward the plane. Elderly men materialized, passed, and vanished into the noise, amazed that the black bomber had flown in from their youth, even though they had expected it would someday.

He waddled out of the dust at top speed. I'd seen that gait before. We spotted each other at once. He skidded to a halt and squinted at me. "Are you here to impede us?" he shouted.

"No. I'm through. . . . D.B.'s waiting for you."

"Yes, I hear him. I'd like you to meet Barnett Osley." He meant the man two steps behind, deeper in the dust. He stepped forward. Half his face rested normally, but some terrible force had twisted the other half into a toothy grimace. The good half smiled and nodded.

"How do you do, Doctor?" Then I introduced the doctors to Sybel and Calabash. Jellyroll sniffed the doctors' shoes. Which one shot Jay Kiley full of air? I didn't think to ask myself that question then. We shook hands all around.

"We'll be going now," said Dr. Keene.

"We don't want to upset Danny Beemon," said Dr. Osley.

The crowd began to cheer. Some people waved shirts and handkerchiefs; others lifted young boys astride their shoulders so that they might see from an unobstructed place:

Danny Beemon standing waist-high out of the top hatch. He waved his Mets cap in a circle over his head, then dropped back into the pilot's seat.

The crowd, us with it, pressed into a semicircle on the port side. Harvey Keene clambered into the belly hatch, then leaned out to help Barnett Osley aboard. One of them pulled the hatch shut. The noise changed pitch. The engines screamed, and the elegant shape began to roll. Heat waves rippled from the wings. D.B. was airborne again.

I knew he'd do it. Everyone else seemed to know, too. He wheeled around steeply and buzzed us. The noise hurt, and the wash rocked us like pines in a storm. We shielded our eyes and watched. Then he was gone, a lingering drone, a speck receding, then nothing. A cloudless blue Florida sky.